When Hearts Are Light Again

When Hearts Are Light Again

Emilie Loring

Thorndike Press
Waterville, Maine USA

Chivers Press
Bath, England

This Large Print edition is published by Thorndike Press®, USA and by Chivers Press, England.

Published in 2003 in the U.S. by arrangement with Little, Brown and Company, Inc.

Published in 2003 in the U.K. by arrangement with Little, Brown and Company, Inc.

U.S. Hardcover 0-7862-5227-8 (Candlelight Series)
U.K. Hardcover 0-7540-7333-5 (Chivers Large Print)
U.K. Softcover 0-7540-7334-3 (Camden Large Print)

The text of this Large Print edition is unabridged.
Other aspects of the book may vary from the original edition.

Set in 16 pt. Plantin by Ramona A. Watson.

Printed in the United States on permanent paper.

British Library Cataloguing-in-Publication Data available

Library of Congress Cataloging-in-Publication Data

Loring, Emilie Baker.
    When hearts are light again / Emilie Loring.
        p. cm.
    ISBN 0-7862-5227-8 (lg. print : hc : alk. paper)
    1. World War, 1939–1945 — United States — Fiction.
2. Undercover operations — Fiction. 3. Aircraft industry
— Fiction. 4. Sabotage — Fiction. 5. Large type books.
I. Title.
PS3523.O645W47 2003
    813′.52—dc21   2003047826

When Hearts Are Light Again

Chapter 1

A little shiver of apprehension ran along Gregory Hunt's nerves as he faced his uncle across the broad desk. Something different in the atmosphere of the familiar office. Nothing you could put your finger on. Nothing in B.C.'s face, though it was more finely drawn than it had been a year ago when he, himself, had left the Clifton Works for the Air Force. More like a faint whisper of warning to look out for trouble. Why sit and wonder? Why not drag the bogey out into the open, if there were a bogey? Perhaps there wasn't one. Perhaps this mild attack of heebie-jeebies was the result of getting back to the factory in which he had spent the eight years since college. Had he been sent home from the Pacific "for a period of rest" to find complications here? Something was up. What?

"Here I am, B.C.," he said; "what's on your mind? Let's have it."

Benjamin Clifton leaned forward in the swivel chair and crossed his arms on the desk. His intent eyes were deeply blue under heavy white brows that had been iron-gray a year ago, his nephew remembered, his large mouth widened in a smile that lighted his eyes.

"First, it's grand to see you, Greg. The story of your heroism, of how you dove six times to secure the rubber boat, of how you pulled four of your exhausted crew aboard under machine-gun fire, of the presentation of the medal, has preceded you. Our workers are very proud of G.H., as they call you."

Greg held up a protesting hand. The lines between nose and the corners of his grim mouth in his thin, bronzed face deepened.

"Let's not go into that, B.C." His tense voice was sharpened by a mental vision of savagery. "I have a hunch that something is wrong here. What?"

"You've asked for it. Here it is without any preamble: You are needed at the Works."

"Here! What's happened to Linc Channing who moved up into my place as Vice President?"

"Passed out suddenly a month ago. I've thought of every alternative to bringing you back. I know you are completely sold on your present job — captain in the Air

Force. You've risen fast, my boy."

"That's because you had the nerve to let me have my own plane when I was twenty-one. I'm sold on it because every man who can pilot a fighting plane is desperately needed, you know that, B.C. I must get back to the show. My bombardier was machine-gunned to pulp." He cleared his voice. "That's a score I mean to write off."

"I know, I know. Sit down, Greg. Let's get at this sanely. We are making plane parts. The factory is running twenty-four hours a day, six days a week including holidays. We have undertaken a job which must be done."

"I know all that, B.C., and I'm proud that I own Mother's share of the Works, but — to return here is out of the question. I'm terribly needed where I am — besides, I like it."

"Not needed so much as you're needed right here, Greg. We must speed up production. There is no one in the organization who can or will put himself into the job as you did. The workers like you, they know that even though you are part owner of the factory, you worked your way up from the bottom. You know every department and are quick to detect slowdowns or unnecessary absenteeism. Even if Lincoln

Channing hadn't died I would have tried to get you back."

"Hang it all, B.C., I don't *want* to come back. I'm crazy over my present job. I didn't need a 'period of rest.' I needed to keep on cracking at the enemy."

"There are numberless men who can take over for you there. There's not a man I know who has had the training to do what you can accomplish at the Works. You'll be serving the nation here, not as spectacularly, but just as loyally as on the front."

"You know me well enough to know I don't give a damn for the spectacular part of it, B.C."

He walked to the broad window and looked out at the gorgeous mid-September world. At the foot of the autumn-tinged hills spread a white blur which was the town. The sky was calm and clear as a turquoise. The river trailed like a blue ribbon edged with the silver of autumn asters through fields and under bridges. Each factory building was set in emerald lawns with gay beds and borders of zinnias. The red, white and blue of the flag on the pole in the center of the court and the Army-Navy E flag beneath it whipped back and forth in the light breeze. Smoke rose from chimneys. The day shift poured out of the doors.

He watched the workers. If he were in the seats of the mighty each mother's son of them would take a turn at the fighting front. When they returned they'd see to it that there were no slowdowns, no absenteeism. They would remember the hellholes where planes were so desperately needed and work their fingers to the bone to provide them.

He looked down at the silver insignia on his tunic. Lord, how he had worked for those wings. He would *not* give them up. Someone else could be found for this job. . . . Was that true? It had taken him years of intensive work to master the intricacies of production. Suppose a man were put in Linc Channing's place who didn't measure up to the job? Production would fall off, the planes for which there was so deep a need would be held up. It must not happen. Was he the answer to that? In the air other lives than his had hung on his quick decision. He said over his shoulder: —

"Okay, B.C. You win." He cleared his throat of a troublesome obstruction. Had he really given up the sense of consecration to a great cause, the excitement and stimu-

11

lation of the service? Committed himself to this mid-New England town until victory was won?

"It will take time to get me out of the Air Force," he said aloud, and thought: "Perhaps I'll have a chance for one more crack at the dirty demons."

"Sit down, Greg. I can't talk to your back, straight as it is in that smart uniform." As his nephew settled into the chair across the desk he went on: —

"It won't take time to secure your honorable discharge. It's being put through now. Sending you back for that 'period of rest' you scorn hasn't been entirely my idea, greatly as I need you. WPB took a hand and ordered your reinstatement here to speed up production. It boils down to the fact that you can't continue in aviation. You're under orders to serve here. I didn't tell you before because I wanted you to decide for yourself where you are most needed."

"Anyone know of this beside you and the omnipotent WPB?"

"No one but my confidential secretary. Why?"

"I brought a ring for Lila. Thought we might get married while I was here."

"Lila Tenny?"

"Why the shocked surprise? She was my girl before I joined up. I'd rather she would hear of the change in my plans from me."

"Of course, of course, Greg. Nothing will be said about your return until you make the announcement. With the whole country mined with saboteur dynamite it better not be known that you were recalled because you are needed here; we'll say it was because of — well, call it a tricky heart."

"I, disqualified because of a physical defect! You're crazy, B.C. I'm sound from head to heels."

"I know, Greg, but later I'll tell you why the reason of your return to the Works must not be suspected. We are at war, remember." He touched a button on a box on his desk and spoke into the interoffice phone. "Bring the WPB file," he said and snapped the switch.

"Have a cigarette, Greg. So many men smoke on the job that I've let up on the NO SMOKING IN BUSINESS HOURS restriction in this office. When I caught Sarah Grand in here one day taking a puff I threw up my hands."

"Good old Sarah. Does Aunt Jane hate your officious secretary as much as ever?"

"Wait till you're married and you'll realize

13

that that isn't a chuckling subject, my boy." The dark-haired girl in a navy crepe frock with snowy collar and cuffs who had opened the door hesitated on the threshold. "Come in."

Greg stared incredulously over the top of the lighter he was applying to a cigarette, snapped it out and sprang to his feet.

"As I live and breathe if it isn't little Gail Trevor, complete with three dimples, feather cut and blue bow in her hair." He caught her hand. "Thought you were the strong right arm of one of the Big Shots in Washington, D.C."

The faint color that spread to the widow's peak of the girl's hair accentuated the brilliance of her dark eyes, the scarlet curve of her lovely mouth. She freed the hand he held.

"You have part of it right, Greg. I was there. I'm here now. I've been drafted too." He wondered what emotion shook her voice. "Here is the correspondence, Mr. B.C."

She laid papers on the desk and turned to go.

"Hey, you can't walk out on me like that," Greg protested. "Have you forgotten that I let you tag me on fishing trips and carry my fly book on your vacations, that I magnanimously loaned you my shoulder to cry on when you got so mad you couldn't talk? That I haven't seen you for two years? Why have you chucked the nation's capital for — Don't tell me you've taken Sarah Grand's job?"

"She has," Benjamin Clifton cut in crisply. "That will be all for the present, Miss Trevor."

Greg stared at the door the girl closed behind her.

"What does Aunt Jane say to *her?*" he demanded.

"Okay. It was her suggestion, when the divine Sarah — that's your aunt's tag, not mine — decided that the Navy needed her. I'll admit I was glad to have her go. She had an exaggerated idea of her own importance. Gail was doing fine in a senator's office in Washington. Then her sister-in-law —"

"You mean Mildred Trevor, Doc John's wife?"

"The same — also decided that her country called and was among the first to join an Auxiliary Corps. She was eligible all right, she started most of the worthwhile organizations in this town. She's a dynamo of energy, what is technically known as 'a live wire.' She left Doctor John, their just fourteen-year-old son,

Billy, and fifteen-and-a-half Cissie-Lou to shift for themselves — except for the colored cook, Petunia, and Hilda Speed, the office nurse, who has no time to look after them."

"I'll be darned, Doc and those grand youngsters need her. They seem like part of our family, B.C. Aunt Jane thinks he's a miracle man and she had the children at Twin Pines whenever she could get them."

"I know, and she has coveted Gail since the first summer she spent with her brother. You remember we lost our little girl. We were as shocked as you are when Mildred announced she was leaving home. She's lost her sense of values, but, in the excitement, so have others."

"What does her husband say?"

"He wouldn't criticize his wife, but if he doesn't save himself a little, he'll crack up. He's the only physician left in town and now he has been informed by the hospital he'll have to take over surgery and obstetrics beside the medical cases there."

"I'd say standing by that family on the home front, with Doc Trevor pressed into constant service and those two growing kids, was serving her country. However, I suppose she's entitled to a point of view. What brought Gail back?"

"Devotion to her brother and love for the children, perhaps also a sense of indebtedness. It's a lovely sight to see her with those youngsters in the church pew on Sunday upholding the Trevor family dignity. They are there, rain or shine."

"She was conscientious as a little girl. If she said she'd do a thing you could count on her doing it."

"She's like that now. When John Trevor was eighteen his father married again. Gail was born of that union. I suspect that Doctor John helped her through college. When she applied to me for the job she said that those youngsters were at a critical age, they mustn't be left to shift for themselves — she'd been reading articles on the increase of juvenile delinquency — that John needed to be looked after when he came home too all-in to eat and dropped asleep in his chair; that Hilda Speed's time was needed by him. Her eyes were flames when she added 'I had planned to be a WAAC, perhaps that's why I get so boiling mad when I think of Mildred walking out on her family.' That's the story."

"Is she good at the job?"

"Good! She was one of the top secretaries in Washington. I was lucky to get her. I didn't know how lucky till she had been here a month."

"She was a mighty lovable, sweet child, with enough quick, flaring temper to keep her from being sugary, and brave as they come. I'll never forget her eyes when I cut a fishhook out of her hand, but nary a whimper. When she walked into the office I realized that in my thoughts she hadn't grown up. I've thought of her and her amusing little ways a lot this last year. It's surprising how often in an inferno like the one I've lived through, you pull out old memory snapshots of everyday living and smile as you turn them over and over. I wondered what put an edge on her voice when she said, 'I was there. I'm here.' Poor little kid."

"I assure you, the 'poor little kid' doesn't need your sympathy. Her brother and the children adore her, and you'd be surprised how often the department heads here and men she knew in Washington feel the need of a conference with me, which they arrange through her. Mark Croston, the new man who came on from the Coast a couple of months ago to take over the department left vacant when Len Small was drafted, appears particularly hard hit."

"I remember. You wrote me that he had

solid gold recommendations. Is he living up to his reputation?"

"Yes. I consider him a find."

"How about the other new department head?"

"Joe Selby is as good though in a different way; the workers like him. We're lucky. There never has been trouble between the front office and the factories." He opened a safe and laid three pieces of metal and a set of prints on the desk.

"These were delivered by hand to me. You and I, and the head of the WPB Department that sent them, are the only persons who know they are here. Take a look at them, Greg."

His nephew picked up a piece of metal and squinted at the inside. Looked at one of the prints. The color under his tan ebbed.

"Imperfect. Our stamp. Where did it come from, B.C.?"

"From a plane that crashed two weeks ago." He nodded toward the other pieces on the desk. "Those came from two other crack-ups."

Greg tried twice before he could produce a voice.

"All three from this factory? What's wrong, B.C.?"

"That's what the WPB wants to know. There's a special agent on the job. A list has been made of all employees who have had access to our assembly lines and each one's background is being investigated. If we have a saboteur in the Clifton Works it's up to you to find him — or her."

Chapter 2

There was a flame-color frock in the shop window. Gail slipped from her wheel and crossed the sidewalk for a nearer view. It was net, glistening with opaline sequins, a honey of a dress, and if the tag was to be believed the price was not prohibitive. She would try it on tomorrow at the noon hour. She hadn't had a new evening costume for two years. She needed one. Now that Greg Hunt had returned there would be all sorts of festivities in his honor.

She walked on, wheeling her bicycle. Drew a long breath of the fragrance of deep purple violets in a basket outside a florist's. They reminded her of Washington and Sebastian Brent. He said it with violets. She stopped to look at a tray of sparkling rings in a jeweler's window, at a display of sensationally gorgeous bracelets. For a town its size the shops were amazingly up to the minute. That was because there were so many beautiful summer estates in the neighborhood and the businessmen were alert to cater to this trade. Now that the defense workers were earning more money, their wives clamored for diamonds and diamonds they bought.

A few minutes later she rode her wheel along the residential street where service stars were displayed in almost every window, where rows of maples blazed with scarlet and gold tempered by delicate green and crimson. She thought of Greg Hunt again and wondered if he knew he was at the Works to stay. She had known for weeks that he would be ordered home, that he was greatly needed. She was selfishly glad to have him back. Would that account for her feeling since she had seen him this afternoon, that something especially nice was ahead?

Her brother's house was charming even in this region of spectacular summer places on the surrounding hills, she reflected, as she approached it. She slid off her bicycle and opened the gate of the white picket fence in front of a garden border, brilliant with zinnias, pink phlox, cosmos, tall asters and blue spikes of late delphinium. It was low and rambling, each ruffle-curtained window had its flower box, rosy with geraniums and spilling over with green vines.

I'll hand it to Mildred for a house-planner

if she's a total loss as a homemaker, she thought, as she opened the front door and stepped into the hall with its curving stairway and white paneling.

From the corner of her eyes she glanced into the Doctor's waiting room, which adjoined his office on the right. Late for patients. Old John Tisdale must be there, there wasn't more than one racking cough like his in town. Rhoda Craven . . . Again! Why had the smartly gowned woman seated on the couch opposite the door come at this time? Why not in regular office hours?

"Miss Gail."

The whisper came from the office beyond. Hilda Speed, the nurse, was beckoning.

Gail followed her into the room and closed the door.

"What is it, Hilda?"

The lines at the corner of the woman's gray eyes deepened. With a big-knuckled hand she brushed back the already satin-smooth salt-and-pepper hair above her left ear. Her thin-lipped mouth straightened.

"That woman is here again."

"What woman, Hilda?" Gail asked as if she didn't know, and pulled off her navy cardigan as she walked to the window.

"That Mrs. Rhoda Craven who leased the largest of Gregory Hunt's cottages on the hill for the summer. It's the one with the green-and-white awnings. See it?"

Gail nodded. But she wasn't seeing the attractive stucco house, she was looking at Twin Pines, the old-time stone mansion above it. Would Greg Hunt live there with his uncle and aunt as he had before he went into the service? She hadn't seen him for two years; in that time his face had aged, bronzed, hardened, thinned. No wonder, after the danger he had faced. His eyes, deep blue like B.C.'s, had a sharp fierceness she never had seen before — until he laughed, when they were gay and friendly as she remembered them. There were two lines between them now, deep as if inked. She recalled the grim set of his mouth when he was fishing, the way it broadened in a laugh when she landed a trout, the steadiness of his fine hands when he detached the flapping thing from the hook because she winced away from touching the clammy body.

"You'll have to do it some day for yourself, Gail; the quicker you learn the better," he had advised. "You won't always have a man round to do the dirty work for you."

24

She had answered with the cocky assurance of her fifteen years: —

"I'm not so sure about that."

"Don't you think so, Miss Gail?" Hilda Speed's stentorian whisper was a magic carpet whisking her back to the present.

"Think what, Hilda?"

"That the Craven woman is after Doctor John? She's trying to get him by making a lot of Cissie-Lou. She's smart as a steel trap. She knows he's crazy about his daughter. I don't wonder she wants him. He isn't exactly handsome with those piercing dark eyes set deep in his head and that big forehead, but his mouth is fine and he has what it takes with women. She's the kind who gets her own way."

"You're imagining it, Hilda. She was a college friend of his wife's. She has been a guest in this house. Besides, he's married." That was a silly answer if ever there were one. How often in these days did marriage halt a predatory woman?

"How much married is he with Herself off in camp parading round in a uniform?" Hilda's eyes and voice were bitter. "He's doing the work of ten men an' she ought to be with him to say nothing of looking after those youngsters who were running wild before you came. I'm as patriotic an American citizen as they come, I'm aching to be off to the fighting front myself, but can I leave with your brother the only physician in town rushed from morning till morning again?"

"You can't, Hilda, dear. You and I are the women behind the man who takes care of the family of the man making the planes. Like you, I'm aching to get into the midst of action — it seems so — so stuffy not to be in the service — but each time I think I'll make the break, I know it can't be done. If this family didn't need me the Clifton Works does. I am more valuable there than I could be anywhere else, just now. . . . This is Petunia's afternoon off, isn't it?"

"Yes, but she left everything ready for dinner. I'll dish it up. All you need do is get those youngsters to the table when I bang the gong. Now who's wanting Himself?" She answered the ring of the telephone.

"It's you, Doctor? Yes. Two patients waiting. I'll tell them you won't be back till late, if then. It's the Gray baby at last? Well, good luck to it — and you." She added the last two words as she cradled the phone.

"Your brother won't be here till late."

26

Her eyes gleamed, her voice dripped satisfaction as she added, "Watch me clear out that office."

As Gail showered and dressed, she thought of Hilda's concern about "that woman." Rhoda Graven was attractive, cultured, and an honest-to-goodness widow. John was a man of integrity, almost Puritanical in his standards of right and wrong, but — he was tragically overworked and he needed his wife. The all-out call for women to the service didn't mean that they were to desert the home front — or did it?

"Hi! Gail!"

She opened her door.

"Here, Billy."

The boy took the stairs three at a time and charged into the room, a red setter at his heels. His fair hair stuck out like wisps of hay, his face was flushed, his brown eyes were clouded with trouble. He was too tall for his going-on-fifteen years, and even the blinding plaid of his shirt, already too short in the sleeves, didn't disguise the thinness which twisted her heart.

The oval gilt-framed mirror above the dressing table before which she sat reflected soft green walls, the purple-and-orchid chintz of hangings and cushions, glints of light cast by lamps on the gold of book bindings, the silver of candlesticks and boxes. It reflected also Billy, as he sank to the couch, plumped elbows on his knees, and plunged his boyishly rounded chin in his hands; the dog as he dropped to the rug beside him, laid his nose on a dusty shoe and gazed up with wistful brown eyes into his master's troubled face.

"Gee, but I'm glad you're here, Gail."

"So am I, Billy." As she looked at the dejected figure she knew that no matter how tempted she was to leave, her job was here. "What's on the little mind, pal?"

She watched him in the mirror while she buffed the rosy enamel on her nails. He clasped his hands behind his head and stretched out his long legs.

"It's that nitwit, Cissie-Lou."

Gail's heart plunged to her gold sandals. What was the self-sufficient Cissie-Lou — properly christened Cecilia Louise — up to now?

"She's exasperating, Billy, but it's a phase. She'll outgrow it. You shouldn't call your sister a nitwit. You know you adore her."

"Sure, I think she's the berries; but if she knew that, there'd be no living with her. I've got to keep her feet on the ground, haven't I? She wows the lads and knows it. She's so darn smart in school. Gets all A's while I have to grind my brain to the bone for a C. 'Tain't fair. She thinks she knows it all. She can't be told. That kid's making a fool of herself, Gail. You and I've got to stop her."

Gail remembered herself at fifteen. Motherless, fatherless, with an inheritance which had seemed a fortune to her inexperience, but which hadn't proved sufficient for her education. A's had come easily for her. Also, she had been allergic to suggestions from interested relatives the summer she had spent in this very house with her brother's family.

"What has Cissie-Lou done that is troubling you, Billy?"

"Will you think I'm a heel to tell tales?"

"Certainly not, pal. Her father has no time to check up on her, her mother is in service, you are the man in her family, it's up to you — if it's serious — to look out for her. Spill it."

"She's meeting that Croston guy on her wheel Saturday afternoons and going riding with him. Gosh knows where they go."

"*Mark Croston!* He's head of one of the departments at the Works."

29

"That's right, and one of your stags. Had a hunch he was carrying the torch for you. Why's that glamour-pants playing round with a kid not sixteen yet? She's nuts about him, just the way she was crazy about Greg Hunt — gosh, he's a captain now, isn't he? — when she was little, always telling him he must wait for her so she could marry him when she grew up. That was okay. He and the rest of us thought it was a joke, besides, he's like one of the family. This is different, she's older and ought to have more sense."

Billy's throat contracted in a sound suspiciously like a sob. The setter rose to his haunches and licked the boy's hand.

"Nice fella, MacArthur." He smoothed the dog's silky ear. "Gee, Gail, we've just *got* to do something about it."

Mark Croston bicycling with Cissie-Lou! Gail visualized his lean, dark-skinned, clean-shaven face, his inscrutable but brilliant hazel eyes, his patrician nose, the flash of perfect teeth between red lips — she'd have to hand it to his smile. He was tall and straight, a sophisticated man-about-town from the West Coast who had been deferred from the service because of his technical training. He had come to fill a responsible position in the Clifton Works.

He knew his job from A to Z. Not to be wondered at that he fascinated Cissie-Lou. She, herself, had fallen for his charm. But why was he spending time on a young girl? It wasn't that he meant to do her any harm. He wasn't that type.

"He's such a darn snappy dresser," the boy flared. "He makes the fellas in her class at High look like thirty cents. Gosh, can't you think of *something* to do about it, Gail, not just sit there like a bump on a log? Talk to her like a Dutch uncle. That ought to do the trick."

"Not the way we want it done, Billy. It would send her hell-for-leather after him. She resents any suggestion from me, told me the other day that I had no right to dictate to her. I wasn't dictating. I was trying to save her from disappointment. I'll think of a way to handle this situation — just give me time. Meanwhile, don't say anything to her — promise."

"Okay, I'll give you a chance, but if you don't put something across darn quick I'll make a try if I have to punch Croston's pretty face. Who's coming, Mac?" The dog was standing motionless. "Look at him, Gail. Keen as they come. He heard someone. I didn't. There's the front door. It's Cissie-Lou's slam. I'll scram. If that

31

hard-boiled kid finds me here she'll smell a rat."

He departed with incredible speed, the setter close on his heels. Gail heard a voice in the lower hall and Hilda's in answer, then someone running upstairs.

"Come in, Cissie-Lou," she called.

The girl stopped and leaned against the doorway in the dramatic pose of a fashion model. Her short hair was a mass of gold curls. Her large eyes were too deep for purple, too light for amethyst; her mouth was young and sweet in spite of a smear of scarlet lipstick; her face was heart-shape. Her hands were lovely, the almond-shaped nails accented with pale rose enamel. She was tall for her age, with no suggestion of lankiness. Gail suppressed a groan of dismay. Why did she have to be so beautiful with only an aunt and young brother to look after her?

"What do you want?" Cissie-Lou's voice, a combination of sulkiness and suspicion, held a hint of music.

"Want?" Gail's laugh was a triumph of will over anxiety. "Nothing, except to ask how the election for the basketball team went."

"I'm captain, of course. I'm getting pretty sick of this kid High stuff. I don't see why I can't go away to school. You did at my age."

"But I hadn't a home like this or a father and mother."

"Lot of good Mother is to me. I'm working my head off selling bonds, taking a Nurses' Aide course and a mechanical course, so when I'm sixteen I'll be all set to drive an ambulance. You can't think I'm unpatriotic when I say that First Officer Mildred Trevor's place is in the home, even if she and Dad did battle every morning because he hadn't accepted that appointment in the big New York hospital."

"Cissie-Lou, you shouldn't repeat private conversations between your father and mother."

"Private! Nothing very private about a breakfast-table fight, is there? Look at Dad." She gave her flair for the dramatic its head; her voice was drenched with tragedy. "Getting thinner and thinner, whiter and whiter, eyes sinking deeper and deeper in their sockets, being worked to death and no one but you to look after him. That doesn't mean I don't think you're good, but you're not Mother." A sound, not unlike the sob Billy had swallowed, contracted her lovely throat.

Gail's heart glowed. The child wasn't hard-boiled. She was vulnerable where her father was concerned.

"You and I must do our best, Cissie-Lou, to keep him rested and happy. Let's conspire. How about a picnic supper by the brook Saturday? We'll leave the receiver off the cradle after office hours and we'll kidnap him if necessary."

"Saturday. Heck! I've got a date."

Mark Croston and a bicycle trip? Was there a way to break that up? There was. Gail wondered and decided in the same breath.

"Too bad, but perhaps Billy and I can manage. It won't be the same for your father, though. You're the light of his eyes, Cissie-Lou. That means that you have the power to make him very happy or hurt him horribly."

"What do you mean by that?" The question was sharp with suspicion.

"Just what I said, nothing more. How about Saturday?"

"Perhaps I can change my date. I'll try."

"Fine. If we go, I'll turn over my turquoise pull-over and cardigan to you. In them, you'll look like a blue-and-gold dream biking."

"That nifty outfit? To keep? Will you

really?" Gail wondered that her ribs didn't crack under the girl's crushing hug. "You can be super when you're not trying to boss me. I'll knock his eyes out in that — Dad's I mean, of course."

"Better get ready for dinner. It's Petunia's night out and when Hilda is cook we have to be on time."

"Or else. I get you. I'm off."

" 'From the time he joined the Army,' " she sang as she raced along the hall to her room.

Gail appraised herself in the mirror. Eyes, not quite black, not quite brown, between long, sooty lashes. Nice nose. Mouth a trifle large, the upper lip a so-called Cupid's bow. The Trevor chin, which in spite of the silly dimple proclaimed that when the owner started for a thing she didn't admit defeat. Cissie-Lou had a chin like that, she reflected, as she pulled two flame-color zinnias from a vase on the dresser and stuck one in her hair and one in the belt of her mimosa yellow frock. She made a little face at her reflection, which set a deep dimple in each cheek putting on its act.

"You've been told you were a knockout in the turquoise outfit, yourself, gal," she reminded the looking-glass girl, "but if it will break up that Saturday date, it's well sacrificed. Who's ringing at this hour, I wonder?" She picked up the telephone on the bedside table.

"Doctor Trevor's house . . . Mrs. B.C. — okay, Aunt Jane, then — your voice sparkles with carbonation — I *know* that your captain is back. Saw him this afternoon. Something to write home about in that uniform, I'll say . . . I'd love it — I'll be waiting. You were lucky to get Mark at such short notice, he's the answer to every girl's prayer in this town where most of the men are in the service. Good-by."

She thoughtfully cradled the phone. Mrs. Benjamin Clifton was asking a few friends in for contract this evening to meet Greg and wanted her. If she could come Mark Croston would call for her, she had said.

That arrangement appeared divinely designed to fit in with her plan. When he came Cissie-Lou would be in the living room. It would give her the chance to slip the first thin knife-edge of suspicion of the man's sincerity into the young girl's mind. Why was he meeting her? The question pricked like a thistle.

She entered her brother's room to open the bed, lay out his pajamas and slippers as she did every night. She looked up at the portrait of a lovely golden-haired woman above the mantel.

"Darn you, Mildred Trevor, why don't you stay at home and take care of your family?" she muttered under her breath before she ran downstairs in answer to the imperative summons of the Chinese gong.

Chapter 3

To refrain from reference to his return to the Works was putting a tremendous strain on his Aunt Jane, Greg realized. During dinner repressed excitement had kept the silver sequins on her ample gray bodice a-quiver. Twice she had been on the verge of leading up to an exultant announcement. Twice her white-haired husband had broken in to derail her train of thought. Now that coffee had been served he would relieve the strain by luring Lila into the garden to tell her of the sudden shift in the plan of his life.

What would she say to it? He thoughtfully regarded the girl in a frosty white dinner frock, seated in a low chair, hands clasped about one knee, looking into the fire. She was lovely. Soft brown hair, parted in the middle and drawn smoothly back into a knot at the neck; skin creamy as a gardenia, a faint touch of pink on her cheeks; perfect nose; clear blue eyes — her mouth, he'd have to admit, had stubborn lines. She had carried on the big summer place as well as the Washington apartment since her parents' death. She would have to be determined, to do that. They were both in the top-bracket-luxury scale. She was like a cool, remote goddess until she smiled, the result was a light at which many men, he among them, had singed their wings. Apparently it left Aunt Jane cold. When he had asked her to invite Lila to dinner tonight she had exclaimed, "*Not Lila Tenny? You're not in love with her,* I hope."

"What's the verdict, Greg? Will I do?" Lila Tenny inquired. "You've been staring at me for the last three minutes." Her low voice lacked vitality.

Her questions set the color burning under his bronzed skin. He laughed and rose.

"Sure, you'll do. That's what I want to tell you. Come into the garden, Maude. How soon are the card-players due, Aunt Jane?"

Mrs. Clifton glanced at the jeweled watch on her plump wrist.

"In half an hour. Gail will be on time. B.C. says she's always on the minute — think of the years he put up with the late Sarah Grand, strolling in when she got good and ready. A new department head at the Works, Mark Croston, is bringing her.

Joe Selby and his sister, Patricia, are coming. He's new, too. He'll be your —"

"Come on, Lila." Greg interrupted his aunt before she could complete the sentence which would reveal the fact that he was back to stay. "Shout when the party is on, Aunt Jane."

A three-quarters moon was spot-lighting paths and flower beds in the garden, turning the water in the lily pool to a shimmering mirror and the white wrought-iron chairs and benches to silver filigree.

"Heavenly night," Lila exclaimed. "Smell the petunias."

"Will you be warm enough?"

"Yes. Glad to be cool. The day has been hot for mid-September. Rather inconsiderate of Mrs. B.C. to ask people in for cards your first night at home, isn't it?"

Of course she was thinking only of him, but Greg resented the implied criticism of his aunt.

"It's her way of killing the fatted calf. She's celebrating my return to civies."

"Greg! What do you mean?" She caught the pocket of his tunic and drew him nearer. "You haven't been cashiered from the Air Force?"

"Not quite so bad as that. I —" he caught back the information that he was

40

needed in the production end. "The fact is, Lila, that — that my heart is a little too tricky to be at the controls of a Flying Fortress. The only other job for which I am as well trained is here at the Works. So, I'm back like a bad penny."

"Greg, it isn't possible. There must be some other way in which you can serve. It would be a crime to take you out of that uniform — you're stunning in it — after the time you've spent earning it."

"It has to be the Works, Lila. I'm sick with disappointment but nothing can be done about it." With tender hands on her shoulders he drew her toward him.

"There's just one thing that makes the change bearable. We can be married and start a home here. All right with you?" He bent his head to kiss her. She twisted free.

"It is *not* all right with me. I intend to be the wife of an officer in the service stationed in Washington, where my interests are, not of a factory department head in this stuffy town for the duration — that's what you'll be. As for saying nothing can be done about the change, that's piffle. Of course some other way of serving can be found if you go to the right people."

"But I don't want another way found. Linc Channing, who took my place when I volunteered, is gone. Now I'll take it again."

"Either one of the new department heads, Croston or Selby, can fill it. I know influential men in Washington. I'll take it up with them. *I'll* find you something."

"No dice, Lila. I'll manage my own life. I take it from the preceding protest that my matrimonial plan goes definitely out the window with my uniform?"

"Temporarily, not finally." The smile for which she was famous drew no response from him. "We'll let the matter rest for the present, Greg, darling."

"No, we won't. You'll answer now. Will you marry me? Yes or no?"

"You've acquired a hands-up-or-I'll-shoot manner with your aviation training, haven't you, Captain?" Her laugh was charming. "How can I answer such a vital question right off the bat, as it were?"

"You knew before I enlisted that I loved you, wanted to marry you. You've had time since to think it over. This is your last chance to acquire one fine young man, warranted steady, perfect digestion, if slightly damaged as to heart, sunny disposition when things go his way and a master mind for remembering birthdays and anniversaries. Yes or no? Going, going —" The gravity of his eyes belied the lightness of his voice.

"Silly." She leaned against him and tipped back her head in invitation. "Of course it is 'Yes.' Doesn't this, quote, 'fine young man,' unquote, I have acquired intend to seal the bargain in the usual way?"

He kissed her and was shocked to realize that the pressure of his lips on hers had left his heart and pulses unstirred, they were jogging along at their accustomed beat.

Had he grown away from her? Had he become another person in this last year, a person with a different sense of values? Probably her disappointment and protest at the change in his plan of life, and the fact that she had expressed no anxiety about his tricky heart, had dimmed the rapture he had been led to believe swept through a man when his girl said, "Yes." He drew a ring from his breast pocket.

"Here's something tangible with which to seal it." The large, round diamond shot out a myriad iridescent sparks in the moonlight as he slipped it on her finger. "Like it?"

She held her left hand with pale, lacquered nails at arm's length and regarded the ring.

"Y—es. Not as modern as an emerald

cut, but it's all right. Shall we tell them when we go in, Greg?"

"All right" was the only praise she could find for a stone which the jeweler had assured him was perfect.

"Why not? We're engaged, aren't we?" A terrified sense that he was balancing on the brink of a precipice stopped his heart for an instant.

"I love you, Greg," her low voice started it quick-stepping.

"Greg—gy!" His aunt's voice stalled his response.

"Okay, Aunt Jane," he called back. "Come on, Lila. Let's get the card party over. We'll talk plans when I take you home."

From the threshold of the living room he took stock of the two new department heads. In these times, particularly after the discovery that imperfect parts for planes had gone out from the Clifton Works, it was imperative that there should be no flaws in the personnel. The tall, dark-haired man, with the cocky lift of his head and the hint of lordly superiority in his smile as he talked to Gail Trevor, probably was Croston. The other newcomer was the old-young-man type. Bone-rimmed spectacles with heavy lenses which masked the eyes behind them; shiny billiard-ball effect in the middle of his thatch of coarse, sandy hair. A determined mouth and aggressive chin made up in strength for what his nondescript nose lacked. The white frock of the pretty red-haired girl beside him was as immaculate as the shirtfront showing between the lapels of his dinner jacket was crumpled.

"Greetings, Greg," Gail said as he crossed the room to her.

He had only time to think how glowingly lovely she was, grown-up, before his aunt asked: "You haven't met Mr. Croston, have you? Mark, this is Gregory Hunt, our nephew, known at the Works as G.H."

"Glad to meet you, Croston." Greg turned to the other man. "Joe Selby, I assume."

"Right the first time, Captain Hunt. This is my sister, Patricia. Now you've met the whole family."

"Too bad there isn't more of it like you two," Greg said and meant it. Croston was all right, looked as if he might be tops at any job he undertook, but he was definitely of the what-a-big-boy-am-I type. Gail had better watch her step if she was falling for him. He was flattering her with his eyes, there was a hint of caress in his low voice when he spoke to her.

"May I tell them now, Greg?" his aunt whispered. "I'm so happy to have you back, whole and for keeps, that I want to shout the news."

"Let them have it," he said. Her announcement would give him a chance to watch its effect on these two men, each one of whom may have hoped he would be picked to fill the position left vacant by Linc Channing's death.

"Greg is out of the service. He has come back to the Works." Jane Clifton's voice quavered with excitement.

"The King is dead! Long live the King!" If Selby was disappointed he was putting on a convincing act. His voice and grin destroyed any suspicion that his plans had suffered a setback. Croston's face registered shock, dark anger, a flash of suspicion before he got it under control.

"What happened, Captain? Been a bad boy that you've been discharged from the Air Force?"

"Greg! Bad! Don't be silly, Mark. He —"

"Something here in need of rest and repair." Greg tapped his left breast as he interrupted his aunt's indignant protest. "A pilot with a faulty engine can't be trusted to take up any kind of plane." Not until victory could it be known that WPB had ordered him back. Otherwise, it might put whoever was responsible for those faulty plane parts hep to the fact that they had been traced to the Clifton Works.

"That's a mean break." Croston's expression of sympathy was convincing.

Jane Clifton clutched Greg's arm. Her large eyes filled with tears that ran over, her plump chin wobbled.

"You never told me you had heart trouble, Greggy. I thought —"

He patted her shoulder.

"Didn't want to worry you, Aunt Jane. My heart may not be sound enough for a pilot but it's plenty good for a manufacturer. I asked B.C. to put my return on the ground that I am needed here. I'll admit I'm sensitive about having been reclassified 4F, not physically fit to serve. Even with that handicap I asked Lila to marry me a few minutes ago. She said 'yes.' Congratulations for me are in order."

He cut short the exclamations that followed his announcement. The good wishes didn't ring true. Was it because he, himself, hated his deception?

"Let's change the subject to cards. How shall we play, Aunt Jane?"

"You and Gail, Greg. B.C. and Lila,

47

Miss Selby and Mark, Mr. Selby and I. How's that?"

"Perfect for me," Joe Selby agreed heartily. "I've heard it rumored that you're tops at contract. Mind if I call you Aunt Jane?"

Mrs. B.C. indulged in a soft chuckle.

"Leave off the Aunt and make it Jane, *Joe*." She wrinkled her button-shaped nose at her husband and proceeded to cut the cards.

Greg and Gail were alone at the other table as he drew out her chair.

"In her youth Aunt Jane was what was then known as a 'trainer,' " he confided.

"I can believe it. She is adorable and has a heart as big as the universe."

"And prejudices as immovable as the Rock of Gibraltar."

"Maybe, but she's a pretty keen judge of human nature. Quick, before Mr. B.C. and Lila come. Is it true about your heart?"

He looked straight down into her earnest eyes.

"For present purposes, *yes*. Get it?"

"I get it. I understand that it is to be known that you left the service because of disability. But — not why you want that reason given."

"Stop wondering. Remember, you're a

48

confidential secretary. Don't ask questions. Be a good little girl and I'll promise to take any fish off your hook that gets troublesome."

"Why so cryptic? I haven't a hook and I haven't a fish."

"No? How about Croston? He hasn't taken his eyes off you since you sat down at this table."

"Why should he?" She dimpled in the way he remembered. "Am I something nice to look at in this mimosa yellow frock — or am I?"

Before he could answer Benjamin Clifton and Lila took their places at the table.

"For a man with a tricky heart — that was the word, wasn't it — you look remarkably vital and — interested, Greg, darling," Lila observed, and cut for deal.

Chapter 4

"How long have you known that Captain Hunt was leaving the Air Force to come back to the production end of the game, Gail?" Mark Croston asked as they were walking home under a sky silver-gilt with stars.

She remembered Greg's direct look into her eyes, when she had asked, "Is it true about your heart?" His voice as he had answered, "For present purposes, *yes*. Get it?"

That meant that neither he nor B.C. wanted it known that the WPB was behind his return. Why? Did they suspect there was a subversive element in the factory? That couldn't be. Only last month the Army-Navy E pennant had been presented to the Clifton Works in an impressive ceremony.

"You're taking your time answering my question," Mark Croston reminded. There was a hint of petulance in his voice. "Hope you're not as slow on a comeback in the office?"

"Me! Slow? I'm a ball of fire, *Mister* Croston. I was thinking how sick with disappointment Greg must have been when he was pronounced 'defective.' He is so keen about flying it must have put another crack in his heart to resign from the Air Force."

"Apparently the glamorous Lila rendered first aid to the break. That engagement was a bomb, too. Altogether, I'd say the evening suffered a news-blitz."

"You've been playing round with her a lot, haven't you? Don't tell me that the 'blitz' shattered your hopes of heaven and matrimony with the devastating Lila?"

"No, but I think Greg Hunt is in luck. Don't like her, do you? Watch out, Gail, or you'll get catty."

"I know it, oh, I know it, Mark, and I hate myself every time I scratch like that. It isn't that I dislike her, it's just that she never rings quite true to me. I used to be considered rather a nice kid — 'sweet' was the word as I remember it. I had heaps of friends in college. But this horrible war — the heartbreak in the world — which I seem to be doing nothing to help —"

"Where do you get that *nothing?* You know that B.C. would part with his right hand before he would let you go. There are five secretaries under you, but he won't allow any one of them to take his dictation or do his telephoning. Right? He couldn't accomplish half he does if you didn't run ahead like a steam roller and smooth the road for him. Sure you didn't know G.H. was returning? It seems unlikely he would make such a drastic turn-about in his plans without consulting his uncle."

Was his quick change of subject designed to trap her into revealing what he suspected she knew?

"Perhaps he did. I wouldn't know. I never open Mr. B.C.'s personal correspondence. Even had I known, I wouldn't speak of it. I'm proud of my job as secretary to a man so important to war matériel production. What's a confidential secretary for if not to clear the road ahead and make sure there are no leaks through her employer's office? Why are you so concerned about Greg's return? It won't make any difference in your job?"

"You never can tell. Something in his eyes as they met mine for the first time told me he didn't like me. He may put the skids under me. Why worry? Plenty of other jobs I can have. Forget it. Perhaps the engagement surprised you, too?"

"Believe it or not, it *did*." Gail was relieved at the switch of subject. The reason of Greg's return was shell-pocked ground, his love affair offered no such hazards. Mark mustn't suspect that the announcement had blacked out the feeling that something especially nice was ahead that had glowed in her heart since she had seen Greg this afternoon.

"G.H. has been in the service over a year and since I've been in town Lila has been reported 'that way' about half a dozen men — all uniformed, nothing lower than a major in rank," she observed lightly. "She's the possessive type. He will have to go her way — or else. It doesn't seem possible that she will settle down with a man in civilian clothes — even so grand a person as Greg Hunt."

"How do you know so much about him?"

"I don't, as he is now. Except for a few days at a time I haven't seen him since the summer I was fifteen when I made my headquarters with my brother John. After that I rarely spent vacations here. Usually I had a summer job. He was nice to me and I adored him. I compared every boy I knew to him and they didn't measure up. I must have bored him to tears. I shiver now when I think how I proclaimed my convictions on any subject on the earth or under it, whether I knew anything about it or not. Remembering that know-it-all stage of my existence helps me to understand and sympathize with Cissie-Lou's delusions of importance."

She hadn't intended to mention her niece but now that she had inadvertently led up to her, this was an opportunity to find out what was behind Mark's attentions to the child. She had been sulky and taciturn when he had tried to make conversation with her in the living room a few hours ago.

"Cissie-Lou is a cute trick. She snubbed me tonight — and how. Wonder why? Give her her head for a while. I've watched her this summer. She handles those eighteen- and nineteen-year-old boys who park on the Doctor's porch like a veteran glamour girl." His indulgent laugh roused Gail's indignation.

"She isn't a glamour girl, she isn't quite sixteen, she's a youngster with a flair for the dramatic, a remarkable voice and an overgrown sense of her own importance. Mind if I sob out my troubles on your shoulder — figuratively speaking? Her father is too loaded down with the problems of birth and life and death to be burdened

54

by them; I've just got to talk to someone."

"Go ahead. Spill it. What's she been up to?"

Was there a hint of alarm in his voice?

"She's been taking bicycle trips into the country Saturday afternoons with a man old enough to know better than to play around with a girl her age."

"Who tipped you off about it?"

"A little I-think-you-ought-to-know bird."

"Did the bird, female of the species indubitably, mention the man's name?"

"No, but he had better watch his step. It was one of those tiny acorns of whispers from which mighty scandals grow. A married man was indicated."

Her misstatements — a more comforting word than fibs — ought to prick her conscience, but they didn't. She was right not to let Mark suspect she knew it was he encouraging romantic dreams in a young girl's mind.

"The man's a fool — probably nothing worse — having a little off-the-record fun with an adoring schoolgirl."

"You can laugh about it, I can't. I know too well how a girl Cissie-Lou's age will dramatize the most ordinary events of life, imagine into voice and words something which isn't there."

"Did you learn that the summer you 'adored' Greg Hunt? That's your own word, remember."

Gail was grateful that the light was too dim for him to see the sudden color that flamed in her cheeks in response to his caustic question.

"If I said 'adored' it was because I regarded Greg as I would a father. I had recently lost mine. I poured out my troubles to him. He would listen and advise as gravely as if they were matters of world-shaking importance. My dream man that summer was a lanky redhead, who called me 'woman' and permitted me to wash his car while he sat in the shade and smoked countless cigarettes."

"Have you taken up the subject of this clandestine romance with Cissie-Lou?"

"Good heavens, no. It would make the matter of too great importance. She'll snap out of it. Someday she'll see a youth in uniform and look back with an indulgent smile on her 'rave' — that's the current word — over an old codger whose hair is doubtless thinning."

She set her teeth in her lips to repress a smile as he smoothed back the hair above his right ear. She filled her lungs with the aromatic air.

"Gorgeous night. That's almost a bombing moon." She shivered as back into her mind swept the tragedy of the battered, battling, bleeding world. Why, why couldn't she do more to help? As if his mind had touched hers Croston asked: —

"What do you hear from your first officer?"

"Enthusiastic letters. Feels that she is serving her country. Perhaps she is. Perhaps I'm all wrong to think that at this moment she should be in my shoes looking after her husband and worrying her head off about her daughter. Let's switch to another station, Mark. I set the ether boiling when I fare forth on that air lane. I've talked enough about my family. Tell me about yours."

"Haven't much of a family to talk about. A mother, that's all."

"Does she live alone? Doesn't she miss you frightfully?"

"Yes, to both questions. She doesn't moan about it, though. She works for the Red Cross, is an Air Raid Warden; now she writes that she is taking a Home Nursing Course."

"Good for her. I considered that last, but decided that Nurses' Aide would fit into my free time better. Is your mother as sensationally good-looking as her son? Subtle,

I calls that last question."

"Thanks for the orchid. I think she is beautiful. She has . . . What's the use trying to describe one's — mother? Sometime I'll show you her picture. Why this sudden raking the leaves of my dear, dead past?"

"Your voice sounds as if you resented it. I had been chattering about my family and its problems, I thought it fair to give you a chance. Here we are. Will you come in?"

"No. Took home some plans from the Works to look over. The Doctor's car is in the drive. I'll scram. He's probably dead-tired, it will be an effort even to say 'Hello.' Good night, Gail."

"Good night, Mark."

Even as she spoke her thoughts were on the man whom she could see through a window, standing with a letter in his hand.

She ran up the steps into the house. On the living-room threshold she stopped to ask eagerly: —

"News?"

John Trevor's face was gray from weariness, his deep-set eyes, dark as her own, burned into her heart as he offered her a page of the letter.

"Read this. Our first officer is a bit peeved that neither you nor I were sufficiently interested to go on to see her receive her commission."

"*Interested!* How could we go?"

"We couldn't. Results have shown that the armed forces can strengthen their fighting ranks if women take over noncombatant duties and free the men. I'm all for it — in some cases — but if ever there was a time when wives and mothers are tragically needed on the home front, it is the present. As I go my rounds every day I am more and more impressed by that fact. Found four-year-old twins, tied up in a yard, today. No one around. Mother and father both working in a factory."

"Poor little things. I wish I were twins so that I might be in two places at once, I could help more."

"You're doubling as it is, Gail. It takes a terrific load from my mind to know that Cissie-Lou and Billy have you to turn to. The twelve-to-seventeen-year youngsters are bewildered emotionally as they are pushed in this turbulent, adult world, into work for which they have no educational or vocational training, in many cases with more money to spend in a week than they've had before in their whole lives. They are in tragic need of affectionate guidance and sympathy from their mothers to help them understand themselves and their problems. They are the hope of the world when this global blitz is over. There is a faint hint in this letter that Mildred may be ordered on overseas service."

"Johnny! She can't go! She can't leave you and the children."

"She thinks she can. She's coming home on leave. I wonder if it ever occurs to her that I might like to break away, shed this growing load, stop just for a little while playing first aid to the stork, folding the hands of the dying, keeping up an incessant fight against the spread of disease among people who *won't* take proper care of themselves?" The fire died from his eyes and voice.

"Sorry for that kid outburst, Gail. Forget it. You know and I know that I wouldn't give up this job for any other on earth. I've had plenty of chances." He brushed his hand across his eyes and picked up his coat. "Don't look so distressed. I'm feeling fine after getting that off my chest."

"You're not going out again. You're too dead-tired. Who wants you?"

"Mrs. Craven on the hill left word I was to come no matter how late. She gets panicky about herself. The Gray baby made its entrance in nonstop speed so I'm home earlier than I expected."

"Have you had anything to eat?"

"Now that you mention it, there's a hollow feeling within that tells me I haven't." He sank into the capacious chair she pushed behind him. "Rustle up something for me, will you? I'll wait."

She shaded the light as he dropped his head back against the chair and closed his eyes. When she returned with a laden tray he was asleep. Her eyes filled with hot tears, as she noticed the gray in his dark hair. She gently placed an afghan over his knees.

You're working for others every minute and no one to look after you, she thought, as she noted the deep lines of weariness and care between his nose and eyes. Memory echoed Hilda's strident whisper: —

"The Craven woman is after Doctor John . . . I don't wonder . . . She's the kind who gets her man."

Not this time. Gail tiptoed into the office and dialed. A woman's crisp, authoritative voice answered: —

"Mrs. Craven speaking."

"A message from Doctor Trevor. He has been detained on a serious case and won't be able to see you tonight."

Her sense of a good deed done was out of proportion to the prick of guilt, she decided, as she soundlessly cradled the receiver. If John's need of rest to keep him fit for his life of incessant service wasn't serious, what was, in this darkly shadowed world?

Chapter 5

"Billy Trevor, you's keep yo' fingers off that choc'late cake," Petunia Judson scolded.

The boy tweaked the colored woman's bright orange apron and gave vent to a laugh of young-animal exuberance. "Keep your shirt on, Pet, I haven't hurt it." He departed from the kitchen whistling with earsplitting shrillness, "I'm a Yankee Doodle Dandy."

"Mis' Gail, you sure look swell in them dark green pants an' matchin' shoes. Ain't yo' blouse what's they call 'shockin' pink'? It's scrumptious, sure is."

Gail glanced up from the picnic basket she was packing at the big, handsome woman who was placing a round chocolate layer cake tenderly in a box. Some quality in the rich, negroid voice set merry-pranks cavorting along her veins. Was this a build-up to the announcement of an approaching marriage?

"Ah's got something Ah want to tell yo', Mis' Gail. Ah's leavin' here in a week or two, soon's there's a defense job ready."

"Petunia! You can't leave. Think how Doctor John needs you. Think how important you are in preparing his meals when he comes home tired."

"Ah knows that, Mis' Gail, Ah don't know how's he'll ever get along without mah choc'late cake, but, Ah has a call to work for mah country. If Ah doesn't, folks'll think Ah's a no-'count."

"How can you work better for your country than to stand back of a man who is keeping hundreds of men and women who are making parts of planes for our fighters well and on the job? He's the only doctor in town, remember, and now he has taken over the hospital work."

"Ah know Ah's important here, but mah friend Magnolia — she's at the Works — has a nice little apartment an' she says if Ah comes to live with her we'd get along fine an' have big pay."

"It will cost you to live. You get a room with bath, board and good wages here. Have you thought of that?"

"Ah has, Mis' Gail. Magnolia, she's a powerful heavy eater an' uses up money fast, but Ah'll take a chance. Ah's sick of housework. Ah want to be free to come an' go, just as Ah please."

Petunia's words echoed and re-echoed

through Gail's memory even while she laughed and chatted on the way to the brook. They recurred as she laid used paper plates on the smoldering coals of the campfire. The voices of her brother and his children, the rustle of leaves they were poking in search of nuts, drifted from the woods.

She poured water on the hot ashes. Repacked the hamper. Dropped to the mossy ground and leaned back against the trunk of a massive oak which towered above the brook like a sentinel. A maple leaf, light as a scarlet feather, twirled down and settled on her dark hair. Minarets of asters. Flames of sumac and maple. Spicy fragrance of balsam. Music of flowing water. Purple columns of smoke rising from the coals. A world so beautiful it made her throat ache.

Her thoughts returned to the practical problems of Petunia. If she departed, who would do the cooking and housework? It wouldn't be easy to fill her place. House-workers were almost an unknown quantity in a town where most of the women who worked outside the home had factory jobs. Would it be one more task for her to take on? She had the sudden sense of smothering helplessness she had experienced as a child when a tent had collapsed on top of her and she had struggled frantically to get free. Petunia shouldn't be allowed to leave her flat. She must stay.

The late afternoon picnic had been a success, her thoughts trooped on. Cissie-Lou had teased and beseeched her father to devote just a little time to her and Billy. When two days ago the girl had jubilantly announced, "All set for the cookout, Gail? Dad's coming," she had answered: —

"That's grand. Hope your Saturday date wasn't peeved at being thrown over?"

Cissie-Lou's chin had come up, her violet eyes had darkened. In the best tradition of cinema drama she had explained loftily: —

"He's ancient history. Poor old duffer — he was pretty smooth but he always had to play it his way. Do I get the turquoise outfit?"

She had worn it with white slacks this afternoon. Her father's deep-set eyes had been tender with adoration as he looked at her and teased: —

"Isn't that rig new, Cecilia Louise? You're almost as delectable in it as the chocolate cake Petunia makes for me. Do I detect an approaching request for an advance of your allowance to pay for it?"

"No, It was a present from a friend."

Later John had said: —

"You are the 'friend' who gave that outfit to Cissie-Lou, aren't you, Gail? Don't spend your money on clothes for her, you'll spoil her."

He couldn't know, she thought, as she watched the faint violet mist of sundown veil a distant hill, that she would have sacrificed more, much more, than a turquoise pullover and cardigan to break off the girl's Saturday afternoon date. He had compared his daughter to Petunia's cake. Suppose, just suppose Petunia departed. There would be no more cakes like that — unless she herself made them — awful thought.

No voices now; only the splash and gurgle of the brook, the shrill of tree toads and the chirp of crickets stirred the air, tangy with the scent of wood-smoke. There must be dozens of purple finches tilting on the branches of the white birch across the stream as they made a stopover on their migration south. That aspen towering above the balsams quivered like gold leaf, if she watched it long —

"Remember me, sleepy head?"

Her eyes flew open. They blinked in unbelief as the laughing face bending over her materialized out of a haze.

"You, Greg? Out of uniform and into gray tweed so soon? I wasn't asleep."

"I know, you were just resting your eyes, as Aunt Jane does after dinner. Why the dickens won't a woman acknowledge that she has dozed?" He dropped to the ground beside her.

"Page 'Information Please.' Now that I've come back with that snappy answer, I'll ask one. Why are you here? This is Dinner and Dance night at the Club. How did you escape your ball and chain, Lila?" His quick look at her sent the color to her face. "Catty," Mark had warned her. What had happened to her that her tongue had become edged?

"She is in Washington. Even if she were here I'm allowed my freedom occasionally."

"You and Petunia. 'Ah wants to be free to come an' go as Ah please.'"

"Don't tell me that stand-by is straining at the leash. She's been at the Doc's for years. Whatever would you do without her?"

"You're asking me! Let's forget it. She may change her mind. It has been known to happen. Why are you here?"

"Expect you and Cissie-Lou will be set to slay me when you know that I've come for Doc."

"Greg! You haven't! We three had planned to lure him to the pictures. Must he go?"

"He'll have to decide that. Louis Pomponi's son has had a bad fall."

"That fat, greasy timekeeper's boy?"

"Greasy he may be, fat he undoubtedly is, but remember that Louis is one of the best men on that particular job we have."

"I know it, but — I hate the man's eyes. How did you know he needed John?"

"He called the Doc's office. Hilda Speed said her boss was away for the evening and refused to say where. Then Louis in desperation came for me; I've helped him out before. I faced the lioness in her den. Made Hilda give."

"You must have hypnotized her. Here they come. Listen. They're harmonizing 'God Bless America.' Cissie-Lou gets her lovely singing voice from her father. You don't know what a load rolls off my shoulders when John laughs, and when he sings the wings of my spirit unfold and take off. Why, why isn't his wife here to look after him instead of leaving it to me?"

"If you don't watch out, Gail, you'll get twisted on the subject of Mildred. Could be. In staying with Doc and keeping on at the Works you're doing what seems right to you, aren't you?"

69

"That's a dumb question. Would I be here otherwise?"

"Mildred is doing what she thinks is right. It isn't, from your point of view; it's infernally wrong from mine; but — give her a break and for Pete's sake don't let it sour you."

"Am I getting sour, Greg? It's an awful thought. From now on, I'll be sugar-sweet."

"Don't be too sweet. I don't like too much sugar."

"You're hard to please, aren't you? Help me up. I've sat here so long I'm cast."

Quite unaware that they stood hand in hand they watched John Trevor and his children, singing lustily, come through the green shadow between the trees. Cissie-Lou's arm was linked in her father's. On the Doctor's other side Billy was beating time with two sturdy broken branches.

The girl was the first to see Greg. Her voice and feet stopped. She tightened her hand on her father's arm.

"If you've come to take Dad to some poisonous patient, Greg Hunt, he isn't going," she flared.

John Trevor's smile faded. Gravity replaced laughter in his dark eyes.

"Hold everything, Cecilia Louise. Did you come for me, G.H.?"

Greg explained, concluded: —

"You may be mighty sure that if the boy wasn't desperately hurt I wouldn't break into your outing, Doc."

"You don't have to tell me that. You and I have worked together over your people too many years for me not to know you from A to Z. Come on, youngsters."

Greg turned as they walked single-file along the trail and caught Cissie-Lou in the act of making a face at him. He stopped.

"So, that's the way you feel about me, sister, and you the gal who used to beg me to wait for her till she grew up?"

Cissie-Lou tossed her head till every curl quivered like the golden leaves of the aspen.

"You didn't wait, did you? Went right ahead and got engaged to Lila Tenny, and now you come butting in on Dad's party. I'm sore."

"Cecilia Louise, you're talking to my best friend, remember."

"I know, Dad, but Gail and Billy and I had a plan to take you to the movie this evening."

"Sorry to break it up, Daughter, but I have a job, remember." They had reached a side road and his sedan parked beside a maroon convertible. "G.H., will you take my family home and save my time?"

"Sure, Doc. I'll take Gail and Billy to the early picture, and a snack at the Club after. I'd like to include you, Cissie-Lou, if I thought you didn't dislike me too much to —"

"Don't be silly, Greg." She was a queen granting a royal pardon. "I canceled an important date this afternoon to play with Dad. I don't intend to be left out on a limb. Of course I'll go."

"Not in slacks, Cissie-Lou. Give the Trevors ten minutes at the house, Greg, to change to what is now known as don't-quite-dress clothes. We wouldn't be admitted to the Club in these."

"Okay, Gail. Wear that yellow thing you had on the night I came home and keep that red leaf in your hair. I like it. Pile in, kids."

The picture had been a convincingly acted chiller with breath-holding suspense, enough comedy to relieve the tension and a finale that sent the audience home in a right-will-triumph mood.

Entering the Club was like stepping into another world. It was brilliant with light, fragrant with the perfume and powder of women in colorful frocks, murmurous with voices and the music of violins and flutes wired in from a central station. As Greg drew out her chair at a round table Gail confided: —

"I feel as if I had emerged from Stygian darkness into the clear light of life, liberty and the pursuit of happiness and the worst of it is, those horrors we saw are true." She shivered.

"You take your movies seriously, don't you?" He took the chair beside her. "What will you have, Cissie-Lou? That pale blue dress makes your eyes look like amethysts in contrast. Go as far as you like. Same to you, Billy. Unless advancing years have killed the hanker, I know that Gail's order will be orange juice with soda. Right?"

Before she could answer, Mark Croston leaned over her. "You said you were devoting this evening to the Doctor, Gail," he reminded sulkily.

"Come on, Billy, let's dance." Cissie-Lou fairly pulled her astonished brother to his feet.

"Gosh, Cis, lay off me. I've ordered a chocolate fudge sundae with marshmallow and *nuts.*"

"It won't run away. Come."

Mark Croston looked after them. His

eyes came back to Gail.

"It is painfully apparent that I'm in the doghouse with your niece. Wonder what I've done she doesn't like?"

Gail wondered too, but she said: —

"Cissie-Lou has views on bringing up Billy. He hates to dance, she thinks he should — consequently he dances when he can't escape."

"She's got the modern slant. Boss the male of the species and make him like it. Come on. This music is too good to miss."

"Not this dance. Gail is here as my guest," Greg Hunt reminded. "She will dance with me first."

"My mistake, boss. How does Miss Tenny like your playing the field?" Croston demanded before he walked away.

"How about it, Gail?"

Curious thing, anger, she thought as she rose; it had reddened Mark's face, it had whitened Greg's until his usually blue eyes looked black in contrast. As his arm went round her she said: —

"Don't mind Mark, Greg. He gets that way if he is crossed. He had some justification for being annoyed. He asked me to come with him tonight and I told him I intended to devote the evening to my brother."

"Are you apologizing for *him*? Arrogant

devil. That's 'My Wonderful, Wonderful Love' they're playing isn't it? You waltz like a dream. Your rhythm is faultless. How's the Nurses' Aide course coming?"

"I have earned my certificate. Now I shall be able to help John in my free time. *Free time!* I forgot. If Petunia leaves there won't be any."

"Let's get out into the air. This room is stuffy."

"For a minute only. Cissie-Lou and Billy will come back to the table and wonder where I am."

On the porch she leaned against a pillar and looked up. "Perfect night. The air is clear as crystal, yet velvet-soft against my face."

He frowned at her above the light he was holding to his cigarette.

"Never have that family off your mind, do you?"

She laughed.

"But, it's such a nice family to have on one's mind. I love —"

"Gail! Gail!" Billy called breathlessly before he reached her.

"What is it, pal? Has anything happened to your father?"

"Jeepers, no. Keep your shirt on. It's Cissie-Lou. She told me that glamour-pants would take her home. I caught her giving him a come-on."

"Have they started?"

"Just going out the door when I made a break for you. We've got to break it up. I don't know what she sees in the guy. What's he got?"

Gail caught Greg's arm.

"Come on, we must stop them. We can catch them this way."

She pelted down the steps, Billy on one side, Greg Hunt on the other.

"I'm all for rescuing a damsel in distress, lady, but will you explain what is up and who goes by the salubrious title of glamour-pants?"

"Mark Croston, Greg. You could see he was furious with me, couldn't you? He is taking Cissie-Lou home to annoy me. He knows I have been worried because she has been meeting him on her bicycle."

"Every Saturday afternoon, the nitwit," Billy cut in angrily. "There they are. She's getting into his super platinum-gray roadster. Hurry!"

Cissie-Lou forgot her woman-of-the-world pose and looked like the frightened youngster she was when a compelling hand was laid on Mark Croston's shoulder. Had a guilty conscience caused

Mark to stiffen under his touch, Greg wondered? Was he secretly putting on a romantic act with a fifteen-year-old schoolgirl? Incredible.

"No can do," he reminded lightly. "She came with me. Get out of that car, Cissie-Lou."

Croston attempted to shake off the fingers digging into his shoulder.

"Stay where you are, Cis. G.H. isn't your guardian. Be a sport. Be independent." He put his foot on the running board. A firm hand drew him back.

"No dice, Croston. Come on, Cissie-Lou." Greg's voice was low and persuasive. "You can't walk out on my party like this."

"Greg is right," she admitted and stepped to the ground with the air of a Queen Elizabeth descending to a red carpet. "I am his guest. Good night, and thanks for the invite, Mr. Croston."

The four stood watching the roadster as it shot ahead. Greg Hunt ran his fingers under his collar as if it had tightened suddenly.

"Cissie-Lou, can't you see that he's merely using you to get back at Gail?" he demanded. "He was burned up because she turned him down this evening for your father and was telling her off. Don't let

77

him fool you. Besides, it isn't cricket to snitch another girl's beau."

Even in the dim light Gail could see the color sweep to her niece's hair, see her blink her long, curved lashes, swallow hard before she declared: —

"Do you think I am so dumb I didn't know he was playing me against my aunt? It has been fun to fool him. Perhaps you think it's cricket for *you* to snitch another man's girl. You brought Gail here tonight, and from what you've just said you knew she was Mark's, didn't you?" She slipped her hand under his arm. "Now that you've spoiled my fun I'll take a chocolate fudge sundae, marshmallow with nuts. Better eat them while the going's good. There's a rumor ice cream is to be rationed."

"Make it two," Billy said. "How about you, Gail?"

The cloyingly rich concoction was a little more than she could bear but in the interest of harmony Gail agreed with convincing enthusiasm: —

"Make it three, Greg — that is, if I'm included in this party." She could see the lines deepen between his eyes as he looked at her. "What's the matter? Don't you w-want me?" Would he notice that silly break in her voice?

"I was wondering if Cissie-Lou was right, if I had snitched another man's girl. . . . You needn't answer. I'd rather not know tonight. Let's go."

Chapter 6

Gregory Hunt stood at his office window in the late afternoon watching the trees bend and writhe. The day shift was pouring out into the court to the distant accompaniment of the whir of machinery, punctuated by the shriller key of rivets, and shouts of laughter as the wind sent hats spinning and bounding like dry leaves in a breeze.

September had blazed and dimmed into the golden russet of October since his return. The Russians were still battling in defense of Stalingrad. Long days of oratory in Congress. Having been granted an extension of time it was still fighting for and against the anti-inflation bill. The uniform of the soldiers at the gate had changed from khaki to olive-drab. From time to time came a rumor that a paratrooper had been seen descending in a township and the inhabitants would turn out *en masse* to hunt, with no results.

He had been back at the Works three weeks and he had not as yet the faintest hint as to the person or persons responsible for those imperfect plane-parts which had been partially responsible for the crash of three bombers. Cautiously, without rousing suspicion, he had examined every piece of that type of mechanism before it went on to the next worker with the explanation that he had been so long away he needed a refresher course. All were perfect. Perhaps his return had made the saboteurs cautious for a while. He answered the interoffice phone: —

"Okay, B.C. I'll be with you in a minute."

He stopped to lock papers into the desk drawer before he passed through the conference room which connected his office with his uncle's, and from which stairs descended to a private entrance. It was furnished with a large table, chairs, couch, cellarette and a lavishly stocked smoker's stand. Benjamin Clifton looked up from a newspaper as he entered.

"It's happened again, G.H."

"What has?" he asked, more to gain time in which to think than because he didn't know.

" 'Five more die as bomber crashes.' Cause unknown."

"Don't look so cut up, B.C. It may not mean imperfect mechanism this time. There's bound to be a certain number of

81

crack-tips as the government expands in air personnel and equipment. Much of the time planes are landing or leaving at the rate of one a minute. Think of the automobile crashes in the years before gas rationing. No one suspected faulty mechanism was the cause. The public calmly accepted the shocking number of deaths and attributed them to fools at the wheel or jay-walkers on the highway."

"Maybe you're right, Greg. You haven't found any flaws as the parts came through?"

"Not a flaw. Whoever did the dirty work either is lying low or has moved on to another field of treachery. Don't worry. We'll get him. Meanwhile, B.C., take it a little easy."

"Easy, with our boys all over the world clamoring for tools with which to fight? How can I take it easy when my heart and soul are in the factory pushing every minute of the time?"

"Sure they are, so are mine, but where will production be if you give out? We send our workers to Florida for winter vacations at our expense when we think the grind is beginning to wear them down. Why not be as good to yourself and let up? I'm here now, fairly bursting with energy — in spite of that heart, the trickiness of which, something tells me, is doubted in certain quarters."

"What do you mean?"

"I have a feeling that Joe Selby suspects I was recalled by the WPB and that Croston knows it."

"How could he?"

"Your confidential secretary handled the correspondence. Croston is the number one stag in her line. I have seen indications that he had hoped for my job after Linc Channing passed out. He's tops in his work, but he's cagey. He might have lured information from her without her realizing it."

Benjamin Clifton spoke into the inter-office phone.

"I want you, Miss Trevor."

"Hey, B.C. Take it easy. I only said that Gail might have given the information unconsciously and —"

"And what information would I give unconsciously, Mr. G.H.?" the girl asked as she closed the door and approached the broad desk beside which the two men were standing. Her mahogany wool frock belted in emerald green accentuated her slenderness. If eyes could burn, hers would have drilled red-hot holes through his.

"Hold everything, Gail. We'll lay our cards on the table. I had told B.C. that sometimes I thought Croston doubted that heart trouble had been the reason of my return to the factory and —"

"Then you said, 'Gail might have given the information unconsciously.' I didn't. Mark Croston has never, since the evening of your return, mentioned it. If that's all, I'll get back to work."

Benjamin Clifton flashed his nephew a now-see-what-you've-done look.

"That ends that, Miss Trevor," he appeased. "Since you have been in my employ I have had no reason to doubt your discretion. G.H. and I are only trying to make sure that there are no leaks in a job which is growing in importance hourly."

The smile which lighted her dark eyes and tipped up the corners of her lovely mouth passed over the younger man and shed its warmth on his uncle.

"You couldn't be unfair if you tried, Mr. B.C., every worker in the factory knows that. Also, they think you're a miracle man."

"Thank you. That's all, Miss Trevor."

Greg followed the girl into her office and closed the door.

"See here, Gail."

"Miss Trevor to you in business hours, Mr. G.H."

"Okay. Now that I've been put in my place stop fooling with those papers and listen." He sat on the corner of the flat desk, selected a red chrysanthemum from the vase on it and drew the stem through the buttonhole in the lapel of his gray coat.

"Snappy effect, what?" He discarded the light touch. "I won't permit a misunderstanding to last between you and me, Gail. I know you are true as steel but in these times information is lured from a person without that person having the faintest idea he or she is giving it."

"And you think the fact that you returned to the Works because of a WPB order has been lured from me, by Mark Croston? It hasn't and never will be. Why would he want to know?"

"I've had a hunch he was expecting to move up as first vice president of the Works when Linc Channing passed out."

"If he did he never has given me so much as a hint of it, Greg."

At her friendly use of his name a load slipped from his shoulders. She had been such a companionable, adoring kid, he couldn't bear to have suspicion and dislike estrange her now.

"Then that's all right. Has Croston been worrying you about Cissie-Lou again?"

"No. Her Saturday afternoons have been devoted to leading her basketball team to victory and much of her free time to practising for the USO concert."

"You give too much thought to that family, Gail."

"Tell me how to give less and yet do what I should to help and I'm all for it. Miss Petunia Judson departs to become a career woman next week. To date I haven't found a person to take her place — except myself."

"Don't tell me you've added housework to the job here."

"With Hilda and Billy and Cissie-Lou to help. It isn't the work, it's the catering and cooking that give me pause. I haven't had experience in planning meals. It's a challenge. I can do it. Wait till you see the rainbow-plaid cotton I've ordered for K.P. duty." One of the three telephones on her desk rang.

"Miss Trevor speaking — Good heavens, Hilda, he is? All right, I know it's your evening off. I'll get there as soon as possible. Tell him to stay in bed." She cradled the receiver.

"Billy is home after a thirty-mile trip on his wheel to a rodeo. He had to pedal back against a high wind. Too many cokes and chocolates added to that have laid him low. If you wish to render first aid, suppose you return to your work and let me tackle mine, so that I may get home to the invalid?"

"It's a brush-off, I'll go." He lingered while Gail answered the interoffice phone.

"He is. I'll tell him." She looked up. "Miss Tenny is waiting in your office."

"Why is she here? She knows I object to social calls in business hours," he protested and hurriedly departed.

Lila, in a moss-green velvet suit with gilt buttons as big as plates in a doll's tea set, turned from the window as he entered.

"I wish you wouldn't keep me waiting, Greg." A minor strain of martyrdom tinged her voice. "My time is valuable if yours isn't."

He thought of the long days he put in at the Works and grinned.

"Mine isn't entirely on the playboy side. Sit down." He drew out a chair for her and faced her across the desk. "Have yourself a time in Washington?"

"I didn't go for what you call a 'time.' I went on business. I've arranged it, Greg." There was an uncharacteristic tinge of excitement in her voice.

"Arranged what?"

"Don't snap. Arranged your transfer from the flying force to the ground force of aviation — and a major's commission!" Triumph in the last sentence.

He cracked down on his temper. This was no time to give it its head.

"That was mighty efficient of you, Lila. But, as I told you the night I came home, it has to be the Works."

Anger deepened the faint pink in her cheeks.

"I've put in hours with influential men getting the commission for you, Greg. You can't let me down now."

"Sorry, but I'm here to stay."

"What will I say to the officers who have helped me? I even had an interview with a consultant in the Secretary of War's department. You will consider it for my sake, won't you?"

"Pos-i-*tive*-ly no, Lila."

"Mark Croston wins," she declared petulantly.

"What do you mean?"

"He bet me a spray of green orchids against a dollar war stamp that you wouldn't leave the Works."

"Have you talked over my personal affairs with a man in my employ?"

"Why not?" Her mouth settled into the

stubborn line which so detracted from the beauty of her face. "The fact that you left the service because of physical disability and returned to the Clifton Works isn't exactly a secret — or is it? I'm going, but don't think for a minute I've given up the fight to get you back into uniform, Greg darling; I know what I want and I *always* get it." She administered a patronizing pat on his cheek and departed.

He backed against the door he had closed behind her and swore under his breath. She had started trouble with a capital T. No knowing where the trail might lead. Had Croston bet those orchids to make Lila a little more determined to win her point, with a view to stepping nimbly into the position vacated by the newly commissioned major? A neat trick — if it worked. This time it wouldn't.

He answered his secretary's voice on the interoffice phone.

"A woman to see me? What does she want? Looks white? Seems desperate? A son in the service? All right, send her in."

Now what, he wondered — a mother trying to get her son off the firing line into the production end, while Lila was working to get her fiancé out of production onto the firing line? The situation had its humorous angle if you were in the mood to appreciate humor. It happened he wasn't.

"Come in."

He was shocked out of thought of personal affairs by the ravaged face of the white-haired woman who entered and closed the door behind her. She came forward blindly with outstretched hands. He sprang forward as she swayed, caught her arm and led her to a chair.

"Sit here, madam. I'll get you a glass of water." She caught his sleeve in black-gloved fingers.

"No. No. I'll be all — right in a minute." Terror clouded the large dark eyes imploring his. "Promise, promise you won't let any — one — know — I'm here until I tell . . . No — one . . . danger . . ." One hand clutched at her left side. Her head fell forward on the desk, her hat slipped off.

For a split second he stared down at the white hair, at the colorless face. What did it mean? Why didn't she want it known she was in his office? He spoke softly into the phone.

"Gail. Come quick. Don't let anyone know where you are. If you've got any smelling salts for heaven's sake bring 'em."

He pulled off the black gloves and rubbed the unconscious woman's slender hands. There were a gold wedding ring and a solitaire diamond on one finger, he noticed.

"I don't own smelling salts," Gail said as she entered. "I've brought aromatic spirits of ammonia. That —"

"Lock the door," he interrupted.

"Who — who is she?" she asked as she saw the huddled figure. She gently raised the white head and loosened the collar of the woman's amethyst crepe blouse.

"Darned if I know. She tottered in. Begged me to promise not to let anyone know she was here, whispered 'Danger,' passed out and frightened the life out of me."

"We'd better move her to the couch in the conference room. Be quick. She must have had an important reason for not wanting it known she was here. She may have come to warn us of treachery in the Works. We're at war, remember."

Greg picked up the unconscious woman and carried her into the adjoining room. Gail snatched off the couch pillow.

"Lay her flat. That's better. Fill a glass with water. That short, hard breathing means a heart attack. As soon as she regains consciousness we'll give her a sip of ammonia."

91

When he returned with the glass Gail was bathing the woman's face with a handkerchief soaked in water. He tried to figure what it was all about. Could she possibly know of those imperfect plane parts? Had she come to warn them of sabotage? Her eyes opened, they were black as obsidian as they met his.

"I'm sorry — to make a scene." Her voice was a faint whisper. Memory returned. She tried to sit up, fell back. Laid her hand over her heart. "It will — stop pound—ing in a minute. It always has. Does anyone — know I'm here?"

"No." Gail slipped a pillow under her head. "Only Mr. G.H. and I and we're the original tight-lips. You're quite safe with us."

"Quick. A tablet — in my bag."

"Your bag is not here, madam," Greg said. "You may have dropped it in the other office. I'll look —"

"No. *No*. It will take time. Not a minute to waste. Give me a sip of ammonia, it is ammonia I smell, isn't it? Anything to keep me braced till I — tell you." Gail held the glass to the blue lips.

"That's — better." She sat up slowly. "Now, if I can — hold my — mind steady — until —" Her voice died away. Her eyes closed. Gail laid an arm about her shoulders.

"Rest against me. That helps the breathing, doesn't it?"

"Thank you." Her eyes were enormous in her white face as she looked up at Greg. "I must talk fast. I — I came here to see my son — who — who was sent to fill an important position in the Clifton Works."

In his mind Greg ran over the names of the men in important positions. There were fifteen, at least. Whom did she mean?

"We haven't much time," the faint, labored voice hurried on. "There's treachery, somewhere. My son's letter made me uneasy. I can't explain — just why. They didn't ring true. He wrote he didn't want me to come — here — at present. So — unlike him — he loved to be with me. I wondered if he were deceiving me about his position. He made me promise before he left not to tell my friends where he was going." She closed her eyes for an instant, clenched her fingers as if to gather strength to go on.

"I imagined he might be out of a job and — didn't want me to know, perhaps — might be — hungry. I came to this factory — today, without letting him know I was coming. I told the soldier guards at the gate whom I wanted to see — they wouldn't let me in — I hadn't realized I would need a pass — one of them said, 'Here comes the man you want now. He'll identify you.' " She put her hand to her throat as if struggling for breath.

"I looked. The name was right, but he wasn't my son —" She rallied her weakening voice. "Something warned me not to speak. I tried to smile, I — tried to say lightly, 'He isn't the man I want. I — I must have the wrong factory.' Just then an army truck drew up at the gate, two soldiers jumped out — and the guards who had stopped me — climbed in, I had been forgotten. I slipped into a doorway and made my way into this building, determined to find someone who would know about my son. I wandered through the corridors — dodging out of sight when I heard footsteps. Saw 'vice president' on a door. I — didn't — know — what — to do. I — only knew I must — get — help." Her eyes were wide with anguish as, hand on Greg's arm, she drew herself to her feet.

"Something is terribly wrong. This *is* the right factory. Someone is pretending he is my son. Sabotage? The man I saw has taken his place. Why? *Why?* Where is my boy?"

Greg laid a tender hand on her shoulder.

"Take it easy, madam. Tell me his name. We'll find him."

"His name! I told the guards — Didn't I tell — you? His name — is —" Her voice trailed to a whisper. Her hand clutched her side. With a long, shuddering sigh she swayed. Greg caught her before she fell and laid her on the couch.

"Look after her, Gail, while I go for B.C."

His impetuous entrance startled his uncle. He hurriedly told what had happened.

"Either the woman is plumb crazy or we have a lead on the source of those faulty plane parts," he concluded.

"We can't take a chance that she's crazy, G.H. We'll assume for the present that she knows of treachery. She didn't give a hint as to the son's name?" Benjamin Clifton's voice was hoarse with anxiety.

"She collapsed before she could get it out. She spoke of a bag. There must be something in that to tell who she is. If there isn't, we'll call in our FBI man. Come on."

As he followed his uncle, he visualized the woman as she entered his office. She had held out both hands as if groping her way. She had had no bag.

"She's still unconscious," Gail said softly as they entered.

"Find anything to tell who she is?"

"Nothing, Mr. B.C. Not money, not even a handkerchief in her pocket. She may have dropped her bag when she dodged the guards. I can't rouse her. I'll send for the infirmary nurse, then try for John."

"Not yet, Gail." Greg caught her hand outstretched to the box on the desk. "If her story is true — B.C. and I have reason to think it may be — it must *not* be known by *anyone* that she is here. The infirmary is out for the present. There's a possibility that the lives of dozens of airmen may hinge on keeping secret what she came here to tell. Call the Doc. We'll get hold of our secret agent. Try once more to rouse her. She may regain consciousness long enough to tell that name. We must get it."

The faces of the two men were lined with anxiety as the girl bent and laid her hand tenderly on the woman's shoulder.

"Come back just for a minute to tell us —" she implored softly. She leaned closer. Straightened. Awe clouded her eyes and hoarsened her whisper.

"She'll never tell now. She's dead!"

Chapter 7

"Hiya! Anyone home?"

Gail twisted round on the bench in front of the dressing table in her room and smiled at the boy and red setter in the doorway.

"Enter my lords. Billy, you might whisper to Mac that there is something on the table I brought home especially for a good dog when he comes to call."

Billy opened the crystal candy-box and grinned.

"Gee whiz! Are these whoppers really chocolate patties or are they an optical illusion?"

"They are real. I bought something large, plump and handsome, knowing Mac's taste and his master's."

"Gosh, I love 'em. Quit drooling, Mac. You'll get yours when you sit up like a gentleman and ask for it." He bit off half of the enormous chocolate, waited for the dog's sharp bark and tossed it to the expectant setter, who caught it deftly.

"That's the stuff. Charge. You've had all

that's coming to you. Quit teasing now."

He stretched out on the purple-and-orchid chintz couch, stuffed a pillow under his head and balanced the candy-box on his stomach.

"Why the war paint?" he inquired through a full mouth. "Stepping out?"

"Right the first time, pal. Dinner and dance at the Country Club." Gail critically regarded herself in the mirror as she clipped rhinestone studs to her ears. "How do I look?"

"Like an outsize poppy with headlights in its ears, if poppies have ears. It's a cinch you'll pass. I'll bet the guys drop their marbles when you walk in. I like you in red, Gail, and I'm sure sold on the cute red feather in your hair." He grinned at her reflection. "I guess you're the woman in my life, all right." His fingers dived into the crystal box. With the other hand he pushed away the dog.

"Nix, Mac. Keep your wet nose out of this. Lie down. Don't you know when you've had enough?" The red setter flopped to the floor and regarded his master through grieved brown eyes.

"Might it be barely possible that you also have had enough, Billy? Far be it from me to drag up the Painful Past but remember the rodeo, my lad."

"Heck, it was the fifteen miles back on the bike against a terrific wind that made me sick as a dog, Gail. I'm chock full of bounce now. I'll never forget that day. I thought I'd be blown off my wheel."

Neither would she forget that day, Gail told herself. She lived over the moments of that same afternoon when Mr. B.C., Greg and she had waited tensely for the arrival of the FBI agent who would tell them how to keep secret the fact that a strange woman had died in the conference office at the Works, a woman who had warned them of treachery. Neither would she forget the man's lean, dark face, his hawklike nose, the wing-shaped black brows and the steel darts which took the place of pupils in his eyes.

His men had taken away the body so quietly that its removal seemed nothing short of magic. Now they were trying to find out whence she came, for whom she had inquired. The soldiers who had questioned her at the gate had departed that very night, destination unknown. It would take time to track them down. Meanwhile, B.C.'s blue eyes were clouded with anxiety and the lines between Greg's brows had deepened. No wonder, with the uncertainty as to whether the woman's story that an impostor was filling her son's responsible position was true, or just a delusion of a mind unhinged by the tragedy of the world.

"Jeepers, life's just one problem after another, isn't it, Gail?" Billy's dejected question derailed her troubled reflections. "What d'you know about Petunia's walking out on us tonight? Found anyone to take her place?"

"No one except myself. I've advertised. Not one answer. You'll have to be my first sergeant, my top kick, Billy."

"Sure, I'll help, so will our snooty Cissie-Lou, or I'll know the reason why. Does Pop know Pet's leaving?"

"Not yet. Why tell him? He'll notice the change in cooking soon enough."

"You should worry. You haven't a real trouble on your mind."

Billy's somber voice switched her thoughts from planning tomorrow night's dinner. He jerked himself erect and sat with elbows on his knees, chin in cupped palms.

"What is it this time, Billy? Not Cissie-Lou again?"

Her voice betrayed panic. She had been so sure that Greg's interference when

Mark had invited the girl to drive home — his suggestion that she was being used to punish her aunt — had hurt Cissie-Lou's pride, that she had written off that complication.

"Nix. I guess glamour-pants gave her the quick brush-off after that night at the Club when G.H. put on the big-brother act. Perhaps she beat him to it and left him flat. Could be. She's a smart kid. Anyone with half an eye can see he's that way about you, and she has two outsize ones on the job every minute. Nope, 'tisn't that. Do you think a fella ought to give up every darned thing he loves to his country?" He cleared his throat noisily.

"What's troubling you, pal? Let me help." Gail sat on the couch beside him and laid a sympathetic hand on his sleeve.

"It's just — I don't know what I ought to do. Mother's in the service, that's okay, even if this outfit was like a haunted house till you came. Pop's never here, always off somewhere doing his part keeping folks well. I've cut out cokes and ice cream sodas to buy war stamps. I've legged miles and lugged tons collecting tin and scrap. I've picked apples till I can't bear the smell or taste of one and now — and now —"

"And now what, Billy?"

The boy's eyes were wide and troubled as they beseeched hers.

"The Government wants dogs to train. Do you think — I ought to give up Mac?"

As if in answer to his name the red setter laid a paw on the boy's knee and looked up at his master with his heart in his eyes.

Gail's throat tightened as she looked from boy to dog. It was a frightening question to answer. If she advised him wrongly it might be one of the mistakes that never could be undone.

"I don't believe it is necessary yet, Billy." His long ragged sigh of relief set tears in her eyes. "Later, it may prove to be one of your 'austerities' — that's the word used in England to express a sacrifice or self-denial which aids the war effort — and you'll square your shoulders and accept it. Why don't you take Mac to the firehouse in the village where the men are training their own dogs in obedience? They might take him as a pupil. Then if he is needed in a branch in the service he will have had some training. Who knows? He may earn a commission in the dog's army."

"Gosh, you've said something." The boy's face was radiant. "I'll do it. Mac's so keen I bet he'd get to be a General like the crack-a-jack soldier he's named for. You're

102

practically in the army now — the home army — young fella." From the doorway he looked back at the girl on the couch. There was a suspicious glitter in his eyes.

"You sure are swell, Gail. Every man needs his woman to tell his troubles to. You're mine. You've got what it takes to boost a guy out of a hole of worry."

Billy's words recurred to Gail later as she was dancing with Mark Croston at the Club and saw Gregory Hunt standing in the doorway. Lila Tenny, in a pale blue frock starred with silver, apparently was arguing with him, for her cheeks were a bright pink and her eyes were brilliant as if with anger.

Was he hearing her voice? His eyes were smoky gray as if his thoughts were far away from the music and lights and the girl beside him. Had anxiety clouded them? Anxiety as to whether a man with an assumed name was filling a responsible position at the Works or whether the story had been the delusion of a mentally unbalanced woman? If only she could boost him out of a hole of worry as she had boosted Billy.

"I'm beginning to believe that G.H. really got out of the Air Force because of his heart," Mark Croston confided close to her ear. "I'll admit I doubted it at first, but this last week his face has looked bloodless under the bronze, as if he were on the way to a physical crack-up."

"He *can't* be! He mustn't let go now of all times," Gail protested passionately.

Croston held her off and looked down into her eyes, his own narrowed in suspicion.

"Anything wrong at the Works I haven't heard of?"

She'd better watch her tongue. Hadn't Greg intimated that she might have given Mark information, unconsciously?

"I'm not clairvoyant," she countered gaily. "How can I know what you've heard? You department-headers get your orders long before I hear of them. You —" Gregory Hunt tapped her partner's shoulder.

"My turn, Croston. I like girls in red frocks — myself."

"Hope I didn't speak out of turn," he said as Mark walked away frowning. "Your special boy-friend growled like a dog who's had a nice juicy bone snatched from him."

"He isn't my special boy-friend," Gail corrected as she fitted her steps to his in waltz time. "And what's more, I object to being likened to a juicy bone even if it's a nice one."

His eyes were no longer smoky gray, they

were blue, lighted with sparks of laughter.

"Pretty choosy, aren't you? Let's get out of this. I have something to tell you."

The windows on the glass-enclosed porch were wide open.

"Too cold for you?"

She shook her head. "I love the cool air." She sniffed. "Smell the pines. Quick, before anyone comes. Have you found out the identity of the mysterious visitor?"

"No. But a woman's black handbag was picked up in the court."

"Really, G.H.? What was in it?"

"Nothing."

"*Nothing?* Not a card or a handkerchief — or a lipstick? Didn't they even leave the heart tablets?"

"Nothing. We've figured that in her excitement when the guards changed the woman dropped it, that either a worker picked it up, stripped it and tossed it aside, or that the man she claimed was impersonating her son — you remember the guard had told her he was approaching — found the bag, realized who she was and destroyed all evidence that would identify her."

"If the last supposition is true, the woman was telling the truth, she wasn't a mental case."

"Have you thought she was? I wish to

God I had. We've got to find out whom she came to see or we'll have more men disappearing. What became of the son the woman was following up? Was he put out of the way? Did a saboteur slip into his job? You'd suppose her relatives would be breaking their hearts with anxiety as to her whereabouts, but no white-haired woman has been on the Missing Persons list. Our secret agent, the FBI man, checks daily."

"If a saboteur is impersonating the son he must be uneasy at the cessation of her letters. Why can't the agent move faster?"

"He has to go slowly. He must be sure of his facts or he might scare the quarry and the build-up back of him into flight. 'Who was she?' — Since the night the woman was carried from the office the words have been going round and round in my mind like a squirrel in a cage. I was selfish enough to try to stop the whirligig by telling you. Instead of that I've frightened you and spoiled your evening."

"You haven't frightened me and the evening hasn't been spoiled. I am as eager to solve the mystery as you are. Even if my job at the Works is but a small part of something of tremendous importance to the nations at war, it's a part. If there is treachery there I'll help run it down."

"Keep out of the mess. It's work for our secret agent and me, not for a girl."

"Don't be selfish, Greg, and try to keep all the fame and glory of discovering a fifth columnist to yourself." Her earnest eyes belied the teasing gaiety of her voice. "We're up against the sort of melodrama on which best-selling spy thrillers are built and you want to keep me out. Try it, that's all, just try it. Please let me help? Why don't you answer? I believe your thoughts are miles away, that you haven't heard a word I said."

"I have." His eyes were a burning blue as they met and held hers. "You want to help solve the mystery. Okay, but you'll take orders from me, understand?"

She raised her hand in salute.

"Yes, Captain. What shall I do, first?"

"Have supper with me? Let's forget tragedy and mystery for a while."

"I came with Mark, but, even if I hadn't, Lila wouldn't like it."

"She has departed, angry because I have again refused to accept a commission."

"What's the big idea hiding out on me?" Mark Croston demanded as he stepped out of the shadow near a window.

Gail's heart stopped beating for an instant and plunged on. How long had he been there? What had he heard?

"We were coming in to look for you," Greg Hunt answered before she could rally to reply. "Mind if I join your table? My girl has walked out on me."

"Pleased as Punch to have you, G.H." Croston's voice didn't sound pleased. "Selby and his sister Pat will be there and a pal of Joe's with whom he worked in Washington. Come on."

He tucked Gail's hand under his arm, possessively. She was uneasily aware of Greg following. Had Mark's sudden appearance set him wondering if their conversation had been overheard?

She was still preoccupied with the question when they stopped beside a table in the supper room. Two men rose. The action derailed her train of thought and brought her back to the present. She nodded to the redheaded girl in sequined black.

"Greetings, Pat. Joe, do you realize that you have cruelly ignored me this evening?" Her glance moved on to a tall, lean, dark man beside him. As his eyes met hers, sharp steel points replaced the pupils. Her breath stopped. Her smile froze. He was the secret agent who had been assigned to solve the mystery of the unknown woman. Whom was he trailing here?

Chapter 8

"Miss Trevor, this is Tom Search, my best friend from Washington," Joe Selby presented the man with boyish affection. He grinned as he added, "He's a grand person if a bum reporter. You've met Mark Croston, Tom. The tall, military person at my right is Gregory Hunt, late captain in the Air Force, now my sub-boss. Tom is here to write up the men who make the Clifton Works click, for a big weekly, G.H."

"But not to write up the Works itself, Captain Hunt," Search corrected quickly as the two men shook hands.

Not a sign in either face to show they had met before. What did it mean? Why was the agent here at the Club? Was he on the trail of the saboteur — if there were one? Search . . . Even the immortal Dickens couldn't have selected a more fitting name for a detective. He drew out a chair.

"Won't you sit here, Miss Trevor? Corking music, isn't it?" Did she imagine it or was there a flash of warning in his eyes? She rated it. She had been gazing at him as if hypnotized since making the breath-snatching discovery that he was the man who had directed the magical removal of the body of the mysterious woman. If his name had been mentioned then, it hadn't registered in her tense preoccupation with the tragedy. Her laugh set her pulses quick-stepping and relaxed her taut nerves.

"From Washington, Mr. Search? I have heaps of friends there. I was the buffer between a senator and his constituents for two years and I mean buffer. Sparkling white grape juice for me, Mark, please."

No one at the table could suspect from her gay voice that she had ever before seen the man at her right. She glanced furtively at Greg Hunt. He was lighting Pat Selby's cigarette and smiling as if he hadn't a care in the world.

"Miss the big city of Washington?" Tom Search asked and engaged her in conversation till Mark Croston tapped her shoulder.

"Break it up, break it up. Let's take a turn, Gail."

"Who's the guy Selby sprang on the party?" he demanded as they danced to the music of "You Are My Guiding Star."

"Search . . . I've never seen the name signed to articles in the big weeklies, and I read them all. Wonder if I'll get a write-up as one of the officials who makes the Works click. I rate it. I work my head off."

"You do, Mark. I know that Mr. B.C. appreciates your interest."

"Perhaps he'll boost my salary. Here's hoping. I thought you had discovered a long-lost brother by the way you and the guy from the big city put your heads together and buzzed. Ever meet him in Washington?"

"Never." Gail was grateful for "in Washington." She could answer that question honestly. "He was describing the crowded living conditions in the Capital. They were bad enough while I was there; apparently they have grown worse."

"Now that a ceiling has been clapped on rents they may improve. Ever wish you were back?" His arm about her tightened. "I'm mighty glad you're not."

"That makes it unanimous. Let's return to the table. Joe's friend had begun to tell of a press conference at the White House when you dragged me away."

"Dragged!" He stopped dancing. "That's telling me."

She laughed and tucked her hand under his arm.

"Don't sulk, foolish. You know I love to dance with you — but — you'll have to

111

admit that a man fresh from the august presence of F.D.R. doesn't drop in on this town every day."

"He's gone," she exclaimed as they approached the table.

"Don't cry about it. His departure is all right with me. G.H. has walked out on us, too. Where's your friend, Selby?" he asked as he drew out Gail's chair.

"Had to meet a man at the Inn. That's the life of a reporter for you. Time's never his own. G.H. offered to drive him over. My gas supply is low, so it was okay with me."

Croston held his glass to the light and watched the bubbles in the champagne cocktail rise.

"What's a Washington reporter doing in this burg?" he inquired.

Why was he pretending he didn't know, when he had said that he rated a write-up in the article about the Clifton Works? Gail wondered.

Selby looked at his sister, whose face flushed softly under his laughing eyes.

"Didn't you hear me say he was here in the interest of research? For an additional reason inquire of Pat."

"My apologies. Patricia, and felicitations." Mark Croston was his jovial self once more. "He looks like a regular guy.

He and Gail had their heads together so long I thought he had designs on my girl."

"If by chance you are referring to me, Mark, this is my cue to say I am not your girl," Gail corrected. "Let's go. It's late. I'm a working woman, remember. Good night, Pat. Good night, Joe."

In the car she protested: —

"Don't say again that I'm your girl, Mark, I don't like it."

"If I spoke out of turn, I'm sorry." His sulky reply exasperated her.

"You act more like a spoiled kid than a grown man, sometimes."

"That's what you think. All right, if my attentions are so distasteful I'll transfer them where they will be appreciated."

"To end the discussion: That will be *quite* all right with me."

They didn't speak again until they reached the door of the house.

"Did you mean we are through?" he asked. "If you did I don't believe it. You don't know what you want." He caught her in his arms and kissed her hard and long on the lips.

With all her strength she pushed him away.

"If I don't know what I want, I know now what I *don't* want," she declared furiously. She opened the door, slipped into the hall and closed it quickly. She leaned against it listening to his footsteps on the path, the whir of the starter, the sound of wheels. She scrubbed her lips hard with her handkerchief.

"Was it as bad as that?" a voice from the waiting room inquired.

"Greg! How did you get here?" she demanded from the threshold. Gregory Hunt rose from a deep chair.

"Hilda let me in after she discovered it was you, not the Doctor, whom I wanted to see. Cerberus, guarding the entrance to the inferno, had nothing on her as a watchdog. She said to tell you there were sandwiches in the icebox. How about a little refreshment?"

"Okay, for me, but it's late to be calling on your uncle's confidential secretary, Mr. Hunt."

"Is that a here's-your-hat-what's-your-hurry hint? Just thought you'd like an explanation of Tom Search's presence at the Club tonight, that's all."

"I would, Greg. You know I would. I'm simply dying to hear," she declared breathlessly. "Come into the kitchen. Don't speak in the hall. Cissie-Lou sleeps with one ear open listening for her father." She looked up the stairs and whispered.

"There's a light in Hilda's room. Her door is open. She's sitting up waiting to see that 'Himself' eats something when he comes in. The beloved man — if ever there was one.

"Now, you can talk as loud as you like," she said as they entered the kitchen.

"One might think I was in the habit of yelling." He glanced about the room with its white cabinets, range, icebox and linoleum floor with a big blue star in the center. "Boy, this place looks like a magazine illustration. Very up to the minute, what?"

"The latest word. Mildred had it equipped before she joined the army. She's on the beam when it comes to material things." She flushed under his quick look. "I know that my voice is edged whenever I speak of her, Greg, but when I see John . . . Let's forget it." She opened the icebox. "Milk or beer?"

"Milk." He reached over her shoulder, drew out a plate and raised the large lettuce leaf that covered sandwiches. "Chicken, tomatoes, mayonnaise and lots of each. Suits me fine. I hate a skimpy filling."

Gail set glasses, plates and paper napkins on the white enamel table.

"Bring them here, then look in that tin box on the shelf."

"Fudge layer cake." He broke off a corner and ate it. "Boy, that's perfect. The cook must have heard that chocolate is to be rationed, and frosted that while the going is good. That wasn't made with corn syrup or whatever it is they use. Where'd you get the sugar?"

"Petunia keeps the rest of the family on short rations that the Doctor may have the cake he loves when he comes in late. What do you think he'd do to a patient if he caught him or her eating that rich concoction at eleven p.m.? All set?" She faced him across the small table.

"Tell me, quick. Is Search really here to write up the personnel of the Works? When I saw him tonight surprise sent my heart into a nose-dive. Is he a friend of Joe Selby's?"

"Not only that, he's in love with Pat. That's why he asked to be assigned to us. The afternoon I phoned we needed him was his first day on the job."

"Joe said he was a reporter."

"He is and a good one."

"Doesn't Joe know that he doubles as a secret agent?"

"No. No one here knows but B.C., I, and

116

now you. I'm trusting you to the limit, Gail."

"I'll die before I betray that trust, Greg."

"You needn't go white about it. I believe you. Drink the milk and eat a sandwich while I talk. That will bring your color back."

"I'd rather listen."

"No eaty, no talky."

She laughed and wrinkled her nose at him.

"The Dictator himself." She sipped the milk and cut the sandwich with a fork. "I'm obeying orders. Go on."

"We have one clue to tie to and one only. The woman said her son had come to fill an important position. There are at least fifteen positions which seem important to B.C. and me."

"Limiting it to that number helps a little, doesn't it?"

"There's only one hitch. The boy — or man — may have been bragging. Remember she said he had made her promise not to tell her friends where he was going? He may have wanted his mother to believe he had landed a more important job than that of a riveter or an oiler."

"If he had been a factory worker the guards would have known him by number, perhaps not well enough to call him by name when he crossed the court."

"Boy, you've got something there! That shoots him back among the upper brackets. Search probably had that figured out days ago. He'll have his first interview for the Weekly with B.C. tomorrow, then he'll go down the line."

"You're sure he intends to write us up?"

"He showed me his contract. I suggested to Aunt Jane that if she were nice to him he might write up her community enterprises to relieve the Government of the what-can-we-do-to-help questions by reviving the old-fashioned habit of neighborly help. She's apt to be a little stand-offish about entertaining strangers — suffers from delusions of social superiority, there was a Declaration of Independence Signer in her family, but that got her. He will be invited to dine soon. He's agreed to give the USO concert a publicity whirl."

"That will be right up Cissie-Lou's street. She'll adore it. She really has a lovely voice but some idiot told her she would make a torch singer and she's on the way to ruining it. She won't tell me what song she has selected."

"She'll be all right. She's so darned pretty no one will know what she sings."

"Her father will. She drew a red circle round the date on his calendar and made him promise to keep the evening free. John is so proud —"

"Did I hear my name?" The pantry door swung behind Doctor Trevor. "Greetings, G.H." His tired eyes brightened as they rested on half of the round cake in the center of the white table, his mouth which had been grim widened in a boyish grin.

"Who's been eating my chocolate cake?" he growled.

"We've left plenty for you, Father Bear," Gail assured him as he sank into the chair Greg brought forward. She filled a tall glass with milk and set a sandwich, thick with slices of the breast of chicken, rich red tomatoes and creamy mayonnaise, before him.

"I wouldn't pretend to cut a portion of cake for you," she teased as she resumed her seat. "I've left the size piece to your discretion, Doctor."

He eyed the luscious chocolate concoction hungrily.

"Ah ain't got no discretion, lady, when it comes to cake." Laughter changed to gravity.

"Glad you're here, G.H. Has one of your workers gone AWOL?"

119

Gail's heart zoomed to her throat. Had it come at last? Was John on the trail of the missing son — if there were a missing son? The doubt steadied her thumping pulses. That was the catch. There was nothing to prove — yet — that the woman hadn't been the victim of hallucination. She stanchly resisted the temptation to meet Greg's eyes.

"Not that I know of, Doc." How could he keep his voice so cool when every nerve in her body was tingling from the excitement of a possible clue? "What's on your mind?"

"This is strictly off the record. Looked in on Pomponi's boy tonight."

"Having a tough time, isn't he?" Greg's voice was still cool but the lines between his eyes had deepened.

"His house across the river is distant from his neighbors. I ought to know it, I've brought the last four Pomponis — I'll amend that: the latest four — into the world. I've called there every day since you came for me at the picnic. The boy is very sick — it's a toss-up if he'll pull through. I'm waiting for a vacancy at the hospital to get him there. Tonight when I was bending over him in the bedroom off the kitchen with his tall, angular mother watching on one side and his fat father on the other, I heard what sounded like a groan overhead, I looked up at the ceiling. 'What's that?' I asked.

"I caught the warning look which flashed from Pomponi's eyes to the woman before he said: —

" 'That noise, Doctor? Emilio, he got a sick dog upstairs in bed with him. He's a funny keed.'

" 'A boy's bed is no place for a sick dog,' I scolded. 'Put him out in the garage.' I went on with my examination of the patient as if that ended it. I could feel the husband and wife relax with relief." He helped himself to a thick slice of cake. "Something tells me that a sick man — not a dog — is being hidden there."

Chapter 9

Gail glanced furtively at Gregory Hunt, her eyes two interrogation points. The slight warning shake of his head closed her lips, which had parted to ask a question.

"They may have taken in a tramp for a slight remuneration, Doc — Mrs. Pomponi is greedy for money — and were afraid to have you know it. It is against the rules of the Works for one of our force to lodge a stranger without first reporting to the office all the facts known about him. I'll get in touch with Louis in the morning and start a check-up."

He rose; laughed, as he looked down at the table.

"We've certainly done right by that chocolate concoction. Hope you are at home for the night, Doc."

"Only one call on the phone pad and that patient is not sufficiently ill to need me at practically midnight. No hint intended, G.H."

"Perhaps not a hint but a masterpiece of subtle suggestion. Better come and lock up after me, Gail, to make sure I don't sneak back to finish the cake. Good night, Doc."

As he stood with his hand on the knob of the front door she demanded: —

"How can you laugh and appear so casual after hearing that the man we want to find may be hidden at Louis Pomponi's?"

"Did he hear a dog or a man, Gail?"

"A man, of course. Johnny wouldn't mistake the sound nor would he imagine the interchange of warning glances between Mr. and Mrs. Pomponi. Suppose, just suppose we've found the missing son?"

"Easy does it. We don't know that there really is a missing son. There are nine chances out of ten that the poor woman was mentally upset, which brings us bang against the question, 'Who was she?'"

"You'll follow up John's suspicion, won't you?"

"Sure."

"Will you report the matter to Tom Search?"

"After I've done a little sleuthing myself. It's hush-hush for the present, remember."

"How would it do to let Mark in on the secret? Louis Pomponi is in his department."

"Mark Croston!" His indignant eyes met hers alight with teasing laughter. "This isn't the time to be funny, Miss Trevor. Good night."

He closed the door before she had a chance to assure him that she knew it was not the time to be funny, that she had tried to switch his thoughts for a moment from that "Who was she?" question which he had admitted kept going round and round in his mind like a squirrel in a cage.

When she returned to the kitchen her brother looked up from a letter.

"Why was G.H. here so late, Gail?"

"He was waiting when I returned from the Club." She slipped a gay green-and-white apron over her red frock, picked up plates from the white enamel table and carried them to the sink. "He came to talk to me about something that happened at — the office."

"Where was Lila Tenny?"

"She had walked out on him." She returned to the table. "He made no secret of it so I am not betraying confidence when I tell you that she is trying to make him return to Aviation. She has obtained a commission for him in the ground force."

"If she has begun to arrange his life already, God help him when he marries her." He cleared his gruff voice and tapped the letter in his hand.

"Mildred writes that Cissie-Lou reported Petunia was leaving."

"Not was. Has. She left after dinner tonight."

"Why didn't you tell me?"

"You have enough on your mind. I considered her walkout strictly in my department. She has taken a defense job at the Works."

"She isn't mentally fitted for that. Found anyone to take her place?"

"Not yet. Total war demands the simplification of living. I can manage with Cissie-Lou, Billy and Hilda to help."

"You won't have Hilda. She is needed at the hospital. So am I. It will save a lot of time and coal to keep office hours there. We'll close the waiting room and office here. I should have done it years ago. Mildred hated having patients come to the house, but I liked it because I could snitch a few minutes with the children. I'll get my meals there until you find a maid."

As if they grew on bushes and I could get one for the picking, Gail thought.

"That will help out; something tells me I'm a better secretary than cook, but I can learn. You'll be at home nights, won't you, Johnny?"

"Yes. There's a postscript to Mildred's

letter. 'Tell Cissie-Lou to put two *l*'s in really.' Pass it on to our Grade A student, will you? Don't get overtired doubling jobs."

"I'm never tired. Is the Pomponi boy too sick to eat?"

"That's the trouble, he should eat but he won't."

"Perhaps I can tempt his appetite. Petunia left chicken soup stock. I'll take a jar to him Saturday afternoon and prepare it myself. It won't be the first time I've been a food-ministering angel to one of the Pomponis."

She spoke lightly for fear he would detect her eagerness to visit the house in which, if his suspicions were correct, a man was hidden.

"It's worth a try. The mother likes you and one of the daughters confided to me that my sister was a 'swell dresser.' As I go my rounds among the factory workers I realize how much more influence a 'swell dresser' has than a 'sloppy' one. That's one reason Mildred could have done an enormous amount of good in this town. She is so immaculate in clothes and grooming. We need a day nursery. In a short time she would have had it running like clockwork. If we can keep the little children of workers happy through the day they won't be so affected by their tired mother's alternating moods of shiftlessness and nervous tension when they return home at night. I'm trying to interest Rhoda Craven in the project, but," he laughed, "she doesn't feel the call." He paused on the threshold to regard her with eyes suddenly turned keen.

"If by chance it is curiosity about the sound I heard at the Pomponis' — not good works — that is taking you there — G.H. didn't fool me for a minute — don't allow it to become evident. Good night, Gail."

"Don't allow curiosity to become evident." Gail thought of her brother's warning as she sat beside the old sofa in the room at the Pomponis' which served as kitchen, dining and living quarters. At one end stairs rose to the floor above. The furnishings were worn but immaculately clean.

The October day had been warm as summer and beyond the wide-open door she could see the sparkle of the deeply blue river. An old black and dirty-white, long-haired dog dozed in the oblong of sunlight on the floor, occasionally opening red-rimmed eyes to blink at the boy on the couch. She had bathed Philippe's face and hands, brushed his hair till it was satin-smooth, had shaken up his pillows and smoothed his wrinkled navy bathrobe before she heated the chicken broth and fed him.

"Good work, you've taken the very last drop, Philippe." She turned the thick cup upside down in its saucer to demonstrate before she carried them to the sink.

"Gee, that tasted great. You're swell to me, Miss Gail. You look awful pretty in that green sweater and plaid skirt. I'm glad you don't wear pants like our girls do."

The boy's weak voice and wistful eyes twisted her heart. If she had made this visit because of curiosity, the next would be from a sheer desire to help pull him back to health, she told herself fervently. Shrieks of laughter, yells of derision outside wrinkled the boy's forehead.

"Gee, them kids make a racket, goes right through my head." He closed his eyes wearily.

"It won't be long before we have you shouting with them, Philippe. Doctor John reported that you were a top-ranking ball pitcher. I'll lower your pillow. Snuggle down and take a nap. I told your mother that I would stay with you while she ran across the field to have a cup of tea with a neighbor." It wasn't necessary to remind him that Mrs. Pomponi had departed only after having ordered two of the small boys to stay with Miss Trevor every minute to help. They had fidgeted to get away and she had sent them to join the ballplayers.

"Where you goin', Miss Gail?"

"To sit on the front steps. I won't leave until your mother comes, I promise. Shut your eyes, dear. Every minute of sleep brings you nearer that ball field, remember."

She closed the door halfway to shut out the patch of sunlight on the floor, motioned to the battling ball-players to move on and sat on the top step. Not a building in sight. Must be poky to come home at night to a house at the dead end of a dark, sparsely inhabited road like this one.

A soft wind came from the river, blew through the branches of a massive oak and set each brown leaf whispering to its neighbor. An old brick chimney, looming among the blackened beams of what once had been a house was the center of a patch of rich, black loam already prepared for a spring Victory garden.

Spring. What would it bring? She thought of the furious battle going on in the Solomons, of Rommel's forces gathering in the East, of the speed, more speed demanded in production. Was she doing all she could to help? It would be silly to question her usefulness to Mr. B.C. More and more he depended on her. Each day she discovered a new way to smooth the road ahead which would help him in his drive for more production. By living at Johnny's she was freeing Mildred to free a man for combat; also, she was freeing Petunia for war work — not that she would be much help.

A sound scattered her reflections. She held her breath to listen. The stillness of the room behind her was broken only by the old dog's heavy breathing. The oak leaves still whispered. The shouts of the distant ball-players came faintly on the breeze. That curious sound again. It came from overhead.

Johnny had said he had heard a sound like a moan on the floor above. This was more like a voice calling. Could she steal upstairs before anyone came? Suppose it were the woman's missing son? Suppose in finding him she found out that treachery was afoot?

She ran down the steps and looked across the field by which Mrs. Pomponi would return. No one in sight.

Heart pounding, ears strained to detect

the slightest sound, she entered the house. The dog opened one bleary eye, regarded her for an instant, thudded a dirty-white tail on the floor and relapsed into slumber.

She bent over the sleeping boy. His breath came easily, his pinched mouth was curved in a slight smile. Was he dreaming of future baseball triumphs?

She stood tensely in the middle of the room, eyes on the wall clock, and listened. If the sound wasn't repeated within five minutes she would be sure she had imagined it. Quiet as the grave up there. Cheery thought. A creak . . . Nothing about that to send an icy chill creeping up her spine. A voice? The chill coasted down. She tiptoed across the floor. Waited at the foot of the stairs.

"Help." Had she heard that strained husky appeal or was it the breeze rattling a window? She would never have a better chance to find out. She set one foot on the lower stair.

"I tell you I left the two boys here with her, Louis. What you makin' such a row about?"

Before the woman on the porch had finished speaking, Gail had opened the front door from the inside and closed it behind her.

"He's sleeping," she whispered and as she saw that the Pomponis, man and wife, were regarding her with suspicion, she added jubilantly: "He took every drop of the broth and said it was 'swell.'"

"Where are those two kids I left to help you?" Mrs. Pomponi demanded. "I'll sock 'em one if they ran away."

"*Ssh,* not so loud. The Doctor wants Philippe to rest. The boys were so noisy I sent them away from the house to play ball. I didn't need them. I've been sitting on the steps until a moment before you came when I stole in to see if he was still asleep." She nodded toward the rich, turned-up earth. "You're getting ready for a wonderful garden there, Mr. Pomponi."

His face, which had been dark with doubt, brightened.

"It will be the finest in the village, Mees Trevor. Already I have made a plan on paper. Would you like to see it?"

"I'd love to, but I'll have to wait until I come again." She glanced at her wrist watch. "I'm cook at home, and my niece and nephew will be ready to eat me if I don't have their dinner on time. I've left some of the broth for Philippe, Mrs. Pomponi. Coax him to take it for his supper."

"I will, Miss Trevor, and we thank you much, for bein' so kind to our sick boy. Don't we, Louis?"

"Sure, sure, we thank her." Pomponi lumbered down the steps and brought her bicycle from where it rested beside the oak. "You have pretty long ride home, yes?"

"It isn't far, but it's a lonely road between here and your next neighbor. Next time I'll come in my small car. Good-by."

She knew that they stood watching her as she pedaled along the road. It took all her self-control not to look back at the upper windows. She hadn't imagined it. She had heard a husky whisper as she listened at the foot of the stairs. Was there a man in that house too ill to make his get-away? Next time she went . . .

"Well, see who's here!"

The voice smashed into her plan and demolished it to unrelated fragments. She regarded the man in the platinum-gray roadster in startled surprise. He was headed toward Pomponi's. Was he going there?

"Don't stare at me as if I were a highwayman about to hold you up," Mark Croston called. "Wait till I turn. I'll bundle your wheel into the rumble and give you a lift."

She watched him curiously as he backed

and turned the roadster. Why was he on this dead-end road?

"Okay. Hop in."

She slipped into the seat beside him. The car shot ahead.

"You haven't spoken since I hailed you," he complained. "Haven't you forgiven that kiss?"

"Forgiven, but not forgotten. Take your arm away, Mark."

"Sorry. My mistake." His gloved hand joined the other on the wheel. "I strive to please. Whence? Whither?"

"I've come from Pomponi's and I'm going home. Doctor John was troubled because the sick boy wouldn't eat. I prepared some of the dear, departed Petunia's broth for him. Now that we are telling the story of our lives, where were you going? To call on the fat and genial Louis?"

"Not on your life. He's one of my time-keepers. I get enough of him at the Works. I came to look for you."

"For me! How did you know where I was?"

"I — I met Cissie-Lou. She told me."

Cissie-Lou couldn't have told him. She didn't know of her plan to visit the sick boy this afternoon. No one knew. The Pomponi house was the only house on the road beyond where Mark had stopped the roadster. If he had been going there, why had he denied it?

Chapter 10

"What's this I hear? Is it true that you are cook and general maid at the Doctor's?"

Gail incredulously regarded Mrs. Benjamin Clifton standing at the other side of the broad desk. She had been so absorbed in the letter she was typing that she hadn't heard her enter the office. She laughed and rose.

"Has my fame spread already, Aunt Jane? It can't be because of the perfection of my cooking. At present it has what Billy calls its 'ups and downs,' but I'm learning."

Mrs. Clifton squeezed her ample self into a chair. The flush on her round cheeks was like the delicate coloring of a banana apple. Her black wool suit was the perfection of tailoring. Her single string of spectacularly large pearls was real and lustrous. Her black hat was an up-to-the-minute model which took years from her face and accentuated the silver sheen of her short hair. Her eyes, almost as dark as her costume, snapped as she drew off her white gloves.

Good heavens, was she preparing to settle down for an afternoon visit? Gail thought of the letters still to be typed from Mr. B.C.'s dictation. She glanced at the clock. Almost time to prepare the cup of tea she served him every afternoon at four. G.H. had fallen into the habit of joining him. Better get it ready now. It would save time if Aunt Jane was preparing for a talk-fest.

"Why are you fussing at that closet?" Mrs. Clifton demanded. "Come here. I want to talk to you."

Gail arranged green-and-white cups and saucers on a burnished copper tray, filled a glass teakettle with water from the cooler in the corner and set it on the electric plate she attached.

"You'll have to talk while I work, Aunt Jane. Nothing stops in this establishment. Leisure has gone to war."

"Getting ready for the Mad Hatter's tea party?"

"Nothing so exciting. It is for your husband. I've discovered that a cup of tea rests him. He's good for two or three hours' hard concentration after it. He'll adore having you join him in his afternoon snack."

"You know better than that, Gail Trevor.

You know that your boss would order me out if I so much as stepped foot within his office. He may not argue that woman's place is in the home, but he made it unmistakably plain to me soon after our marriage that he was mighty sure it wasn't visiting in her husband's office. What have you done to your hand, child?"

"This?" Gail indicated the ugly red welt that ran from the top of the thumb of her right hand to the wrist. "I got gay with the electric range. It will serve as a look-before-you-touch warning for some time to come. I've learned that a college degree doesn't necessarily equip one for household efficiency."

"Have you tried to find a maid?"

"I have. Those whom the Works and the Hospital haven't taken get enormous wages, and their meals, for dishwashing at the cafeterias in town."

"Bid higher. Your brother can afford it."

"No use. Like Petunia, they all wants their freedom." She sliced a lemon with a thin-bladed knife. "Can't say that I blame them. The person who first observed that woman's work is never done said it all. The inventor who comes across with a general housework robot will qualify for a solid gold niche in my Hall of Fame."

She answered the telephone. Made an appointment for an important conference with Benjamin Clifton for the next day. Cradled the phone.

"Tea is ready, Aunt Jane. Shall we beard the lion in his den, the Douglas in his hall?"

"*Hmp*, easy to see where Cissie-Lou gets her flair for the dramatic. Straight from you." With an effort Mrs. Clifton extricated herself from the tight-fitting chair.

"I'm taking my life in my hands, but I'll carry in that tray. Time those two men realized how they are driving you with all you have to do at home."

"Driving me! *This* is my job, Aunt Jane. Adding a little housework won't hurt me. Think of the thousands and thousands of women working who are returning at night to carry on at home. When I read of what our men in the service are doing and sacrificing, I'm ashamed if I'm not dead-tired, even when I tumble into bed early."

"You won't put on the early-to-bed act tonight. You and your brother are dining at Twin Pines, remember. Lila Tenny phoned to ask if she might bring an officer friend who is at the Inn, and that newspaperman is coming. Greg suggested that I might get material from him to put pep in my speech to the Women Voters."

"You will, he's most interesting. All set for the lion's den? Here's the tray." She opened the door of Benjamin Clifton's office.

"A lady to see you, Mr. B.C."

"What in thunder are you doing here, Jane?" she heard him exclaim before she closed it.

Gregory Hunt, who was taking papers from the file behind his uncle, turned in surprise.

"See who's here! Welcome to our city, Aunt Jane." He took the tray and set it on the desk. "You don't honor us often."

"Often! You know very well that I haven't been in this office before for years, Greg." She sank into a chair and regarded her husband defiantly as she filled a cup. The diamonds on her fingers were no more brilliant than her eyes as she declared: —

"I can't stand by and see a willing horse worked to death by you two slavedrivers. Here's your tea, B.C."

"You've got your metaphor mixed, Jane, but I get your drift. Who's working a willing horse to death and who's the horse? Damnation! Why didn't you tell me this was hot?"

"Where there's steam there's likely to be heat, my love. Tea, Greg? Do you also depend on the cup that cheers to recharge your mental battery every afternoon at four?"

Greg laughed.

"You've said it." Plate and cup in hand he perched on the corner of the desk. "How about that horse we are killing? Give the defense a chance to be heard."

Mrs. Clifton surreptitiously slipped the third lump of sugar into her cup.

"It's Gail. She's doing a man-size job here and general work at home. She has a burn on her hand long as the amendments to the Constitution."

"Who told you that?" Benjamin Clifton cautiously sampled his tea. "I know about the tremendous job she is doing here — she's my right hand and part of my brain — I mean about the burn and the work at home?"

"I saw the burn. You must be blind if you haven't noticed it. Hilda Speed told me about the housework. Doctor John has moved his office to the hospital and taken her with him. I talked with her yesterday when I attended the Board Meeting. She said that not only was Gail doing the housework but was adding visits to one of the Doctor's patients to her schedule."

"What patient?"

"Goodness, Greg, don't be so explosive. You made me jump so my tea splashed in my lap." She dabbed at her black skirt with a paper napkin. "Hilda didn't tell me the name. A sick boy, I believe."

"A sick boy!" Greg echoed his aunt's words. Had Gail gone to Pomponi's in the hope of finding out the truth about the mysterious sound her brother had reported?

"That isn't all Hilda Speed had on her mind. This is going to be good." Jane Clifton's throaty chuckle snapped his attention back to her.

"She hinted that a certain beautiful widow had a covetous eye on a desirable physician. Beautiful! *Hmp.* I still say that make-up is God's best gift to woman."

Greg Hunt shouted with laughter.

"What long, sharp claws you've got, Grandmother."

She chuckled in sympathy.

"Stop laughing at your aunt, Greg, it isn't respectful. I knew to whom she referred. It gave me a jolt when I remembered that I had invited them both to dine with us tonight. I felt as if I were conniving at a love triangle. Hilda apparently was frightened after she told all and made me swear never to repeat it."

"You swore, of course?" Benjamin Clifton inquired dryly. Without waiting for an answer he seized his wife's hands and drew her to her feet.

"Jane, I love you, but not here. This country is at war, remember. These Works are loaded to the muzzle with defense contracts. Gossip is out for the duration." He opened the door. "So are you. Scram."

She tweaked his imposing nose as she passed him, lingered on the threshold to prophesy: —

"My love, I'll bet a twenty-five-dollar war bond that you two men get busy with the aforementioned gossip tidbit as soon as I exit. Good afternoon."

He bent his white head and kissed her swiftly. "Be a good girl, Jane." As Benjamin closed the door behind his wife, Greg said: —

"When I see you and Aunt Jane together, B.C., my belief in matrimony is recharged. You two uphold those lines of the marriage service, 'To have and to hold from this day forward . . . to love and to cherish till death do us part.' "

" 'According to God's holy ordinance and thereto I plight my troth,' " Benjamin Clifton quoted. "Believe it or not, Greg, there never has been anyone else since I met her. Jane is my wife, loved and desired and will be for all time." He shrugged as if throwing off a spell and returned to his desk.

"Great Scott, here we stand sentimentalizing and there's a war on. Jane's report that Hilda Speed is worrying about Doctor John's love life started it. Who's the woman? Your aunt said she was dining with us tonight but I never know who's coming."

"I have a suspicion she referred to my tenant, Mrs. Craven. She and Mildred Trevor were roommates at college. To revive an old friendship was the reason the charming Rhoda gave for settling here. I'd say that nurse was crazy to start a yarn like that."

"Remember she swore your Aunt Jane to secrecy. Do you believe there's any truth in her suspicion?"

"That Rhoda Craven is in love with Doc? I don't know why not. She knew him when he became engaged to Mildred. She calls him 'Johnny.' He's got what it takes to attract the female of the species. That he would divorce the mother of his children to marry another woman I can't believe and she's not the type to be satisfied with anything less than a marriage certificate."

"Mrs. Craven is fascinating, beautiful and persistent. She hammered at me while you were away to let her have the house you didn't want to rent. John Trevor hasn't seen his wife for weeks. Add that up and what do you get?"

"Not unfaithfulness on the Doc's part, B.C. Something tells me you owe Aunt Jane a war bond. We didn't lose a split second after the door closed getting our teeth into that juicy morsel of gossip, did we? Let's forget the Doc and his problems. What can we do about Gail? Call her in now. Let's find out just what she is doing. Okay?"

His uncle nodded approval. Greg saw Gail shift her notebook to cover her right hand as she entered in response to the summons.

"You're on the carpet, Miss Trevor," Benjamin Clifton announced. "Why did you send my wife here with tea? Didn't you realize you were throwing sand into the gears of the Works? She accused G.H. and me of working you to death."

"She said that to me, Mr. B.C. I took it as a joke. Had I suspected she intended to pass that nonsense on to you she would have entered this room only over my dead body."

"Sit down." As Gail perched on the edge of the chair in which she sat when taking dictation, he asked, "Then you don't think we are?"

"Are you serious? You can't be. Working me to death? Of course not. I love my job here. I wouldn't change it for a WAAC officer's uniform and that's saying an awful lot. This isn't a diplomatic approach to firing me because of what Aunt Jane said, is it, Mr. B.C.?"

"Not at present. I would as soon think of chopping off my right hand. I want to check on this housework you've taken on."

"Oh that." Relief set stars of laughter in her dark eyes. "I can take care of that with one hand."

"With the hand you're hiding under that notebook?" Greg suggested. "Hold it out." As she looked inquiringly at Benjamin Clifton, he agreed: —

"G.H. is the junior boss. Obey orders."

"It's nothing," she assured as she exposed the burned hand. "Accidents happen to the best of cooks. Not that I've reached that shining peak of excellence yet, but if electricity and rationing don't let me down I'm on my way.

"A girl, who bore, mid snow and ice
A banner with the strange device,
Excelsior."

146

Benjamin Clifton chuckled.

"You're letting your real, gay self out of captivity, aren't you, Miss Trevor? A self I haven't seen since you've been my secretary, you've taken your job so seriously."

"Business for business hours was impressed on my mind when I was training for secretarial work." She rose. "It is still good medicine. I have heaps to do before the mail closes. If I may be excused —"

"You'll be excused only to go to the infirmary and have that burn taken care of. G.H., watch her. See that my orders are obeyed."

"Really, Mr. B.C. My hand isn't painful. I don't need — I'm going," she capitulated, as she met his stern eyes; "but — I *don't* need to go under guard."

Greg opened the door.

"Make it fast. I'm a busy man."

"I don't need you. I —"

"Orders is orders. Step on it."

As they waited for the elevator he asked, "What was your real reason for going to Pomponi's, Gail?"

"How did you know I went there, Charlie Chan?"

"Hilda Speed told Aunt Jane. Give. Let's have your real reason."

"I went to —" The elevator door

opened. Lila Tenny stepped out.

"Greg," she exclaimed and tucked her hand under his arm. "I have something very important to tell —"

Gail stepped into the elevator. "To the infirmary," she said quickly and smiled as she glimpsed Greg's annoyed frown before the door closed.

Louis Pomponi was waiting to go down as she stepped from the car. With his black hair slicked to oily smoothness, he looked a bit more greasy than usual.

"You're not here because Philippe is worse, are you, Mr. Pomponi?" she asked anxiously.

"No, No, Mees Trevor." He puffed out his fat cheeks. "I come to see the nurse. Down." The elevator door clanged behind him.

Silly question to ask, Gail thought as she entered the infirmary. Philippe would have been taken to the hospital, not here.

"What can I do for you, Miss Trevor?" inquired the red-haired nurse in a voice as crisp as her white uniform. Even her capable hands were covered with the freckles that went with the skin that went with her hair.

"Mr. B.C. didn't like the looks of this, Miss Walsh." Gail held out her hand. "It doesn't amount to anything —"

"Are you telling *me?* Sit in that chair. I'll put on a dressing."

From the window Gail could see fields and hills, glowing like rosy copper in the late afternoon light. Her eyes came back to the room with its snowy equipment. She rested her head against the high back of the chair and drew a long breath.

"Heavenly peaceful here, isn't it? Have many patients?" she inquired, as the nurse drew up a small table.

"Not many. This will smart for a minute."

"You've *said* it. Ooch! All right now. I met Mr. Pomponi in the corridor. Had he had an accident?"

"No. He was here asking for chloroform."

"Chloroform! What did he want *chloroform* for, Miss Walsh?"

"Just a minute more and I'll be through the dressing. There."

"Did he get it?"

"Who? Get what? Oh, you're talking about Pomponi and the chloroform. You bet he didn't get it. I told him he'd have to have a prescription even if all he wanted it for was to put a sick dog out of his misery."

Chapter 11

"You still refuse to accept that commission, Greg?" Lila Tenny demanded impatiently.

She turned from the window where her slim figure had been silhouetted against the crimson afterglow and took a quick step toward the man whose hand gripped the back of his desk chair. His eyes, shadowed with annoyance, met hers steadily. A white line settled about his mouth.

"I do." His voice was grim. "I've just given you another chance to argue your case, but it's the last. What's more, it's time for a showdown between us, Lila. I shall stay on the job here. If you marry me next month as we had planned, it will be with the understanding that the subject of rejoining the Air Force is never to be raised again. Otherwise, our marriage is off."

"Then it's off, forever. I'll make the announcement. Here's your ring."

"Just a minute." Greg answered the buzz from the box on his desk. "Hunt speaking."

"Greg! Greg! I must see you at once!"

Gail's terrified whisper. Had the burn proved serious?

"Greg, do you hear me? I must —"

"I'll be free in about five minutes." He snapped off the connection.

"That was Gail Trevor, wasn't it?" Lila Tenny was drawing on her left glove. Greg saw the flash of a diamond before it was covered. "She should be more discreet. I could hear her demand to see you at once. The five minutes you allowed to close this interview must be about up. I'll go." As he opened the door she turned on her famous smile.

"I was merely testing you, Greg. Of course we'll be married next month as we planned, the day before Thanksgiving, darling. Your conscience will allow you that week end for a honeymoon, I hope. I'll see you at dinner tonight at Twin Pines. Until then," she blew him a kiss as she crossed the threshold. "Don't forget me."

He leaned against the door he had closed behind her. Darned queer that a man who had loved a girl enough to ask her to marry him should feel as if he had suddenly been shackled with ball and chain, that Thanksgiving was terrifyingly near. What had changed Lila's mind? She had declared she wouldn't marry him, had

151

begun to pull off her engagement ring, then Gail had called. Gail! Her voice had been frightened.

"What is it? What's happened? Your hand? Is it serious?" he demanded as he entered her office.

"*That* little burn? Goodness, no, Miss Walsh said I needn't keep on the dressing. I thought you ought to know at once that Pomponi tried to get chloroform at the infirmary."

"Boy, is that all? I imagined that something terrible had happened to you."

"Don't you understand, Greg? He told the nurse he wanted to put a sick dog out of the way. Remember that Johnny heard what he thought was a groan and that Louis said —"

"You needn't go on. I remember. Just a minute before we assume that the fat Louis is up to mischief. Doc suspected a man was hidden there. We don't *know* it."

"I do. The afternoon I took care of Philippe, I'm sure I heard a husky voice call, 'Help.' Don't stand there like a robot. That man may be the missing son, he may be the clue to treachery in the Works —"

"What do you know about treachery here?"

"I have a brain, haven't I? I know there's

nothing wrong with your heart. A top ranking pilot isn't ordered out of the Air Force unless — Take your hand off my mouth, I shan't say any more. Why are we wasting time? Suppose Pomponi gets that chloroform somewhere else and —"

"Take it easy, Gail. Go home, please. That burn must be painful. I told Search of the Doc's suspicion. He and I will take care of this."

She glanced at the clock.

"I usually work an hour longer, but I have finished Mr. B.C.'s letters. If he doesn't need me —"

"He doesn't." He held her dark fur jacket. "Put this on. Make those kids get their own supper tonight and go easy with that hand. You're dining at Twin Pines, aren't you?" He caught her blue beret by its silk pompom and crushed it down on her hair.

"Here's your hat. What's your hurry?" Her voice rippled with laughter. "I'm going. Wait till I put away my papers." As she locked her desk she reminded anxiously: —

"Things may be happening while we're wasting time here, Greg."

"*I'm* not wasting time, lady. You're the one. Soon's you are out of the way I'll get into action."

153

Later, at home in the white kitchen, she glanced at the clock. One hour since she had left the office. In that time she had changed to the rainbow-plaid short-sleeved cotton frock; laid out John's dinner clothes; and prepared a casserole with chops, mushrooms and green peas, now in the oven.

Had Greg contacted Louis Pomponi in time, she wondered as she tossed a salad of pale green lettuce, watercress, and paper-thin slices of cucumber in French dressing. He hadn't appeared to take the man's request for chloroform very seriously. If he had heard the sound she had . . .

"Gosh!" Billy in the doorway sniffed approval. "Something smells good. Stay outside, Mac. You know this cook won't let you in the kitchen. Go back to the living room. What's cooking?"

Gail told him.

"Will you and Cissie-Lou mind having your dinner in the kitchen?"

"I like it. It's kind of cosy. I'll set the table. Hey, what'd you mean, me an' Cissie-Lou? Where you going?"

"Your father and I are dining at Twin Pines."

"Heck. It's no fun when you aren't here. . . . That's a lousy gripe for me to

154

make when you put in so much time slaving for us. I'm sorry."

"I don't slave and I'm crazy about you, pal. If you would like currant jelly with the lamb you'll have to get a fresh glass from the preserve closet downstairs."

"Okay, what's for dessert?"

"Look on the serving shelf."

"Lemon meringue tarts." He broke off a bit of flaky crust. "Gosh, I love 'em. Did you make those?"

"Not I. I bought them on my way home. There's the phone. Answer it, will you, Billy?"

She was adding squares of mild cheese to the dessert plates when he returned.

"It was Pop. Said he wouldn't get here in time to dress, for you to go ahead without him and he'd go to Twin Pines as soon as he could. What's the matter? You look queer."

"I was mentally shifting costumes. I had counted on wearing white, your father had said he would take me in his car. Looks like hiking for yours truly now: I can't walk up the hill in white shoes, my runabout is at the garage being tested and a taxi at this time of day isn't to be had." She glanced at the clock. "Means less time to dress. The casserole will be ready in five minutes. Will you take it out of the oven, Billy?"

"Sure, you run along." A door banged with a force that rattled the teakettle on the electric range. "Hi, Cissie-Lou," Billy shouted.

With her golden hair blown into a halo, the jacket of her gray-and-green plaid suit open to show a pastel-pink blouse, the girl paused in the doorway, hand on her hip.

"What do you want, Billy? Howdy, Gail."

"Want! Cut out the *Vogue* pose, nitwit, and get down to work. Gail's going out to dinner. She's late. Peel off that coat and help. Put this on."

Had her mouth been one degree less lovely Cissie-Lou's expression would have been a pout. She pulled off her jacket and slipped into the huge white bibbed apron her brother was holding.

"Oh, all right, smart aleck. It was bad enough when we had to cut out the second maid, but to be without any is poisonous. When I have a house *I'll* never get caught without a cook. What do I do first, Gail?"

"Butter the bread on the loaf and slice it, you like it that way. By the time you have the glasses filled with milk the casserole will be ready. Thanks a lot, pals, for helping out."

156

"You're thanking us!" Billy's tone was gruff. "What would we do without you with Mom gone?" He twitched his sister's hair. "Why don't you speak up, little orphan Annie, and tell Gail she's a hunk of all right?"

"Of course she is, but she's an easy mark." Cissie-Lou was expertly buttering and cutting bread into dainty slices. "*I* wouldn't have let Petunia go. I'd have told her that just because she could cook didn't mean she'd be a burst of speed in a factory. It would have proved true, too. Mother wouldn't have let her go, I bet."

"I'll bet Mom couldn't have stopped her any more than Gail could," Billy championed. "You'd better scram, Gail. How long will it take you to dress?"

"I'd like an hour but as I'll have to walk I can't allow more than three quarters in which to turn myself into a triple threat." She slipped out of her enveloping white apron. "Why, Billy?"

"Thought I'd do some mumbo-jumbo stuff and have Cinderella's pumpkin coach and four at the door. If you can squeeze into the basket I use for bundles on the front of my wheel, I'll land you at Twin Pines in style — and how."

"Thanks a million, Billy, but I'll walk.

Will you two get on all right if I go now?"

"For Pete's sake don't treat us like morons, Gail, of course we'll get on all right." Cissie-Lou waved a bread knife threateningly. "Skip."

Cissie-Lou was right, Gail thought as she touched her ears with perfume, Mildred wouldn't have allowed Petunia to go. She thought of the many facets of gracious ways of living which a world at war was sweeping into the scrap heap of useless things. Desperately as she had tried to fit it in, there had been no time in her busy day to polish the silver saucers and frames for the delicate porcelain cups in which coffee had been served after dinner in this house ever since she could remember. There was no maid in cap and apron to bring them into the living room on the huge antique Sheffield tray. What did those niceties of life matter when there was a war to be won? And of course it would be won if it took the last full measure of sacrifice.

She critically regarded herself in the long mirror. Not too bad. The white velvet jacket with silver sequins and the black crepe skirt were adequate for dining at Twin Pines. The velvet bag and the huge piece of glass, pinch-hitting for an emerald in her costume ring, matched the bow in her hair. The heels of her green sandals were not too high for walking. She slipped into her fur jacket.

"Hey there!" She opened her door in response to Billy's hail. "The pumpkin waits, lady."

She laughed as she started down the stairs.

"Billy, you weren't serious about packing me into that bike basket? Of all the crazy — Greg! Where did you come from?" She had never seen his eyes so blue as when they laughed up at her.

"Heard that the Doc had let you down, and as I was passing —"

"Passing!" She was beside him in the hall now. "You are dressed for dinner. How —"

"If you stop to argue we'll be late and you know Mrs. Benjamin Clifton's opinion of a guest who isn't on time. Step on it, gal."

"Coming." She turned swiftly and kissed the boy grinning at her. "You're the best thing in my life, pal." She cleared her husky voice and reminded, "Don't forget the currant jelly. Good night."

As the roadster shot ahead she guessed: —

"Billy phoned you I was walking, didn't he, Greg?"

"Take the goods the gods provide and

don't ask questions. I dropped in at Pomponi's."

"Really? What excuse did you give for going there?"

"Looking for the Doc and as good luck would have it, there he was."

"Is Philippe worse?"

"No, I'd say he was better. I told Louis that someone had been hurt and needed Doctor John. Then I said, 'The nurse at the infirmary reported you were on the hunt for chloroform today. What's up?'

" 'There's a sick dog round' — he puffed out his cheeks — 'I want to get rid of.'

" 'Where is he? I'll take care of him, Louis,' your brother offered quickly.

"Pomponi shrugged his fat shoulders. 'When I couldn't get the stuff I gave him to Mr. Search, he's my good friend. He said he'd put the cur out of the way.'

" 'Sure he's not upstairs?' the Doc suggested.

"Louis' enormous eyes bulged with grieved reproach. 'Would I lie to you, Doctor John?' He gestured grandiloquently toward the stairs, 'You like to go see?' He was convincingly in earnest. If a man has been hidden there, he has been spirited away."

"We must find him, Greg."

"We will, I have views. The Doc told me he would phone Search after he left the Pomponis'. The sick dog worried him. I got in touch with our secret agent immediately after you left the office. He agrees with me that there's a chance that Louis' mystery may be tied up with the death of the woman at the Works. . . . Let's sign off on tragedy. Grand night, isn't it?"

"So beautiful it makes my throat ache."

The moon was a plaque of silver. The stars were twinkling gold sequins. The sky was purple velvet. The crystal-clear air was keen with frost.

"It was a night like this; no wind; I can smell the musty odor from decaying vegetation now," Greg's voice was low, tense, as if he were reporting what he was seeing. "We were on a mission to intercept a formation of Mikados and Kawa 95's speeding southward. We were over water and had engaged them when one of our outfit radioed that our tail was in flames. Lord, how we worked to put out the fire. No use. We got the life raft off. Stepped out and dropped into the sea. We drifted for a week. One after another of the crew died of machine-gun wounds, until only the radio man and I were alive to be rescued."

A passing car honked impatiently. The spell of memory was broken.

"Sorry, Gail, that I should have reminisced after suggesting that we sign off on tragedy."

"If only you had kept on, Greg! I've so wished you would tell me about it."

"No can do. It's too terrible. I try to work off a little of the hate which makes me see red when I allow myself to remember, in pushing production. What happened to my men is only a millionth part of the horrors of this war. Here we are at Twin Pines. Sorry I let myself go. This is a party, remember."

Gail couldn't dismiss his experience so easily. She would never forget the restrained ferocity of his voice and eyes. As she threw off her fur jacket in the Chinese-red powder room, she was still under the spell of a moonlit night, musty with the odor of decaying vegetation, its silence being shattered by the splutter of bullets directed at the struggling men in the sea.

"You look lovely, Miss Gail." The voice of Mrs. B.C.'s elderly maid who had been in the Cliftons' employ for years brought her back to her surroundings.

"Thanks, Sarah." She laughed and glanced in the hall mirror. "It's the green

162

bow in my hair. Color does something for me. Sets me on top of the world."

On the threshold of the living room she paused. There was a tall crystal vase of huge golden-yellow chrysanthemums standing on the floor beside the fireplace and a ruddy copper bowl filled with smaller mums of the same color on a table. The air was slightly tinged with the aroma of fine old sherry. She looked at the hostess, glittering in black sequins, at auburn-haired Rhoda Craven, in shimmering silver lamé talking to her white-haired host, at blond Lila Tenny gazing up at a tall man in Air Force uniform standing back to the room. Would the sight of that uniform submerge Greg in a bitter tide of disappointment?

Greg's hand lightly touched her sleeve. "As I reminded you before, this is a party. Snap out of it or I shall think I scraped off the icing from the evening cake with my saga of the Pacific."

"Did I look that mournful?" She laughed. "If you'll promise not to tell I'll confess I was wondering if I had allowed time enough for the lamb chops to cook in the casserole I left behind me."

Of course she hadn't been thinking that, equally of course he mustn't suspect what

163

thoughts the sight of the uniform had conjured.

"Who is the major? I can just see the gold leaf on his shoulder."

The officer, as if feeling her interest, turned and looked at her. It was Sebastian Brent, Sebastian who said it with violets.

He met her halfway across the room and caught her hands in his. His dark eyes were alight with something deeper than pleasure, color surged under his olive skin as he pressed his lips to one palm and then the other.

"Gail! To think it should be you."

The instant of surprise having passed she was uncomfortably aware that she and Major Brent were occupying stage center, that conversation in the room had ceased, that the attention of host, hostess and guests was focused on them. Her face burned.

"You didn't tell me you had a friend here, Sebastian."

Never had Gail been so glad to hear a voice, a voice iced in Lila Tenny's best manner. It slashed like a keen rapier between two pairs of hands. Major Brent turned and bowed with his characteristic air of devotion. Hers hadn't been the only female heart in Washington his manner had fluttered, Gail remembered.

"I did not know Miss Trevor was here, Lila. I did not know that I would find her when I followed the trail of a woman who has mysteriously disappeared."

Chapter 12

"Do you play poker, Miss Trevor?" Tom Search inquired as he offered Gail a blue Sèvres cup of coffee in the living room after dinner.

"No. Would you advise it?"

He took the other seat in the turn-of-the-century tête à tête near a lamp-lighted table strewn with books.

"I'd advise anything which would train you to keep your expression under control."

"I understand. I'll struggle to acquire not only a poker face but what is known as a dead pan."

"I'd hate to have you do that, yours is so lovely, but, you are part of a critical situation. You must not reveal your thoughts in your expression as you did when the Major spoke of the disappearance of a woman. Quick, before he steers this way. What's the low-down on him?"

"Spanish mother — bred-in-the-bone New England father. Educated in America. Stars and Stripes to the backbone in spite

166

of the foreign manner he affects. On the way to stardom in Hollywood. Came the war and a commission in Washington."

She smiled at her brother, who was approaching. She recalled Hilda Speed's description of him: "He isn't exactly handsome with those piercing dark eyes set deep in his head and that big forehead, but his mouth is fine and he has what it takes with women."

If Rhoda Craven's expression as she looked up at him was to be believed, he had. Blue-green eyes, upswept bronze hair, a classic nose, a scarlet mouth above a determined chin, a figure for which professional models would starve or stuff, an eager interest in life, that was Rhoda Craven.

"Johnny, at last. Have you had anything to eat?" she inquired anxiously. After a word of greeting Search crossed the room.

"I have. When I went home to dress I found Cissie-Lou and Billy feasting on lamb chops *en casserole*. I horned in on the party and topped off with chocolate cake, you having thriftily provided but two lemon meringue tarts. Next time make it three. I like those, too. Go ahead and tell your story, Rhoda."

"As her mother isn't here to do it, I want

to give a party for Cis, Miss Trevor."

The criticism of Mildred in her voice was nothing one could resent, yet it was there. She's undermining his wife's hold on him. Like a termite she keeps quietly, steadily, on the job, Gail thought.

"Her sixteenth birthday comes next week," the smooth voice carried on. "That's a date in a girl's life over which a fuss should be made if ever there was one."

"I had planned to invite some of her best friends in for a buffet supper."

"You have enough to do, Miss Trevor. The town is buzzing with the details of your achievements as cook, general maid and doubling as secretary to the world's busiest man."

"There's a war going on which ought to divert attention from my domestic career. You make me feel like Cinderella escaping from the kitchen to a ball." Gail was immediately sorry for her ungraciousness. "You are most kind to suggest the party. I know that it would be perfection. I am not the one to decide. Ask her father."

"You will say, 'Yes,' Johnny, won't you?" Rhoda Craven pleaded. "You always do say 'Yes' to me, don't you?"

"I hadn't realized that I had degenerated into a yes-man." Color mounted under the

Doctor's dark skin. "If that is so, it's time to break the slate. I vote for a celebration of Cissie-Lou's birthday at home. It has been indicated that a wrist watch — *with* diamonds — would be an acceptable token of parental affection. I'll talk with you about selecting it on the drive back, Gail. This time I won't fail you. Come on, Rhoda. The card tables are being set out. I'll have time only for two or three hands."

As he turned away Gail crossed to the deep bay from which she could look down into the garden, silver-plated now with moonlight. For one tense moment she had feared he would consent to Rhoda Craven's request to give the party for Cissie-Lou. That would have started gossip. Maybe it would have been better if he had said "Yes." Maybe critical comment would have jarred his wife awake to her responsibilities.

"I'll bet you a twenty-five-dollar war bond you're thinking of your sister-in-law," declared a low voice beside her.

"Greg, I was. How did you know?"

"Your face tells tales. Watch your step, lady, or you'll become Mildred-fixated."

"You've told me that before. I don't know why she exasperates me. She has, ever since Johnny married her. Whenever we are together she leaves a splinter in my heart. I can't think it's a case of sister-in-law-itis."

"Forget her; if you don't, anger at her may sometime land you in a trap from which you won't escape in a hurry. The next time she riles you go slow. You don't like Lila, either."

"You've guessed it, I don't like Lila. Not very nice of me to acknowledge that about your fiancée, but you asked for it. Curious that my two special aversions should be in the same town. I like women as a rule."

"And they like you. I heard you were voted the most popular girl in your college class."

"Jess Ramsay, my best friend, and I shared the honor. The Inseparables, they called us. Perhaps Mildred and Lila aggravate me because I think they are being unfair to the two men for whom I care the most."

"Meaning *me* as one of them?"

"Why the surprise? You *know* I'm fond of you. You're family. You seemed like a father to me when I was fifteen."

"Help! A *father!* I'm not that much older than you."

"You're just seven years older, Mister. I wasn't referring to age. Sometime I'll learn not to show what I think or feel. Only a few minutes ago Mr. Search advised me to acquire a poker face. When Sebastian Brent announced that he was on the trail of a woman who had disappeared I registered startled surprise. I thought at once of our mysterious visitor."

"By the way the dashing Major held your hands and kissed them I suspected you were the woman he was trailing. I'll bet his first name is Romeo. Like him a lot, don't you? Why are you grinning?"

For some inexplicable reason his voice, tense as it had been on the day of his return to the Works, had dispelled the fog of her anxiety.

"That 'grin' to which you so gruffly refer has been called an 'adorable smile,' in case you're interested."

"The romantic Major's line, I assume. Here he comes. Let's try for some light on the woman he is hunting. I'll get a wireless across to Search to join us."

The FBI agent must have been watching for a signal for he strolled across the room a moment after Sebastian Brent had joined them in the deep bay window.

"You must be psychic, Major," Gail welcomed. "We were just talking about you. Were you in earnest when you declared you had come here to trail a woman who had disappeared?"

"Didn't you know I would follow you to the ends of the world until I found you, beautiful?" he reproached theatrically.

"Something tells me that's one of the lines from the picture which sent you soaring among the stars, Major. Having duly impressed me with your declaration of devotion, tell us about your quest. Mr. Search is a writer and at all times a writer is keen for human interest stories. He might help you."

Sebastian Brent dropped the role of foreign romantic and became straight American.

"Perhaps you can, Search. Perhaps you can take the hunt off my shoulders. I don't like it. I don't like mysteries, but this was forced on me by a friend on the West Coast."

"Mysteries are right up my street. What's the story?"

"The friend who pulled me into the mess had a neighbor whose son came East to accept a responsible position in a factory doing defense work. What's the matter, Gail?"

"Why, because I caught my breath? I thought for a minute I was about to deliver one of my shattering sneezes." She couldn't tell him that the sound he had heard had been a suppressed "Ouch" occasioned by a sharp nip of Search's fingers on her arm. The excitement caused by the words, "came East to accept a responsible position in a factory doing defense work," must have shown in her face.

"You had gotten as far as the boy who came East to accept a position," Greg prodded. "Let's have the rest of the story. We may be able to help. Had you seen the woman?"

"No, I have her photograph among my traps at the Inn."

"What did she look like?" Gail asked. She denatured the eagerness of her voice with indifference as she added, "Sorry I interrupted. Like Mr. Search, I'm a pushover for any type of human interest story. Tell us why she disappeared."

"Her neighbor wrote that she became uneasy about her son — something in his letters that didn't seem like him — and started East to see for herself if he really had a job, or was telling her he had one to keep her from worrying. She had been away three weeks; no word had come from her, though she had promised to write as soon as she saw the boy. Meanwhile his letters kept on arriving. My friend thought that was queer — anything could happen these days — and wrote me to check on her. He didn't want to report to the police, it might mean headlines in the papers, and if she was safe publicity could upset her plans."

"I'd say the word 'queer' was a masterpiece of understatement," Search observed. He lighted a cigarette. "What brought you to this town? A clue?"

"*No.* We've traced her as far as Chicago, where she changed cars for the East, then lost her. I asked for a short leave to check on the factories with war orders in New England. I met Miss Tenny in Washington. She told me of the Clifton Works, so here I am and to my amazement I find Gail, who left the Capital without giving me her address."

"I consider that last anticlimactic," Gail protested. "I was like a hound on the scent, nose to the ground on the trail of that mysterious woman, and you lose her, Major. You won't leave her lost, will you? I just couldn't bear it. I'm a crime story fan. All mysteries must be solved."

"Then someone else will have to do it. I've used up my leave. My friend wasn't enough of a friend to pull me into this mess because of a mere neighbor. I'm through."

"Like Miss Trevor I hate unfinished mysteries," Search declared. "If you really intend to wash your hands of it, if you will tell me the woman's name and give me what data you have, I'll make a try at locating her."

"Name's Edwards. The job's yours."

Edwards, Edwards . . . Gail mentally repeated. There was no department head named Edwards. The Major's mysterious woman couldn't be the person who had died in the office.

"Okay, I'll take over," Search agreed, "but only with the understanding that if there *is* a story there — something tells me the woman has reached home again and is serenely knitting — I may use it for a pulp yarn, of course substituting fictitious names."

"All right with me. The missing neighbor of a friend is nothing in my life. I'll turn the little material I have over to you. Where shall I reach you?"

"I'm at the Inn, you said you were staying there. I'll run you back tonight."

"That suits me. Get your wrap, Gail, and come into the garden. I've a lot to say to you, beautiful."

Instinctively Gail's eyes sought Search's. She knew from his barely discernible nod that he would welcome her removal of Sebastian Brent that he and Greg might confer. She glanced from the window.

"Hollywood in all its glory couldn't duplicate that moonlit setting, Major, even the trees have been dipped in silver. I'll get my jacket and join you on the terrace. Greg, explain to Aunt Jane that I'm personally conducting the Air Force about her garden, will you?"

"Sorry to break up the plan but I have been sent to announce that you are needed, Sebastian." Lila Tenny's voice, cool, clear as her ice-blue frock, arrested all movement. Her slightly mocking eyes glanced from one face to the other, came back to Brent's.

"I know you hate cards, Major, but Doctor John has had a hurry-up call and is leaving. You are needed to fill his place. This hostess expects every man to do his duty, so don't look so pathetically at Miss Trevor."

Reprieved, Gail thought. The garden interlude would have staged Sebastian Brent's renewed pleading for her to marry him.

"Sorry to miss our talk-fest, but I promised to ride home with Johnny, Major," she apologized and explained in the same breath. "It's a chance to discuss and plan family affairs with him that comes once in a Blue Moon. Good night, everybody."

In the sedan beside her brother she confided: —

"I hope I was a perfect lady and said good night prettily to my hosts, Johnny, but after Lila told me you were ready to leave, my one thought was not to keep you waiting."

"I didn't notice any lapse of manners. That hurry-up call was an excuse to get away that we might have time to talk. I'm overdue at the hospital now. I've got a tough job to hand you, Gail."

His grave voice set her heart thumping like a tom-tom. A tough job . . . Did it mean that he intended to break with Mildred, that he was in love with Rhoda Craven? Why should that decision affect his sister? Would he expect her to stay with the children if he married again? It was their mother's job, not hers. She swallowed her heart, which appeared to have stuck in her throat, kept her eyes on the low-swinging Dipper as she asked: —

"What is it?"

They passed a few dimly lighted houses

which bordered the road, now a silver ribbon in the moonlight.

"I'm sending Hilda back to stay at the house."

"To help me? You need her much more than I do. Is it because of this silly burn on my hand? Aunt Jane made a fuss about it. Did she tell you?"

"It isn't the burn. I have a patient there for her to care for."

"A patient. You mean to *live* there?"

"He'll be more likely to live if his being there can be kept off the record. I talked to Cissie-Lou and Billy tonight, told them that a man had been brought to the house because the hospital was full to the brim — that's true. They immediately jumped to the conclusion that he was a wounded soldier back from the war. I didn't correct them. I don't know that he isn't. I warned them that because he might have information of value to the enemy, his whereabouts must be kept a secret."

"They are pretty young to be expected to keep it, aren't they?"

"Young, but both are patriots to the core of their hearts. The load is coming on your shoulders as housekeeper. Hilda will have her hands full with the patient. He's not only sick, he's mentally upset. G.H. and I may be all wrong, but we have a hunch that if between us we can pull him back to sanity, we may be serving the nation as surely as if we were on the firing line."

"Who is the mysterious patient? Don't keep me in suspense. Tell me."

"It's the 'sick dog' at Pomponi's. The man whose voice you heard muttering 'help.' "

Gail suppressed a startled exclamation. Had the missing son been found? It was an effort to keep her voice steady as she asked: —

"When will he come, Johnny?"

"He is at the house now, on the third floor in the two-maid suite which the late Petunia occupied in lonely state."

If he suspected the treachery and danger which the finding of that man might disclose — that word "might" was the catch — would he speak so lightly?

"How and when did you get him there?"

"Hilda and I picked him up on that little-used road between the river and the hill. That's the reason I couldn't take you to Twin Pines."

"Hurry and tell all, unless you want me to burst like a toy balloon from excitement. Tonight Greg told me he saw you at the Pomponis' when he went there from the factory, that you offered to put the 'sick dog' out of his misery and that Louis had said that when he found he couldn't get chloroform himself he turned the animal over to Tom Search who offered to put it out of the way. *Please,* carry on from there."

"Search has managed in the short time he has been in town to become friendly with the Pomponis. He's had them on his mind since Greg reported to him that I heard a groan upstairs which had been attributed to a sick dog."

"Then you know why Joe Selby's friend and Pat's fiancé is here?"

"I know nothing about him, except that he has come to write up the personnel of the Clifton Works."

"Thanks for reminding me that he is a reporter, nothing else. How did he persuade Pomponi to turn over the sick man to him?"

"Louis was mighty glad to get rid of him, if the yarn he told Search is true. About a month ago at midnight he went to his front door in response to a faint tapping. When he opened it a man fell forward and lay helpless on the floor. His clothes were dripping as if he had come from the river. There was an ugly scar above his right ear. Pomponi and his wife carried him upstairs, he was so attenuated he wasn't much of a weight, to the one vacant room they had. They stripped him, wrapped him in blankets, but couldn't restore consciousness."

"Why didn't they call you?"

"That's what Search asked, and Louis answered, 'There were no papers, no marks of identification,' and that he did not dare tell anyone because in the morning the man began to mutter, 'This is the place. There will be help and money here to carry on.' It was at the time of the trial of the relatives who had helped the German saboteurs and Louis was terrified for fear the man who had staggered into his house was one who had escaped detection and that he, himself, would be imprisoned, perhaps executed if a spy were found on his premises."

"But the Pomponis have been naturalized, have been citizens of this town for years."

"When Search reminded Louis of that, he said, 'My name is against me. A leetle whisper an' I lose my job at the Works, me with my beeg family, me, who loves this country wheech has given me an' my keeds so much. Mees Gail came one day, I know she hear something by her eyes. I asked for chloroform today at the infirmary, said it

181

was for a sick dog I wanted it, then I think, "No use, we can't fool her." We tell our good friend, Search. He take him away.' "

"And he dropped him on your shoulders, Johnny?"

"On ours, Gail. You're in this thing up to the neck. We don't know why the man came here. From his mutterings Search and I suspect he may be an enemy paratrooper who came down in the river and, starved and chilled, had been wandering in the woods for weeks."

Apparently Greg had not told him of the missing son whom the mysterious woman had come to the Works to find. It was much more likely that the man was a saboteur, his reference to "help" and "money" made that probable.

"The situation doesn't seem real. I feel as if I had been at a movie watching the story unfold on the screen. What part do I play in the chiller-thriller?"

"To carry on the house as usual — even if we could find a maid it wouldn't do to take her in now — and to scotch curiosity about our affairs whenever it rears its head. In short, to paraphrase one of our generals, 'Get your teeth in the secret and keep them closed.' Hilda has come back, presumably to help you."

"Makes me out a weak sister. Never mind, I can take it as part of my job. Does Louis know you are caring for his late visitor?"

"No, Search played up the possible danger to him and his family if the man turned out to be a spy and the Government discovered that he had harbored him. Believe me, Louis won't talk nor will his wife or children. Here we are at the house. Remember, you don't know there is anyone on the third floor. Keep away from it."

"You may be surprised, Johnny, but the less I know of what goes on in the suite of the late Miss Petunia Judson, the happier I will be."

Chapter 13

Followed days of weather so perfect that flowers still bloomed in protected corners of the garden. Gail glanced at the calendar beside the vase of tawny russet chrysanthemums on her office desk. November first and the global war was approaching another crisis. The Japs intensified their attempts to eliminate the footholds of the Marines in the Solomons, the Germans diverted their main effort to the Caucasus plains and passes, and the British Eighth Army in Egypt pushed ahead slowly through enemy minefields in a preliminary phase of a showdown struggle for the Mediterranean. In her own little corner of the universe, B.C. and Greg drove the Works to unprecedented speed to do their full share in the production of the five thousand planes rolling off the assembly lines of the country each month, and the mysterious patient still occupied the suite of the late Petunia.

She thought of her assurance to Johnny that the less she knew of what went on there the happier she would be. She hadn't realized then how subtly curiosity about the occupant of the third floor could undermine distaste. It was like being given the key of a Bluebeard closet and being forbidden to use it. It had been given to her the evening Sebastian Brent had come back into her life, she remembered. He had gone again that same night, but he had not allowed her to forget him. She glanced at the fragrant bunch of deep purple violets thrust into the belt of her navy serge skirt. They were perfect against her soft yellow blouse. She had written and begged him not to send them but they came each week.

"Come in." She answered the tap on her door.

"Mark, when did you return?"

Croston dropped into the chair opposite her. The strong light of the late afternoon sun brought out fine lines which hadn't been there when she had seen him a week ago, revealed a curious pallor under the skin drawn tight over his Slavic cheekbones. The change added a certain romantic appeal to a face which had been extremely good-looking before. His coming had set her heart glowing. Was her feeling for him warmer than friendship?

"Miss me?" he asked.

She had missed him. She hadn't realized

until he went away what a large share of her thoughts and time he had occupied. It wouldn't do to let him know it.

"Yes and no. I've been terrifically busy. I've come back to the Works several nights to get off letters."

"So Cissie-Lou told me."

"Cissie-Lou!" She realized the dismay in her voice and laughed. "Charge my surprise up to the fact that I thought my niece was at Mrs. Craven's practising for her musical debut at the concert the night after Thanksgiving."

"Got through early, she said, I saw her on the street, picked her up and dropped her at the house. What's happened to the kid? When I suggested that I come in and wait for you, she acted as nervous as if she suspected I was Raffles, modern model. She assured me hurriedly that you wouldn't be home until late, you would have dinner to prepare and that you, I quote, 'pos—i—*tive*—ly *loathed* having anyone underfoot in the kitchen,' Unquote. She and I were pals. You haven't turned her against me, have you?"

It was difficult to meet his eyes narrowed in suspicion, when she was wondering if Cissie-Lou had had the patient on the third floor in mind and feared Mark

Croston might suspect his presence if he came into the house. She and Billy were taking the secret entrusted to them seriously.

"You're so long answering I believe you have," he accused.

"Don't be foolish, Mark, *I* like you. Why shouldn't Cissie-Lou? Tell me about your trip. Did you find your mother well? Although you didn't admit it, I had a feeling you were anxious about her."

"I was. Three thousand miles is a long distance away from a person to whom you have been very close. She was fine. Has a couple of student army officers quartered in my rooms, and is having the time of her life showing them round, which proves how silly it is to worry, doesn't it?"

"Not to me. I think it's sweet for a son to have his mother on his mind enough for him to fly to the Coast and back to make sure she's all right."

"She is, double all right. Who's been sending you violets while I was away? I don't like it."

"Don't you? I love it." Unnecessary to tell him that when he entered she had been planning how to stop more of them coming. "I'm terribly glad you're back."

"Why? Anything wrong in my department?" He was on his feet frowning down at her across the desk.

"Goodness, no, don't be so temperamental. It's just that each one of us should be on the job as never before. Mr. B.C. has grown a little whiter and G.H. is getting to resemble no one so much as the lean and hungry Cassius. I suspect he's torn between his urge to get into the fighting at Guadalcanal and the surety that he can do more to help here than there."

"I assume he's not so rushed that he won't take time out for his wedding. Date still the day before Thanksgiving?"

"I haven't heard of a change." She placed a fresh sheet of paper in her typewriter. "Now that we have finished our gossip-fest I suggest you run along. I have a lot to do before I leave, if you haven't."

"How about dining with me at the Club?"

"Sorry. The answer is 'No' — with thanks of course. I'm always the perfect lady. I have dinner to prepare at home."

"Okay, it's your turn to invite me to dine."

"Not tonight. Didn't plan for a guest. In my effort to conserve, Billy says I'm penurious. I'm not, but I budget my housekeeping minutes to the second. Time is of the essence. I'm not sure just what that means but I've had a yen to use the expression, so here goes."

"You're in one of your twinkle-twinkle moods, aren't you? It couldn't be because I'm back, could it?"

"Could be, but is it? I don't know. Sorry to erase that devastating smile, but the truth must be told."

"Not always. By the way —" his tone was elaborately casual — "suppose I were called to another job — suddenly — the Government can shift me — would you go with me at a moment's notice?"

Was he asking her to marry him? He'd have to be more definite than that. Her pulses picked up to double-quick. She strove to keep her voice as casual as his.

"Can't tell till the time comes. You might be so eloquent you'd sweep me off my feet into matrimony. That's what you implied, wasn't it?"

"Inference correct. Forget the sudden-shift stuff. I'm staying here. To return to the present, can't you whip up enough food for one more tonight?"

"It hurts to admit it, but I'm no whipperupper, Mark. I make out menus for a week, market for them and put them through as planned. Believe it or not, I have to budget my office time too."

"I get you. Arrange your budget to include dining with me tomorrow night, will you?"

"I'd love it. Now, if you —"

"Don't say it, I'm going." He stopped at the door. "You're beginning to show the strain of your double-life program, office and housework to be explicit. Your always outsize eyes are enormous. Anything on your mind I can help about?"

"The only thing on my mind at present is getting off these letters. If you really want to help —"

" 'Nuff said. I'll be seeing you."

As the door closed behind him she glanced into the mirror. Was Mark right? Was she showing the strain of packed-to-the-brim days, three evenings a week as Nurses' Aide at the hospital, a secret in the house and wakeful nights? Had he intended marriage when he had asked if she would go away with him suddenly? He had shifted the subject quickly when she had flatly asked his intentions. Marry him? Did she love him enough for that? Did she love him at all or was what she felt for him merely attraction?

"Come in," she called in answer to a tap on her door.

"Now what?" she wondered as it slowly

opened. A head in a black feather turban was projected into the room and a voice, shaking with mock terror, inquired: —

"Safe for me to enter?"

"Aunt Jane! Come in." With a profound sigh Mrs. Clifton sank into a chair. "What's on your mind this time?"

"Greg."

"*Greg!* Why? Has he been *hurt?* Is he *ill?* Is he —" Aware, from the curious expression in the eyes watching her, that her voice had been rising in panic, Gail caught at her self-control and laughed.

"Of course it isn't any of those things or I would have known it. What *is* the matter?"

"I don't like the idea of his approaching marriage, the day is getting frighteningly near. To come out with the truth, I don't like Lila Tenny. I don't want her to have my pearls. Of course they will go to Greg. She's tricky. I don't trust her."

"He does. As you won't have to live with her — they are to occupy that vacant house of his on the hill, I understand. A little bird told me he had positively refused to move to that colossal mansion of hers — it won't make a lot of difference if you don't like her, will it?"

"But, I *am* to live with her — or she with

me. Since the oil shortage, even though we have converted to coal, B.C. and I have decided we had no right to run our big house for two of us. He suggested to Greg and Lila that this winter they occupy the ell suite. It has living room, two bedrooms each with a dressing room, and a first floor entrance with stairs leading to it. They'll be quite on their own."

"I remember it. Mr. B.C. had it built on for Greg's mother after her husband died, didn't he?"

"Yes. She didn't live in it long, poor soul. I've had the time of my life having the apartment done over. No priorities yet on furnishings. Lila's rooms are as deluxe as a Hollywood stage-set and a lot more artistic. I've yearned for a daughter to dress. I'm quite sure Lila won't like it — it's too glamourish for her — but I ordered the most adorable white velvet housecoat with a whopping cabochon of green glass in the buckle of the wide gold belt, and sandals to match, as a surprise present for her. How does the costume sound to you?"

"Like a *Vogue* dream. What did Lila say to doubling up?"

"To my amazement she gave her unqualified approval. Our servants from butler to kitchen maid are too old to get other jobs — they'll stay with us till they are pensioned — the prospect of house-keeping with the present difficulty about help didn't appeal to her."

"Does Greg approve?"

"He approves of anything which will leave him free to give all his thought to the Works. I'm the one who is scared. Can you imagine Lila and me living in the same house without fireworks?"

"Of course you can. You're tired. You are working too hard, you've been at the Red Cross for hours every day and I suspect you're dieting strenuously. The Gremlins will get you if you don't watch out. Haven't had a bite since breakfast, have you?"

"No, but I've lost four pounds this last month." Triumph gave way to longing. "I presume you served tea in the boss's office an hour ago?"

"I did, but it won't take a minute to prepare a cup for his famished wife."

Apparently Mrs. B.C. had come with a purpose. Better let her get it off her mind. As Gail filled the glass teakettle she cast a wistful glance at her typewriter. Why worry? The letters could be finished at home after dinner.

"B.C. won't listen — he declares that

Greg's love life isn't our business," Mrs. Clifton pursued the subject of her concern. "Love life! I believe the boy doesn't know what real love is. It isn't only physical attraction that keeps a marriage off the rocks, it's loving a person so much that just being together spells happiness, respecting one another's dislikes as well as likes — hasn't Lila been nagging him to get back into the service, when he has told her time and again that his place is here? Why am I telling *you* facts that only years of marital partnership can teach? Because, if you believe your fiction, one of the jobs of the modern secretary is to listen to the troubles of her boss's wife. I'm so worried I've got to talk to someone."

Gail sidetracked the train of thought which had been rearranging her evening time-schedule to provide for typing the letters.

"Worried about what?"

"I told you. Greg's marriage."

"Oh, that." She measured tea and sliced a lemon. "I'd like to be helpful, Aunt Jane, but I don't see what can be done about it at this late date."

"I thought you might do something."

"*I!* What can I do?"

"Make a play for him yourself."

Gail set down the saucer and cup on the desk with a little crash.

"You have such wonderful ideas, Mrs. Clifton! You'd be a veritable gold mine for Hollywood."

"Don't be sarcastic, young woman. Remember I'm the wife of your boss."

If you weren't, you would have been out of this office minutes ago, Gail told herself. Aloud she said: —

"I haven't forgotten. If I weren't too busy to make a play for anyone, I have other views as to matrimony."

"The man who says it with violets? He has good taste, they are perfect against your yellow blouse. I suppose it's Mark Croston. I met him in the corridor just now. He's fascinating with his you're-the-only-woman-in-my-life line. He even tries it on me. Stop grinning. I know I'm fat and over forty, but I'm the wife of his boss and say it who shouldn't I give excellent dinners."

"I was smiling at the disdain in your voice when you said, 'even tries it on me.' I know he sincerely likes you."

"I like him, but when I'm with him an inner voice warns, 'Watch your tongue.' What do you make of that?"

"Nothing, except that 'Don't talk. Information may help the enemy' is being hammered into one's consciousness from morning till night. Drink the tea, that's a dear. Nothing like it when one is low in one's mind."

"I know you're laughing at me, but I'll take it, if you'll listen. You must have noticed how thin and tense Greg is. It would be a tragedy if he is heading for an unhappy marriage. He never whistles now. Before he enlisted I used to listen for his whistle in the morning while he dressed, and after he came home at night. It warmed my heart." Her plump chin wobbled, tears brimmed her eyes. "Perhaps I'm silly to be so anxious but he's the only child B.C. and I have, he was all ours after his mother died when he was ten."

Gail blinked wet lashes in sympathy. She had attributed the change in Greg to his burning urge to get at the facts behind the story of the missing son of the mysterious woman, not to dissatisfaction with his fiancée.

"Everyone is tense now, Aunt Jane, and will be till the time comes when hearts are light again."

"When hearts are light again. That's a thought for anxious days and wakeful nights. Just the sound of the words lifts the weight from my spirit and reminds me that the skies always clear. But, I still want to know what sends Greg out at midnight to prowl the streets if it isn't the realization that he will make a hideous mistake if he marries Lila Tenny."

"Greg is an Air Raid Warden. Doubtless he goes out at night to familiarize himself with his district."

"With the district in which he has lived all his life? Think up another reason if you want me to believe you're as brilliant as my husband declares you are."

"That's telling me. I give up. I —" The opening of the door of Benjamin Clifton's office cut off the sentence. Greg Hunt laughed as he entered.

"Here again, Aunt Jane? Tea-drinking at the Works isn't getting to be a habit, is it? If it is, it's a nice one." He glanced from one face to the other. "What was Gail about to give up, when I stepped into the picture?"

Mrs. Clifton rose. As he followed her to the door she said: —

"She had given up trying to explain the reason of your tenseness and loss of flesh, Greg."

"What's your answer, Aunt Jane?"

"Mine?" She looked up at him and laid a

tender hand on his sleeve. "I think you know you are making a tragic mistake in your marriage, my boy. I don't believe you really love Lila, not with the kind of love that makes a man take a desperate chance to get the woman he wants."

Gail had expected him to laugh; instead he repeated gravely: —

" 'A desperate chance.' You think that's a proof of real love? If I am worrying about my approaching marriage, Aunt Jane, what would you advise me to do about it?"

"I've already prescribed. I advised Gail to make a play for you and draw you away from Lila." She ignored the girl's stifled, *"Aunt Jane!"* "But — she declined, replied snootily that her heart has been bestowed elsewhere. Page the violet man. Good-by."

Chapter 14

Backed against the door he had closed behind his aunt, Gregory Hunt asked gravely: —

"Has your heart been bestowed elsewhere, Gail?"

"*Elsewhere!*" Indignation sent a wave of delicate pink to her hair. "You wouldn't expect it to be left at your door all tied up with rose-color ribbon, or would you?"

"No. No such luck." The color had come back to his face, the sparkle to his eyes. "I might like to find it there but I wouldn't expect it. Who is the lucky man? Croston? Aren't the violets a recent tribute? I've never seen you wear them before."

She could stop this questioning by admitting that Mark had not asked her to marry him, though he had expected the privileges of a fiancé. Or had he tentatively proposed a few moments ago? Why admit that the violets were not from him? Why admit anything? Why not keep others guessing as Mark was keeping her?

"What's the answer?" Greg frowned at her across the desk.

"About the violets? That I adore them, somebody knows it. Who can it be?" she teased. "Sounds reasonable doesn't it? My question: See that notebook full of dictation? I must get those letters into the evening mail. First, Mark Croston appears for a 'welcome home' greeting, next Aunt Jane. Now you. A desk in the village square would be cloistered quiet in comparison to my office this afternoon."

"I get you. In other words you are too busy to listen to what we have discovered about our mysterious visitor."

"Of course I'm not, Greg." She leaned forward eagerly. "Don't be so maddening. Tell me, quick."

"The power of curiosity. I was an intruder, now I'm as welcome as the flowers that bloom in the spring, tra-la. Sit back and take it easy." He dropped into the chair across the desk; the third person to occupy it within the hour, Gail thought, before she reminded: —

"I'm waiting."

"I see you. There is a little curl in the middle of your forehead and a slight smudge of carbon on your chin. They add to your glamour. I'm not blind, did you think I was?"

She started to answer, "According to

Aunt Jane you are, about Lila," thought better of it and substituted: —

"Don't waste time asking foolish questions. I'm tingling with excitement. What have you found out about our mysterious visitor?"

"Remember that your heart-throb —"

"Mark Croston knows nothing about her. I —"

"So, he is your heart-throb? I was referring to Major Brent."

Gail's cheeks burned. By her eager denial she had practically admitted that Mark Croston was the man in her life. She started to go to town on the subject of this cross-examination, thought better of it and laughed: —

"Pretty lucky to have two heart-throbs in these manless days, I'll say. What am I to remember about Major Brent?"

"That he had a photograph of the person whom he was trailing." He left the chair for the corner of her desk.

"I remember. I remember also that her name was Edwards. We haven't an Edwards in the organization — or have we? Is it a picture of the woman who came here?" Her voice had dropped to a whisper.

"Yes. There can be no doubt that the woman Brent was trailing and the woman who died in our office were the same person. It doesn't prove, though, that the son had been bound for our defense job. We haven't an Edwards here."

"What will you do about it?"

"Search has flown to the Coast to talk with the neighbor who started Brent on his quest and to fingerprint some of the son's letters. We've had a lantern slide made from the photograph. When he returns we'll throw it on a screen and invite the men who occupy responsible positions in the Works to view it."

"What reason will you give for showing it?"

"The same story Brent told, that she has disappeared and that all factories with defense orders have been asked to show the picture that the son may know his mother is missing."

"Will you say that she — died?"

"Not at first. I'm telling you so you won't be caught off guard. B.C. and I know we can count on your loyalty and courage, but the man who has been writing to her, who is posing as her son — always supposing that this is the plant for which the boy was slated — was selected for the job because he has the cunning of a fox."

"There's one department head you needn't invite to the picture-show."

"*Who?*"

"Good heavens, Greg, that word went through my head like a pistol shot!"

"Let's look." He leaned forward and gently pushed back the hair at her right temple. "No hole there."

"Why be so literal? Don't you recognize a figure of speech when you hear it? To answer your explosive question, I was referring to Mark Croston."

"Why so cocksure our picture-show won't interest him?"

"Because he flew to the West Coast to check on his mother. He has just returned. He told me only a few minutes ago that she was fine, had a couple of army officers quartered in his rooms and was having the time of her life."

"In spite of the fact that he has seen his mother recently, we'll invite him to the picture-show. Might look queer if we didn't."

"Don't worry so about it, Greg. If the substitute for the woman's son is here, we'll catch him,"

"How can I help worrying? Here's a great industrial plant, throbbing with vitality, a young giant of war production —

for whose growth and usefulness I am partially responsible — with a mystery we haven't yet fathomed threatening its continuing usefulness if not its life."

"Life seems made up of mystery these days. It's a great adventure no matter where you are. I understand your anxiety, Greg. Aren't you wasting valuable time waiting for the return of Tom Search?"

"No. We need all the facts before we make any sort of move. Dated for tonight?"

"No. Why?"

"The Doc invited me home for dinner with him."

"He *did!* How like a man. I didn't know he had planned to dine at home. You can't come. There won't be enough dinner."

"Don't tell me your hospitality bump is frozen for the duration."

"It isn't. Billy and Cissie-Lou entertain their friends as often as they like. All I ask is to be forewarned that I may provide enough for a hungry horde."

"If that's all that's holding up my coming, I'll bring a steak — this isn't a meatless day, is it?"

"No, but —"

"If I can't get steak there is always chicken. I'll come early and help. I'm a knockout in a chef's apron."

"Where's Lila? Why aren't you dining with her?"

"In New York getting clothes. Good Lord, she has more now than she can wear."

"Why not have what she likes — if she can — while the going's good? Any day now they may be rationed. I'm sold on the up-to-the-minute fashions. They certainly are exciting."

"You girls are all alike." He glanced at the clock. "My car is here. Suppose I call for you in an hour? We could go to market together?"

"No."

"Who's shooting off a word now? I'll be at the house in time for K.P. duty." He closed the door, opened it quickly to ask: "Any idea where Croston's mother lives?"

"No."

"Okay. Until six-thirty. *Adios.*"

When Gail reached home the lace-covered table was set in the mahogany paneled dining room with the choicest Trevor china and glass. Cissie-Lou, with cheeks as pink as the carnations which spattered her smock, was arranging a bowl of small feathery-white chrysanthemums.

"Silver candlesticks! Do my eyes deceive me, or is that a beautifully polished coffee

205

set on the buffet?" Gail demanded theatrically from the threshold. "Something tells me that a party is indicated, or am I wrong?"

"You're right, all right." Cissie-Lou stepped back to appraise the effect of the flowers in the center of the table. "Dad phoned he had invited G.H. to dinner and then along came the chrysanthemums in a box with a sensational spray of yellow orchids for you and two super gardenias for me from Greg. They're in the icebox." She thrust out her wrist to look at a watch in a setting of infinitesimal diamonds.

"Don't stand there with your eyes bulging like black marbles. You've got the dinner to cook."

"My eyes are bulging from frenzied computation. How can I stretch a broiler to serve five persons, two of them men, not to mention Billy, who, when it comes to appetite, figures up to three more?"

"You should worry. A huge prewar steak came with the flowers — I thought for a minute it was a mirage — also frozen asparagus and the biggest, whitest, plumpest mushrooms you've ever seen."

"Manna from heaven."

"As a cook wasn't dropped with it, it's up to you to get busy preparing said manna instead of standing there staging a dramatic act, Gail. When those men come, they'll be hungry and you know when Dad's hungry he's cross as a bear until he's fed. Before I marry I'll find out what sort of a disposition the candidate has when his meals aren't on time. It will be nix to him if he's a grouch — if he's the only man in the world. I don't intend to fight my way through matrimony. Marry! Fat chance I have of having a beau for years, with all eighteen and nineteen boys to be taken into the service and nothing but the fifteen-to-seventeen kids left."

"The new draft law does thin your stag-line, doesn't it? I hadn't thought before of what it would mean to girls of your age."

"We can take it if you older girls can. Scram. The eats have got to live up to the flowers and silver. I about broke my arm polishing it. It had to be done, couldn't let Greg think we live hand-to-mouth style. Pretty noble of me as this is rehearsal night and I'll have to study till dewy dawn to make up the time."

Judging by the contented postures of Doctor John and Greg Hunt as they slouched in deep chairs beside the living-room fire, smoking in companionable silence, the dinner had matched the appointments, Gail decided. She released a sigh which was half satisfaction and half fatigue, as she curled up at one end of the broad couch in a pale blue bodice and short black velvet skirt, with the soft yellow orchids at her shoulder.

It was difficult to realize that somewhere the earth was shaken by the thunder of battle lines forming and reforming, that the heavens were being rent by the shriek and whistle of bombs, that men were fighting, dying, when the room was so heavenly peaceful. Shaded lamps glowed. Burning logs purred and fell apart softly. Within glass walls Billy's goldfish twins flashed flaming shapes through crystal clear water. Sheet music lay on the top of the small grand piano. From the kitchen ell drifted an occasional exclamation or a high giggle. Cissie-Lou and Billy had ordered her out when she entered the pantry to help clear up; it was their job, they insisted, hers was to return to the living room and be a perfect lady.

"Why are you smiling, Gail?"

She glanced up at Greg Hunt looking gravely down at her.

"I was thinking what dears Cissie-Lou and Billy are. They never shirk —" she laughed — "that is, hardly ever. Where's Johnny?"

"Answering the phone. I hope he isn't called out. You could see the lines fade and the color come back into his face at dinner. He adores those kids, doesn't he?"

"I've never seen a father who didn't. Fathers as I've observed them are something very special. Thanks for the sensational orchids, Greg. I feel as glamorous as a movie star on a bond-selling tour. Hilda! What is it?"

The white-faced woman in the doorway tried twice before her stiff lips moved.

"Where's Himself?"

"At the phone. He —"

"What's up, Hilda?" Her brother interrupted Gail's explanation.

"It's the patient on the third floor, Doctor."

"What's happened to him?" The two men spoke in unison. The nurse looked from one to the other, her eyes flashed back to John Trevor.

"I came down to get my own dinner and prepare his tray as I always do. I left him asleep in the big chair. When I went back he was gone."

"*Gone!* Where?"

"If I knew I wouldn't be standing here, would I?" Hilda was recovering her poise, the snap had returned to her voice. "The window above the ell was wide open. I looked out. The red tail-light of a speeding car flashed on the back road and disappeared."

Chapter 15

For a split second after Hilda's announcement John Trevor and Gregory Hunt regarded her incredulously, then took the stairs to the third floor two at a time.

"Wait here," the Doctor called when the nurse started to follow them.

"What do you make of it, Hilda?" Gail inquired anxiously.

The woman nervously smoothed back the salt-and-pepper hair above her left ear.

"It stumps me, Miss Gail. Half the time the patient has slumped in a big chair staring out the window. He appeared in a daze. If he spoke, the words would be disconnected. Has he been fooling me all this time?" Her eyes narrowed. "Now that I think of it, he has eaten everything I served him — as you know, that's been plenty — and his color has been better, a lot better." She dropped into a chair beside the fireplace as if her knees refused longer to hold her up.

"If he has made a fool of me after my years of experience it's time I gave up nursing and retired to a home for the feeble-minded."

"Perhaps he wasn't putting on an act, Hilda. Perhaps someone came in and carried him off."

"How? Pull him out on the ell roof and order him to jump, or drag him down the back stairs with me and the children in the kitchen? No. That man escaped under his own power. That comes from letting Billy's dog stay at the firehouse. If he'd been here no one could have got in or out." As John Trevor and Gregory Hunt entered she asked tensely: —

"Has he really gone, Doctor?"

"Gone and taken my best loungecoat with him."

"What became of the clothes he wore when Search brought him here, Hilda?"

"They were so dirty and ragged I burned them, Mr. Hunt. Doctor's orders."

"They appeared to have been lived in for weeks. I had planned to buy new ones for him when he was well enough to leave," John Trevor explained. "He got a jump ahead of me. Several jumps, as my dark blue suit is missing."

"How could he get it?" Hilda Speed's cheeks burned red as stoplights. "I haven't been out of this house since he was brought here and when I've taken my daily nap I've slept with one eye and both ears open."

"Not so open as you thought, apparently. Don't blame yourself, Hilda, he has out-witted us all. What's the next move, G.H.?"

"His escape nails him as an undesirable person to have on the loose. We've got to find him. If he is an enemy paratrooper, as we suspect, he'll contact fifth columnists, then prepare for trouble. We've thought he couldn't talk while all this time his mind was keen enough to aid in planning his get-away."

"Has anyone tried to see him, Hilda?"

"Not a living soul, Doctor."

"If he could get to your room for your clothes why couldn't he have used the tele-phone beside your bed to call someone, Johnny?"

"You said something then, Gail. What do you think of that as a solution of our mys-tery, Doc?"

"Good as any, I presume, G.H." John Trevor backed against the mantel and clasped his hands behind him. "It's a mess whichever way you look at it. We've lost a man who must not be lost. Answer the doorbell, Hilda. Our late patient may have returned."

It wasn't the late patient. Rhoda Craven, in a short mink coat over a pale gray frock, brushed by the frowning nurse and breezed into the living room on a fragrant air-wave of choice perfume. With a disapproving sniff Hilda disappeared.

"I've come to take Cis to the rehearsal. I — Johnny!" The emeralds on the hands Mrs. Craven clasped in startled surprise matched to a tint the perky bow in her bronze hair. "Are you real or a ghost?"

"I'm in no mood for histrionics, Rhoda. Why shouldn't I be here?" he answered impatiently. "I have an occasional moment at home."

"It isn't that. I passed your car in the village. Started to hail you. I thought you might be taking Cissie-Lou to —"

"Billy!" Greg Hunt shouted in the hall.

"Coming up, Cap," the boy called back. "What do you want?"

"See if your father's car is outside." He waited on the threshold. A distant door slammed. Rhoda Craven looked from one man to the other.

"What have I said or done to make such a commotion?"

"Are we making a commotion?" Gail evaded. "One of the neighbor's boys is everlastingly pestering the Doctor for the use of his car to run to the village and he just as steadily says 'No.' He must have snitched it and —"

"It's gone," Billy announced breathlessly from the hall. "Someone's stolen —"

"I've told you, Johnny, you should watch that Slippy Curtis —"

"Why should Pop watch Slip Curtis, Gail? What's the big idea? He wouldn't —"

"Billy, you've fronted for that boy too often. This is the showdown. Tell Cissie-Lou that Mrs. Craven is here. Please — or they will be late for rehearsal," she insisted as he looked at her as if suddenly she had lost her mind.

"Okay, I'll go, but you've certainly gone nuts, Gail, when you accuse Slip —"

"Billy! Call Cissie-Lou!"

"Yes, sir. Yes, Pop." He departed hurriedly.

"If you have gone 'nuts,' Gail, it is tremendously becoming." Rhoda Craven's approval was tinged with sarcasm. "Your eyes are brilliant as brown diamonds, your cheeks are the color of very pink roses. Brunettes are more effective than blondes when they are angry — aren't they, Mr. Hunt?"

"I really wouldn't know, Mrs. Craven. Haven't had much experience with angry gals. Hi, Cissie-Lou," he hailed, as the girl entered. A gay kerchief was tied over her golden hair. Two gardenias adorned the lapel of the plaid topcoat hung on her shoulders, under which she wore a turquoise blue skirt and cardigan. "Work hard on that song and do us credit at the concert."

"Where do you get that 'us,' you won't be there to hear it, Mr. Gregory Hunt."

"And why not?"

"Why *not?*" Cissie-Lou's eyes were glowing amethysts of surprise. "You're to be married the day before Thanksgiving, aren't you? You'll be on your honeymoon, won't you? Poisonous of you to plan to be away when I'm making my debut, Greggy."

"There's something in what you say, Cissie-Lou. I'll have to see what I can do about it."

Rhoda Craven's laugh tinkled with innuendo.

"Come, Cis. We'll leave the ardent bridegroom to plan a postponement of his wedding day. Won't the bride be pleased?"

John Trevor followed them into the hall and opened the door.

"Don't be late, Cissie-Lou. Good night, Rhoda."

"Good night, Johnny. If I see your stolen

216

car I'll seize it in the name of the law and bring it back to you."

Her slightly raised voice and the laugh that followed drifted back to the living room. Close beside Greg at the fireplace Gail whispered: —

"Do you believe Rhoda did see the car?"

"Why not? It is not outside. Someone has taken it. That woman's a pest. I'll bet I opened Pandora's box and let a lot of imps of mischief loose on this village when I leased my house to her."

"She was snippy about your marriage, Greg, but you rated it when you proposed postponing your wedding."

"Why shouldn't I postpone it if I want to?" He was the tense, tautly strung man of the day of his return to the office. "After all, there are two parties to a marriage contract, aren't there?"

"Greg!" Gail regarded him in consternation. Had the escape of the patient worked him up like this? "Easy does it." She laughed. "You've said that to me times enough. We'll get the man again. What good are Search and his minions if they can't find him? We'll —"

"Hi, Gail!" Billy hailed from the threshold. "What'd you mean saying Slippy Curtis stole Pop's car?"

"I didn't say he stole it, I said he might have borrowed it."

"He wouldn't do it. I'll bet it was the man who came to the back door —"

"What man?" With the simultaneous exclamation Gail and Greg Hunt closed in on the boy.

"When did he come?"

"For Pete's sake, what's all the shootin' about? He came while Hilda was eating her supper in the pantry."

"What did he say? What did he *do?* Where did he *go?*"

"Keep your shirt on, Gail. He just said, 'How's that patient upstairs?' and when I stalled and asked, 'What patient?' he winked and whispered, 'I'm one of Search's men.' "

"Was he?"

"I don't know, Cap. Didn't know Search had any men. Thought he was a reporter. Then the guy said, he talked kind of thick, 'Ask the old lady in there if I can see him.' I guess he heard Hilda scraping dishes in the pantry. She'd have been fit to tie if she'd heard that 'old lady.' I went to speak to her. When I came back he had vamoosed. I beat it to the door, thought I must be seeing double for two men were running down the drive."

"Running?" The telephone in the office rang. Gail heard her brother answer it before she asked, "Are you sure there were *two?*"

"Sure, I'm sure. Say, what's it all about? You two look as if you'd been called for and couldn't come."

"It's about the third-floor patient, Billy. He's made his getaway in your father's car *and* his blue serge suit."

The boy dropped to the arm of a chair.

"No kidding? I told Hilda I saw him coming out of Pop's room one day and she shushed me and said I was seeing things." He stared thoughtfully into the fire before he said, "Know what I think, Cap? I'll bet my hat she's covering up for the guy."

"Nonsense, Billy, here comes your father. We won't worry him with your suspicions about Hilda — yet. Any news of the car, Doc?" Greg asked as John Trevor entered.

"Cal Conway phoned it was parked in front of the Town Hall. My bag of instruments is in it. Billy, hop on your wheel and bring it back. I've got to wait here for a hospital call or I'd go myself."

"I haven't a license, Pop, but if you think I'd get away with it I'd be gosh-darned glad —"

"Of course you can't drive it," John Trevor interrupted the eager offer. "Sometimes I forget you are not older than you are." He laid his hand on the boy's shoulder. "You're such a good sport, son."

"I'll get the car." Greg Hunt tossed a cigarette into the fire. "My convertible is here. Gail can come with me and drive your sedan home."

"I'll get a coat and be back before you can say El Alamein," she agreed eagerly.

In the corridor outside her room she barely escaped collision with Hilda Speed. The nurse followed her in.

"Where are you going, Miss Gail?"

"After the Doctor's car. Didn't you hear Mrs. Craven say she saw it in the village?"

"I didn't wait to hear anything that woman said. The perfume she uses is downright sinful. It makes me sick. Are you sure it was Himself's car she saw?"

"It's gone from the drive where he always parks it and to make it more certain Cal Conway phoned a few minutes ago that it was outside Town Hall. I'm going there now to bring it back. The red light on that must have been the one you saw disappearing when you looked out the window."

"If I had thought he'd steal I wouldn't have let him go —"

"Who would steal, Hilda? Where wouldn't you have let him go? Did you know the patient was planning to escape?"

"Of course I didn't. What d'ye mean accusing me of double —"

"Gail! Hurry!" John Trevor called from the hall below. "What kept you so long?" he demanded as she pelted down the stairs.

"Hunting for my license. Ready, Greg."

"There was no use telling Johnny that it wasn't my license that was holding me up, that I was too stunned by Hilda's rambling remarks to move," Gail confided as the car shot forward under a sky silver-gilt with stars. "Perhaps you can make sense of them." She repeated the conversation with the nurse.

" 'If I had thought he'd steal I wouldn't have let him go —' " Greg repeated. "Sounds as if Hilda knew the patient was skipping, doesn't it? Even so, it doesn't make sense. She idolizes Doc. I can't see her messing up a plan of his — and it was his plan to keep the man at his house until he could talk."

A bell in a church solemnly told the hour. She counted: —

"Only nine! I can't believe it. This day

has seemed years long, so much has happened."

"What specifically?"

"I'd say it began with Mark Croston's return," she said as if she were trying to marshal her thoughts into line.

"Does he mean so much to you, that his arrival can start things happening?"

"That's just the point, Greg. I don't know, I only know that I was terribly glad to see him."

"Go on with your saga of the events of this epoch-making day. After Croston, what?"

"Your aunt followed Mark. You know what she talked about."

"I remember she said your heart had been bestowed already. What else?"

"She told me that you and Lila were to live at Twin Pines. That was a surprise as I'd heard you were to move into your vacant house on the hill. Aunt Jane is wondering how the arrangement will work out."

"She's not wondering half as hard as I am. However, doubling up in this instance seems to be not only the sensible, but the patriotic, thing to do, so we'll hope for the best. Here we are and here's the Doc's sedan. I didn't really believe we'd find it."

A man standing in the lighted doorway ran down the steps of the white marble building as the convertible stopped.

"Howdy, Miss Trevor. Howdy, G.H. Come for the Doc's car?" His voice was thin and high.

"Yes. Hop out, Gail. Perhaps you know how it got here, Cal? You town clerks are supposed to know everything."

"Not about stolen cars, we don't. Haven't got an idea. Saw it out front, thought 'twas a queer place for the Doc's car to be, he wouldn't be likely to have a patient in this neighborhood. Phoned his house to ask if 'twas okay it's bein' here? Seems it wasn't. I've kept an eye on it since. I've been swamped with applications for marriage licenses today. Left the office for a coke a few minutes ago an' saw the sedan. When are you plannin' to step up for your license, G.H.? They do say the big time's set for the night before Thanksgivin'."

Greg, who was flashing an electric torch round the inside of the sedan, said over his shoulder: —

"I'll be along for it in plenty of time." He snapped off the light and thrust his left hand into his coat pocket. "Suppose I didn't turn up till the last minute? Would I get it?"

Cal Conway thumped his shoulder affectionately.

"There ain't nothing you wouldn't get in this town, how and when you want it. I guess we know what to do for our hero." He cleared the gruffness from his voice. "Don't squirm, G.H. I ain't goin' to say no more, just wanted you to know they do say there ain't anything too good for you. If you want a license at one-hour notice, day or night, give me a ring an' you'll get it. An' that goes for you too, Miss Trevor. Always supposin' I approve of the guy."

Through Gail's memory echoed Mark Croston's voice, "Suppose I were called away suddenly — would you go with me at a moment's notice?" Curious that Cal Conway's offer of a marriage license while you wait should follow so quickly. She laughed in response to the twinkle in the Town Clerk's friendly green eyes.

"Thanks, Mr. Conway. That relieves my mind. No knowing when I may decide suddenly to go off the deep end. Shall I take the sedan now, Greg?"

"No. I have a better idea. Town Hall door unlocked, Cal?"

"Sure, it's always open. Why? Ain't thinkin' of savin' time an gettin' your license now, are you? Might be a good idea.

You've got everything you need right here — and how." He winked at Gail.

"I'm going in to phone the Doc. Don't take your eyes off those cars." Greg ran up the steps. A door clanged heavily behind him.

"Great guy, what?" Conway approved. "They do say it's fellas like him that are goin' to win this war for us. I don't mean because he's educated an' has family an' fortune behind him, it's the stuff he's made of that won't let his kind fail."

"The power within," Gail said softly and wondered where the phrase had come from.

"You've said it, only some folks call it 'guts.' Papers say the greatest naval battle of history was pulled off last week. Kind of encouraging that the war'll be over soon, don't you think?" He had two sons in the service, Gail remembered.

"I do, Mr. Conway." She responded fervently to the wistful eagerness in his voice, "In spite of what I read and hear, the hope of an early peace persists in sending out tendrils, very delicate, but very tenuous."

"*Hmp*, guess it's best we're not all that hopeful, we might stop workin' an' get licked. They do say —"

"Cal!" Greg sent his voice ahead of him

as he ran down the steps. "Will you drive my convertible to Doc Trevor's? He needs it, p.d.q. He'll drop you at your house."

"Me drive that classy car? Will a cat lick up cream? Lead me to it." He was behind the wheel before he finished talking. "Remember about that license, G.H. Any day, any minute. We won't keep you waitin', no *sir.*" The red light disappeared like a shooting star.

"Why the shift of cars, Greg?" Gail asked.

"Remember the Doc said he'd left his bag of instruments in the sedan? It's gone."

"Gone!"

"Not so much as the smell of antiseptics left. Hop in front. I'll drop you at the house. I'm taking the car to the hospital."

"Hospital. At this time of night! Why?"

"I want the Doc to give it the once-over with me." He drew out the hand he had kept in his pocket. "See that? The rug in the back was damp."

Even in the dim light of the street she could see the stain on his fingers.

"It isn't —" Her voice caught in her tight throat.

"It is. Blood. Stop shivering. Whoever was hurt isn't in the car now."

"Do you suppose the patient was kid-naped and — and — k-killed because he knew too much?"

"Darn sight more likely that the patient did the killing."

Chapter 16

Gail dropped the morning paper on her desk and glanced at the wall clock. She would have to work fast to make up for the time she had spent reading it. How could she have resisted following the glaring headline, CREWS SCRAP THE FRENCH FLEET? She couldn't and she hadn't. Thanksgiving tomorrow would be a real day of thanks for the United Nations.

The day before Thanksgiving and Greg's wedding day. She hadn't seen him since the night, days ago, when he had left her at her brother's door, before he drove on to the hospital with the bloodstained sedan. She had served evenings as Nurses' Aide at the hospital. There had been a round of informal parties. Each time news of a battle came a neighbor would plan a get-together in the hope of easing the tension of the mothers and fathers whose sons were on the battlefront. Greg had not appeared at any of them, Mark Croston had been her devoted escort.

Each time her office door opened she

had looked up eagerly hoping that it was Greg. Didn't he realize that she was fairly aching to hear the next installment of the mystery? The cause of the stains? If the missing patient had been located? She had given Johnny several opportunities to open the subject but each time he had dexterously shied away from it. Why hadn't Greg come here or to the house to tell her? Of course he and Mr. B.C. were straining every nerve to increase production. Even so — the door opening! Had he come at last?

"If your radiant smile is an indication, you sure are glad to see me, Gail." Mark Croston's satisfied voice didn't jibe with the uneasy expression of his eyes. Why explain that her welcome was not for him?

"I haven't seen you for almost twenty-four hours, Mark. That's a long time between friends." Of course she was talking nonsense; equally of course, he would understand that her fervent voice was plain theater. Or wouldn't he? His brows were drawn in a frown as he faced her across her desk.

"That's one thing I'm here to talk about," he said and became absorbed in stabbing a fountain pen into its ink holder.

"I assume you're going to the Tenny-

Hunt wedding this afternoon? Guest list limited to family and *very* intimate friends, I understand. The Trevors will qualify if anyone in town will."

The sudden switch of subject startled her. She had expected something else, had begun to wonder how she would answer if he asked her to marry him. She liked him tremendously, her pulses picked up when she saw him, they had fun together, but, were liking, accelerated pulses and fun a basis for marriage?

"You are going, aren't you?"

The emphasized question brought her eyes to his.

"Certainly I'm going and that isn't all. When I leave here at noon to array myself in a pastel blue, sheer wool frock and matching hat to do honor to my sub-boss's wedding in church, I start on a week-end vacation, the first since I took this job. I feel guilty about taking the time off but Mr. B.C. insists that I've earned it."

"Where are you week-ending? There are stars of anticipation in your eyes."

"They would be in yours if you had been general maid for weeks, trying to do a better catering job with less material and variety, a whole lot less — but, quote, 'the home must be maintained at all costs,' unquote. Aunt Jane, Mrs. B.C. to you, has invited Cissie-Lou, Billy, Doctor John, whenever he can come, and yours truly, to spend the week end at Twin Pines. The bride and groom won't return until Sunday afternoon to take up residence there . . . Just a minute."

She answered a phone call. Made an appointment for a conference. Spoke into the box on her desk, listened to a voice and snapped the switch.

"Pretty busy, aren't you?"

"Too busy to be entertaining a caller at this time in the morning, mister."

"Go on about your week end."

"No planning of meals. No cooking. No housework for three whole days. Result, happiness, to borrow from Mr. Micawber. Breakfast trays in our rooms. No wonder my eyes shine. The coachman came for our bags this morning. Mrs. B.C. has reverted to horse and station-wagon locomotion. I've packed enough in my wardrobe-case for a month's visit, one really needs as much in three days as for a month. And that, dear children, is my story."

"You are on top of the world, aren't you?"

"Perhaps I'm whistling to keep up my courage. It's at a new low when I think of

Greg." Her voice and eyes were grave.

"What d'you mean? You're not in love with your boss, are you? It has happened before."

"Of course I'm not, foolish, but I've been terribly fond of him since I was a little girl and I can't believe that Lila will make him happy."

"Why not? I admit she wilts with women but I think G.H. is getting a break. She has what it takes. Beauty. Influential friends. Family background and a tidy fortune. That combination can do spectacular things for the man she marries."

"Is that wh-what you want in a wife, Mark?" Had the treacherous catch in her voice tinged his dark skin with red? His eyes met hers for an instant and shifted back to the pen.

"It is, just what I want. I came here to put my cards on the table, Gail. I was afraid you might take seriously my little joke when I asked, the other day, if you would go away with me at a moment's notice. I like you more than any girl I ever met, but we've been going out together pretty constantly, especially this last week, and it's only fair to tell you that you haven't what I must have in a wife, the material things, I mean."

Brains didn't burst from rage — they didn't, Gail assured herself, even if hers showed all the symptoms. Had she really heard him turn her down or was it just nightmare? She plunged her teeth hard into her lower lip and winced. That hurt. She was awake. She was too boiling mad to cry, which had been her childish method of throwing off anger. She must answer him. Something light, of course. Would the sound she made pass for a laugh?

"Nice of you to let me know where I stand." That was wrong. Cut out sarcasm or he will think I care. "We have been good friends, haven't we? Why the past tense? We'll continue to be, won't we?"

"It's sporting of you to take it this way."

"But how would I take it? I'm not sure I want to marry. Marriage is apt to be presented as pure happiness, not for what it is, an adventure of incalculable risk. You didn't think I expected to marry you, an industrialist, did you? I'm convinced that I'm divinely designed to be the wife of a senator. I adore Washington life. There's the noon whistle."

As she rose he came round the desk and caught her hands.

"Gail, do you mean you're in love with that Washington boss of yours? Did the vi-

233

olets come from him?"

She smiled up into his angry eyes.

"If I am, if they did, it's a secret, Mark. Now, having settled matters to our mutual satisfaction I'll remind you that I have several letters to get off before I start on my vacation."

"There's no one like you, Gail. You're so gay, so sweet —" He caught her in his arms and kissed her. "If only —"

She twisted free and drew her hand lightly across her lips.

"If you've finished the Great Lover act, I would like to get to work."

"Okay, I'm going." As he paused with his hand on the doorknob, she thoughtfully regarded the inkwell. If she were sure of her aim, sure it would spatter — "This won't make any difference in our having fun together, will it?" he pleaded.

She discarded the idea of the inkwell. Even hurling that at him wouldn't relieve her feelings sufficiently.

"Silly, why should it? We'll have *more* fun. We'll both feel so *safe*."

"I'll phone you for a date."

She stood at her desk staring at the closed door. Was it true? Had she let him tell her he didn't want her without slapping him down with all her might? There were times when letting oneself go had self-control beaten to a frazzle for results. Her eyes and thoughts returned to the notebook on her desk.

"I can't tackle those letters now. I'll drive home, dress, come back here and get them off before I go to the wedding."

Her thoughts went round and round as on a treadmill as she drove her runabout home. Furious anger with herself that she had shown her liking for Mark so plainly that he had had to warn her off, that was what "putting his cards on the table" amounted to: a warning that she must not expect him to marry her. Lila had just what he wanted. Why hadn't he cut out Greg and married her?

She reached that question and the house at the same time. As she opened the front door she thought, "I must cool down. No sense in letting fury get me." Johnny's voice in the living room. What could have brought him home this time of day? Was either of the children ill? As she crossed the hall she heard a woman protest: —

"Not very patriotic of you to make such a fuss about my being away, John."

Mildred! Mildred had come. For an instant surprise paralyzed Gail's locomotive muscles.

"Lack of patriotism! That's a joke, Mildred. I've gladly shouldered the work of five men that they may serve on the firing lines. I'm fighting disease on the civilian front. I need you to help me carry on my tremendously vital job here."

"Why? You have Gail to run things."

"Gail is my sister. The children need you. This town needs you. I need *a wife* to whom I can turn for uplift and encouragement when I'm battling the stealthy demons of disease and death. The health of this whole county rests on my shoulders. You think of service in terms of change, I think of it as standing four-square to the nearest responsibility."

"Why didn't you say all this before? It will be impossible for me to get a discharge now."

"I said it but you wouldn't listen. You can get your discharge. I've inquired." He drew a letter from his pocket. "Listen to this: 'According to regulations, a discharge from an Auxiliary Corps will be issued at the convenience of the Government for the following reasons: Upon request of the applicant in case of utmost emergency . . .'

"There are other reasons listed which do not interest us. I consider your case one of utmost emergency. A big job doesn't necessarily call for a uniform. Think it over."

The gruff earnestness of her brother's voice roused Gail to the realization that she was listening to an intimate conversation. She attempted to steal by the door unobserved.

"Come in, Gail," he called. "Mildred is here." As she stood on the threshold he added, "Our first officer is something to write home about, what?"

She was; she was beautiful, Gail admitted as she glanced at her sister-in-law. She was perched on the arm of a chair, her perfect legs in beige nylons crossed in a most unmilitary attitude to keep her balance. Her tilted cap accentuated the golden sheen of her smooth hair. Wind and weather had not dulled the translucent quality of her skin, nor coarsened her finely drawn features. Her greenish eyes were slightly tilted, the brows above them were clean-cut black arches, the nose below them perfection, the lips were softly red. Her uniform with double silver bars on the shoulders was immaculate and complete even to the gloves drawn through the brown leather belt. She waved her hand, a cigarette between long, capable fingers.

"Greetings!" Then as Gail waited for the

feeling of dislike which always submerged her to subside, she added, "Don't worry, I haven't come to take your job."

"Haven't you? That's a break." Gail hoped for her brother's sake that aversion hadn't been noticeable in her voice.

Mrs. Trevor rose, tossed her cigarette into the fire and backed up to it. As her husband went to the hall to answer the phone she complained: —

"John has been lecturing me on my duty. He thinks I should be serving the nation at home."

"That seems to be the town consensus."

"Does that mean that my neighbors are not *proud* of what I am doing?"

If it were anyone but Mildred I'd think that break in her voice was emotion, Gail told herself, before she answered: —

"You'll have to ask them."

"I shan't." First Officer Trevor was her cool, assured self again. "At least I will be here long enough to get this house straightened out. It's a mess."

She'd better watch out, this was the second time this morning she had gone hot with fury. Two such attacks might do irreparable things to her brain, Gail warned herself.

"I thought the house looked quite or-

238

derly and respectable. What's the special mess?"

"Not special. General. Dust. Dust. *Dust*."

Dusting was Cissie-Lou's job, but her mother need not know that.

"My parlormaid evidently agrees with the poet who called dust 'the bloom of time.' "

"You may think it funny, I don't. Why has the silver been put away?"

"For the excellent reason that I haven't had time to clean it, and tarnished silver is my pet peeve."

"You shouldn't have tried to do the work yourself. You shouldn't have allowed Petunia to go."

"*Allowed!* I'd like to see you try and stop her."

"I would have. You're too easy to make an efficient housekeeper, my dear."

Gail thought of the thrill and excitement of the job in Washington she had given up to help Johnny, and she thought of the hours she had spent cooking and cleaning here because no woman was to be had to help. Before she could answer, her brother's slightly raised voice at the hall telephone interrupted: —

"I have asked you before not to phone the hospital to ask where I am, Rhoda.

Sorry. Can't take you to the wedding. Our first officer is here."

"What does that mean?" Mildred Trevor demanded.

Gail shrugged.

"That a fascinating woman is trying to get your job on the home front."

"Is John in love with Rhoda Craven?"

"Page him for the answer. She's terribly attractive, warmly sympathetic with his problems *and* determined to get her man. Johnny's strength and endurance are stretched to the snapping point. He is neither wood nor stone and is hungry for a woman to whom he can take his hopes and fears, his triumphs over death and his defeats. Figure it out yourself."

"He wouldn't be unfaithful."

"That's what you think." She was as sure as that the sun would rise tomorrow that he wouldn't be, but it would do his wife good to wonder.

"You were right, Mildred, when you said I am too easy. Now, if you have no other complaints I'll run up and dress for Greg Hunt's wedding. I have work to finish at the office before I can go festive."

"You mean you won't wait and get luncheon for your brother and me?"

"How quick you are. That's just what I

mean. I'll be seeing you — at the wedding."

She stopped on the stairs to call.

"Johnny would love pancakes and sausage for his lunch — in case you've forgotten."

Chapter 17

Curious that the numb feeling of anger didn't wear off, Gail thought, as back in the office she slipped a sheet of paper into the typewriter. She had showered and dressed in her gala clothes feeling as if a stranger, a girl she didn't know, were looking back at her from the mirror. The girl's eyes were brilliantly dark, her skin as colorless as ivory, her pastel-blue sheer wool frock with jet and sequins on pockets and cuffs, the matching toque with its touch of glittering black and shoulder-length veil, pale as an azure mist, thrown back from her face now, were as up to the minute as they came, but for some reason only her eyes seemed alive.

She'd better snap out of this comatose state and finish the work if she intended to get to the wedding. Wedding . . . The ice within her began to crack. "I think G.H. is getting a break," Mark had said. What had he said next? Her fury at Mildred had driven the preceding anger from her mind. It was coming back, what he had said about his fear that she would take his joke seriously about going away with him; that Lila had just what he wanted in a wife; that while he liked Gail Trevor more than any girl he'd ever met, it was only fair to tell her that she hadn't the material things he needed.

Her cheeks burned, hot tears stung her eyes. How had he dared? Why had she listened? Why had she let him get away with it? Why had she allowed Mildred to get her down? Why, why was Greg marrying a girl who was bound to make him unhappy? The last question broke up the ice in her heart. A freshet of anger swept away her control. She swung her chair and dropped her head on her folded arms on the desk.

Suppose Mr. B.C. were to come in and find her sobbing as if her heart were broken? He wouldn't. He was at home dressing for the wedding. Never mind who came, she'd cry this thing out. It had been piling up for weeks. Of course she was tired, but, who wasn't these days, tired from heartache at the agony of the world? Of course she had been tense ever since the woman had died in the office, what excuse was that for her to go to pieces? Of what significance was the death of one woman when men were dying by the thousands? When —

"Gail! What's happened?"

She looked up. Greg Hunt stood in the doorway of his uncle's office, an open letter in his hand. Had he heard her crying, had that drained the color from under his bronzed skin? Silly, of course not. She drew a long ragged breath and dabbed at her eyes with her fingers.

"I'm s-sorry, G-Greg. I — I'm terribly ashamed. I — I went h-home and Mil—"

"Stop talking. Look up." He came behind her chair and patted her eyes with a fine linen handkerchief. "That's better." The tender protectiveness of his voice flooded her eyes. "Hey, don't let the tears come again." He dabbed at two big drops on her checks. "Don't talk." He seated himself on the desk in front of her.

"I — I c-can talk now, G-Greg."

"Okay, what's the story? Got pretty mad about something, didn't you?"

She swallowed a sob and shut her eyes tight to keep back a fresh tide of tears.

"I — did. I'm terribly ashamed."

"You needn't be. You had it coming to you. Aunt Jane was right, we have driven a willing horse too hard."

"It isn't that, Greg, honestly it isn't. I've loved every minute of my work. Something h-happened here and then I went home and Mildred was there and she s-said the house was a m-mess and —"

"Easy does it, Gail. Get your breath. Now, what else did she say?"

"That the silver wasn't clean — that I shouldn't have let Petunia go —" She was on her feet now challenging him with defiant eyes.

"I'm never going back to that house, Greg, *never*. She can stay and keep up the domestic morale on the home front, take care of her family. I'm through. I suppose you think I'm a quitter, and unpatriotic. I don't care if you do."

He was looking down at the sheet of paper he was holding. Her eyes followed his.

"Why are you clutching that note, Greg? Something about the missing patient? I've been on the verge of a nervous breakdown while I *waited* and *waited* for you to tell me what happened the night he escaped."

"The letter is not about him. I'll give you a full report later."

"Someone not coming to the wed— The wedding!" She glanced at the clock. Her eyes widened in dismay. "Greg Hunt, *why* are you here listening to my silly troubles? You're still in your blue serge. *Why* aren't you at home dressing?"

"You're dressed for the fracas, aren't you? Honey outfit. That gauzy stuff on the hat looks like the sort of thing bridesmaids wear on their heads. Let's see how it goes." He carefully drew the veil over her face till the edge encircled her shoulders, "It's a knockout."

"Greg, stop talking to me as if I were a child to be comforted. For goodness' sake, go home and dress. Wait a minute." She threw back the veil which made a misty setting for her dark hair to answer a call on the interoffice phone.

"You, Mark? Of course what you said this noon didn't make me cry. The hoarseness may be a cold starting. You're sorry. That's all right — You do want to? Is this a *bona fide* proposal? No fooling? I'm all excited. It isn't sarcasm. I'll take it under consideration. Sure, I'll dine with you tonight — if I can eat anything after Aunt Jane's spread for the wedding. I'm terribly busy. Good-by until dinner. I'll be ready at seven-thirty as usual — just a minute — I shall be at Twin Pines. Come there for me." She snapped off the switch.

"That was Croston asking you to marry him, wasn't it? I couldn't help hearing. Why was he sorry?" Greg inquired.

"He dropped in this morning to assure

me that you had all the breaks in getting Lila, that his attention to me was not serious." Her breath caught. "Evidently he thought it over."

"He proposed to you, didn't he?"

"That makes the second time. The other day, he asked me if I would go with him at a moment's notice if he were shifted suddenly to another job, if you can call that a proposal."

"*He* — asked you that? You wouldn't, or would you?"

"Greg, don't take it so seriously. I'm not sure whether I would or not. I more than like him. It would be a simple way to straighten out the tangle at my brother's if I weren't there. Mildred would be at home — Johnny says she's terribly needed in this town — devoting herself to her husband and civilian front activities." The wall clock struck the hour. "Stop thinking of my silly troubles. Go home and dress for your wedding."

"There won't be a wedding. Read this. It came ten minutes ago."

She looked up into his eyes, gray now, inscrutable, before she took the letter he offered.

"Read it aloud. I want to be sure it isn't an optical illusion."

Her voice showed husky traces of her emotional storm as she read: —

"Dear Greg,

"After you told me last evening that you would be unable to leave the Works even for a week end honeymoon I decided we'd better call off our marriage before, rather than after, the ceremony, for a break was bound to come.

"*Greg!* At this late hour! She can't mean it!"

"Go on! Read."

"My wishes, what I want, have been secondary with you and I won't stand for it. I am enclosing your ring. I shall leave for Washington when you receive this.

LILA

"I just can't believe it," Gail whispered. "I don't blame Lila for being disappointed about the honeymoon, but to break up her marriage for that reason is incredible. Why couldn't you get away?"

"New directives, and Search wrote he'd be ready for the picture-showdown Saturday."

"You mean — the mysterious woman?"

"Yes." His voice was as hushed as hers. "B.C. and I talked it over, I *must* be here this week end. I didn't know about the directives or the showdown until last night. Anyway, how can I leave with every man at the Works giving up his holiday for rapid-fire production?"

"Why did she wait until now to tell you?"

"You're asking me. I suspect it was her intention to leave me waiting at the church, then lost her courage because of what people would say."

"Perhaps writing that she was going to Washington was a bluff. Perhaps she hasn't gone. Perhaps she's just testing you. Perhaps she's dressed waiting for you to give in and come for her or telephone. Hurry. There's still time."

His laugh had no mirth in it.

"Then she'll be disappointed. I have no intention of giving in."

"Greg, what will you do now? In less than two hours the guests will begin to arrive at the church. How can you reach them? Do Aunt Jane and Mr. B.C. know?"

"No one knows — but you. I came here to ask you to cancel arrangements for me. I found you sobbing your heart out and suddenly a solution slashed through my mind like a bolt from the blue."

"I'm ashamed now. Terribly ashamed. Two persons had made me furiously angry. You know me, when I get good and mad." Her lips trembled in a smile, laughter flashed between her drenched lashes. "The storm is over. Let's get busy. I made out the list of guests for the reception. I have it here."

He caught the hand with which she was opening a drawer in the desk.

"Just a minute. Why cancel? Why not let the festivities proceed?"

"Greg, dear, I know you've had a terrific shock, but get hold of yourself. It isn't fair not to stop arrangements as soon as possible. There isn't anything else to do."

"Oh, yes there is. You can take Lila's place. Hold everything. Don't talk until I finish. Just a few changes in the marriage license — didn't Cal Conway assure us he would accommodate at a moment's notice — and you and I walk up the church aisle to the strains of 'Here Comes the Bride.' That's the way Lila had planned it: no attendants, no one to give the bride away. You're dressed for it, 'something blue,' even to the veil. Think what a boon to the community! For a few hours their minds

250

will rest from war headlines while they discuss us."

"Greg!" The word was a shocked whisper. "Now I *know* you're crazy."

"What's crazy about that proposition? It will be just one more wartime wedding. Men and girls all over the country are falling in love, going off the deep end at a moment's notice. I found you here sobbing out your heart, declaring you will never return to your brother's house. Next, you say you're tempted to marry Croston to escape. Neither B.C., Aunt Jane, the Doc nor I want you to marry him. We've talked it over plenty. We don't know enough about him. The solution of your situation and mine flashed like a caption on a screen. MARRY. Let Mildred work out her own family problems. If you hadn't rushed in to fill the breach perhaps she wouldn't have gone into the service. She can do more good in this town than she can where she is. Her war job is right here." He glanced at the wall clock.

"How about it? Afraid?"

"I'm not afraid of anything — except you, when you've gone haywire as you have now."

"I've not gone haywire, never was more sane in my life. We're both on the same job, up to our necks in it, we've got to see this through. We're the best of friends. Ever since you were a youngster I've felt that to a degree I was responsible for your safety and happiness. Now I want to take over entirely. I don't like the way you've been running round with Croston, I don't like —"

"*You* don't have to like it. I'm the one. Mark dropped in this morning to tell me that though he admired me more than any girl he'd ever met, I didn't come up to specifications financially. I was furious with him all the way home, then I walked in on Mildred —"

"So, Croston started the cloudburst? Love him so much he made you cry?"

"I don't know whether I love him or not."

"If you loved him, you'd know it. When the real thing hits you, there's no doubt. It's like a — a bolt from the blue. Remember what Aunt Jane said in this very office, that real love would make a man take a desperate chance to get the woman he wants? I know now that she's right."

"Are you giving me the benefit of *your* experience?"

"We'll go into that later when there's more time. You haven't answered my question. Will you marry me at four? We'll have time to get the license *and* a wedding ring before we go to the church. Yes or no?"

Then we'll have time for things like wedding rings . . .

The line from a current song hummed through Gail's mind as she glanced at the clock. Marry him in just one hour and fifty-five minutes? At least he didn't intend to use the ring he had bought for Lila. Suppose she said, "Yes." Maybe he was right, maybe it would straighten out Johnny's home problems if she were where she couldn't keep house for his family. Where would she — she caught her breath —

"You don't mean for me to live at Twin Pines, do you?"

"Where else if you were Mrs. Gregory Hunt?"

"I can't do it. I can't."

"Okay. Aunt Jane expects you for the week end. Don't let my change of plan upset that. Get out the list. We'll cancel. Can't you imagine Lila's gleeful satisfaction when she reads the glaring headlines, 'Pacific Hero Left Waiting at the Church'? I haven't been forgotten quite yet, you know."

"Greg. It mustn't happen." She stood very near him and looked up.

"You don't mean this to be a real marriage, do you? I — I couldn't."

"To preserve the dignity of marriage is one of the things for which we are fighting those libertine devils, isn't it? I don't want a wife without her love. That gives you a rough idea of what marriage means to me."

"How about *your* love? Were you planning to marry Lila Tenny without really loving her?"

"It seems to add up to that. I must have been living in a sort of hangover from the nightmare of war. I'm wide awake now. I know I don't love her. I can't bear to see those spectacular lashes of yours wet." He tenderly wiped her eyes. "Come on, be a good girl. Smile for the guy, lady."

"You haven't answered my question."

Color burned under his dark skin. His eyes were brilliantly blue as they met hers.

"I thought I had when I declared that I didn't want a wife without her love. Suppose we start out as the pals we have always been and leave the rest on the knees of the gods? Sounds like an interesting experiment. Yes or no?"

"Y—" Her breath caught. "Yes," she whispered.

Chapter 18

Of course she would wake and find it a hectic dream, one could live a lifetime in a few minutes in one's sleep, Gail told herself. She wasn't really walking beside Greg Hunt up the aisle of the small church. Yet — the harvest decorations, the magic and the music of the Wedding March from "Lohengrin" setting the air vibrating softly, and the rainbow of colors pouring through the stained glass of the west window on the clergyman's head seemed real. The low exclamations of the wedding guests as they rose, turned and saw her instead of Lila, were terribly real. "It will be just one more wartime wedding," Greg had said, or had he? Perhaps that was part of the dream, also.

"Dearly beloved, we are gathered here together in the sight of God . . ."

The voice shocked her out of her daze. What was she doing? What tragic mistake was Greg making? Why had she laid her hand in his? It mustn't stay there. She tried to withdraw it. His fingers closed over it in a grip which hurt. He looked at her and smiled and she stopped struggling. She couldn't let him down after going this far. She would be as contemptible as Lila. She'd see it through until after the reception at Twin Pines — then . . .

She was signing her name in the registry. Greg's face was colorless even as he smilingly explained to his grave aunt and uncle and to her brother and his wife.

"Lila changed her mind at the last minute. Seemed a pity to cheat you people out of a wedding, so Gail stepped into the breach." As he told it, it seemed the most natural arrangement in the world. After the first shock of surprise would the guests accept it in that spirit?

Later at the informal reception at Twin Pines, her brother drew her into the library. She wondered if forever after when she smelled the fragrance of red roses she would remember tall silver vases of them against mahogany paneled walls, hear a string orchestra playing, "I'm dreaming of a White Christmas"; see Johnny's tired face, hear his grave voice asking: —

"Why did you do it, Gail? Has Croston disappointed you? Was it because of Mildred's tirade about the house? I heard it. Resentment is a tricky foundation on which to build a marriage."

"I don't know why I did it, Johnny, honestly I don't. Perhaps Greg and I both had a brainstorm. Less than two hours before the time set for the wedding he came to my office with Lila's note in which she refused to marry him. It hurt unendurably to think he would be humiliated —"

"That's the wrong word. No one could humiliate G.H. Certainly not a woman like that." He smiled. "If it has 'hurt you unendurably' to see him turned down at the last minute, you've made a wise decision."

"What do you mean by that? It isn't to be a real —"

"Oh, here you are," Greg Hunt interrupted as he entered. His eyes flashed from one face to the other. "Hope you're not sore because we didn't consult you, Doc?"

"You're both of age. I only pray this won't prove a case of marry in haste and repent at leisure."

"It won't, you old croaker. I meant it when I promised to honor and keep her, in sickness and in health and all the rest of the marriage vow, as long as we both shall live. That make you feel better, Doc?"

"Greg!" The warm gravity of his voice forced the whispered protest through Gail's lips, stiff from the smile she had kept on them since the ceremony. The repetition of that promise made the marriage seem real, and he had said —

"Hey, Gail!" Billy dashed across the room. His love-pat on her shoulder rocked her on her feet. His embarrassment burst into laughter. "You sure put one across this p.m.! Did you know you were going to be married when you bought that nifty blue get-up?" His eyes and voice sobered.

"Pop says Mother's coming home has knocked our week end here into a cocked hat. I can bear that, but it isn't true, is it, that you'll live at Twin Pines instead of with us? Heck, who'll I have to talk to?"

"I'll be here for a while, pal, and then —"

"Why are the bride and groom hiding out?" Cissie-Lou demanded from the threshold where she posed with self-conscious charm. Her dark blue velvet frock and beret accentuated the gold of her hair, the delicacy of her skin, the violet of her eyes. "Guests are leaving. The girls are waiting for you to throw your bridal bouquet, Gail."

"I haven't —"

"Sorry, I forgot." Greg's disturbed voice interrupted her admission. "The bride didn't even have an orchid to wear." He lifted the red roses from a silver vase, wrapped his handkerchief around the wet stems and laid them in her arms.

"Bridal bouquets provided while you wait. There you are, Mrs. Hunt. Throw them from the stair landing. Come on, Cissie-Lou, get in the front row, maybe you'll catch it."

"Lot of good it would do me — just sixteen and all my boy-friends gone or going into the service, only kids left." She sighed with dramatic intensity. "Poisonous of you not to wait for me, Greg."

"You told me, didn't you, that I must be at the concert to hear you sing? You see how neatly I've managed it. I'll be there."

"Greg, you're the sweetest thing, I'll sing right to you, if you have left me flat."

"Hey, Cis, cut out the movie stuff," Billy interrupted. "He's snitched the woman in my life and I'm not grouching. I forgot —" He drew a letter from his pocket. "This came to the house for you, Gail, and I brought it along. Come on and chuck those roses," he prodded as she tucked the letter into one of the jet-and-sequined pockets of her frock. "I want to see who gets them and I've got to corral Mac at the firehouse before I go home."

"Oh, here you are, Johnny!"

Rhoda Craven, in a ravishing black costume complete with diamond-and-emerald clips and bracelet, crossed the room and slipped her hand under Doctor Trevor's arm.

"You will take me home, won't you?" Tone and eyes were wistful. "I'm weak from surprise after the shift in brides and due for a nervous breakdown if I don't talk it over with someone. Besides, I haven't seen you for *twenty-four* hours."

"That's just too bad, Rhoda," Mildred Trevor icily condoled as she entered. Mrs. Craven's hand dropped from the arm against which she had been leaning. "John, if you can spare the time, I'd like to talk over home arrangements with you, now that Gail has deserted." In her olive drab she was quite as feminine and attractive as Rhoda Craven in her smart black.

"Desertion" is the word for what I have done, Gail thought later, as she sat before the fire in the library with Mr. and Mrs. Clifton. I shouldn't have left Johnny and the children, they need me. Sitting before the fire after her wedding reception sans bridegroom . . . To add the last perfect dramatic touch she should be playing solitaire, her thoughts trooped on. That would be funny if there could be any humor about the situation which more and more was taking on an *Alice in Wonderland* un-reality.

"This is always the best of the party to me, talking it over after the guests have gone." With a sigh of relief Mrs. Clifton, in the black velvet frock and the matching turban with its diamond eagle she had worn at the wedding, a double string of lustrous pearls about her plump white throat, kicked off one high-heeled satin sandal after the other, and flexed her toes in her gossamer-thin stockings.

"Little I thought when I invited the Trevor family for Thanksgiving dinner to-morrow that it would turn into a celebration of Greg's marriage to you, my dear. Your sister-in-law's arrival is most timely. She assured me she wouldn't upset my plans by insisting that they dine at home; they'll come."

"Billy and Cissie-Lou — to say nothing of Mac, I understand he is included in the invitation — would have been bitterly disappointed if your plan had been given up, Aunt Jane."

"They are adorable youngsters. I love them as if they were my own." She waved away the butler, who offered a silver tray heaped with fruit-shaped ices.

"Don't tempt me, Parrock, you know I

mustn't eat them. Pass them to Miss Trevor — my mistake, Mrs. Hunt. She must be starved."

The tall, white-haired servant smiled as he approached the girl by the fire.

"It will take time for me to think of you as Mrs. Hunt, Miss Gail. You'll excuse me saying it, I've always thought you and Mr. Greg belong together. I wish you happiness from the bottom of my heart."

"Thank you." The realization of the mad step she had taken was rising and rising like an irresistible tidal wave threatening to choke her. She wasn't hungry, she couldn't swallow — but why advertise the fact? "That peach ice with the very pink cheeks will be perfect, Parrock," she said.

From the servants' quarters came a radioed baritone singing, "Praise the Lord and pass the ammunition, and we'll all stay free." *Free* — how carelessly she had flung away her freedom. As clearly as if it were being broadcast she heard Greg's voice warning: —

"Forget Mildred; if you don't, anger at her may sometime land you in a trap from which you won't escape in a hurry." A trap. "This is it," she told herself.

"Tell us what it's all about, my dear," Mrs. Clifton's eager voice smashed head-on into her troubled reflections. "I'll confess I was so tense I could have screamed in that awful silence which followed the clergyman's challenge, 'If anyone knows of any reason,' and so forth, for fear Lila would appear and seize Greg."

"Then you aren't angry because of the change, Aunt Jane, or you, Mr. B.C.?"

Benjamin Clifton's face registered honest surprise. "Angry? I am very much pleased. Great Scott!" His shift of expression and voice was ludicrous. "This — this marriage doesn't mean that you'll quit your job, does it — that I'll lose my secretary?"

"Of course she'll quit her job, my love. Why should Greg's wife —"

"Of course I won't, Mr. B.C.," Gail contradicted. "I'll be on hand tomorrow morning as usual."

"But you were to have a week-end vacation before this sudden marriage broke. Why not now?"

"Because it will be business as usual for most of the workers, Aunt Jane." No sense in confessing that she must be busy to keep from thinking of this crazy marriage. "You'll need me, won't you, Mr. B.C.?"

"I need you at all times, but I'll stick by my promise of the week-end vacation."

"Of course you will, Ben Clifton. Even if the child didn't need a rest it's ridiculous to think of a bride —"

"What's that about a bride, Aunt Jane?" Greg Hunt inquired as he entered and crossed to the fireplace.

"B.C. wants his secretary at the office as usual tomorrow and I protested."

"What do you say to that, Gail?"

"I shall be there, Greg. I think you owe it to your aunt and uncle to tell them how this — this —"

"Marriage is the word you're hunting for, isn't it?"

"Marriage happened."

"Happened! How do you know it isn't one of those made-in-heaven arrangements?"

"*Don't* joke about it. Tell them. I'm so ashamed of my own part in the brainstorm that I just can't bear not to have them know."

"You're not sorry so soon?" His stern question sent little shivers of ice along her nerves.

"I don't know what I am." She looked from Benjamin Clifton to his wife and back to the man in front of the fire. "You are all so real it can't be a dream, so the ceremony must have been real too, though

264

I still can't believe it." She touched the diamond circlet on her left hand. "That ring feels real. But, I wish, how I wish from the bottom of my heart that it hadn't been. Tell them, Greg, why we did this crazy thing."

It seemed rather as if nothing else could have happened, as if the substitute bride had been divinely ordained, as he gravely told the story, omitting her tempest of tears, Mark Croston's and Mildred's part in her devastating attack of nerves.

"I was pretty mad that Lila should walk out on me at the last minute when I had given her plenty of excuse to do it before and then I felt an overwhelming sense of relief, as if I had been flying through an impenetrable fog and had emerged into dazzling sunlight, for I have tramped the streets many a night when I couldn't sleep, trying to convince myself that marriage to her wouldn't be a mistake."

"Great Scott, boy, if you felt that way why go on with it for a day?" Benjamin Clifton demanded.

"Because I had asked her to marry me. We were tentatively engaged before I entered the service. I thought I loved her then. When I was in the midst of horror I idealized her. Memory of her cool beauty

265

would relax my taut nerves. Perhaps she changed. I know I did. I asked her once to call it off. She refused. Don't mistake me, I have liked being with her." Color tinged his face. "She can be alluring when she chooses."

"Did you never think what life would be in the long stretches when she didn't choose?"

"Yes, Aunt Jane, but I argued that when we were married, it would be different. My thoughts and time have been so taken up with production and complications that I haven't given much attention to personal problems. It took the shock of her note at the last minute to show me what was really in my heart. You can't condemn me more than I condemn myself. I was drifting into marriage. Being given a chance out by a woman who could have dragged me over red-hot coals of publicity, had I reneged, is better luck than I deserve."

"Drifting? Is plunging any better? What sort of a mess do you think you've made of your life now?" Gail demanded passionately.

"Mr. Mark Croston," the butler announced.

She felt as a sleepwalker might who had been awakened suddenly as she looked at the man entering the room. She had promised to dine with him tonight, had told him to call for her at Twin Pines, and here he was. Hadn't he heard?

Color flushed Croston's lean, dark-skinned face as his eyes met hers. Was he mutely apologizing for what he had said in her office this morning? He bent over Mrs. Clifton's hand with his characteristic air of devotion.

"Good evening, Mrs. Clifton. I passed the caterer's van going out the drive as I was coming in, so I knew the festivity was over. Ready for our date, Gail? Never have seen you in pastel blue before. I like —" His eyes widened in surprise as Gregory Hunt stepped forward from the fireplace.

"G.H.! I thought you'd be on your honeymoon by this time. Where's Lila? Will I get a chance to offer my felicitations to the bride?"

Gail's heart stopped. What an unbearable situation. He hadn't heard. Even if he had been contemptible this morning she hated to see him hurt and his phone apology had shown that he did care for her. She had allowed Greg to think her weak-spirited enough to consider marrying a man who had calmly told her he didn't want her, when she hadn't had the slightest intention of doing it. Would he speak now or would he leave the explaining to her?

"I'm sure the bride will be glad of your felicitations, Croston," Gregory Hunt answered. "She is here to speak for herself."

"Here!" Croston's eyes flashed from one to the other. "I don't see her. You haven't her up your sleeve, have you, G.H. — or maybe you do it with mirrors?"

"I'm, I'm the — the bride, Mark." It was with difficulty Gail forced her voice from her tight throat.

"You! *You!*" He stared at her incredulously, looked from Benjamin Clifton to his wife. "Overwork hasn't upset her mind, has it, or is this a joke?"

"It is neither an aberration nor a joke, Mark," Jane Clifton's assurance oozed satisfaction. "The explanation is simple when reduced to the lowest denomination. Lila stepped out at the eleventh hour and Gail stepped in. To say that I am pleased at the change would be a masterpiece of understatement."

Mark Croston appeared not to be listening to the exultant declaration. His burning eyes were on the girl.

"Is this true?" he demanded.

"Y— Yes. For the —"

"Sorry to have intruded on this scene of

marital ecstasy," he lashed before she could add the word "present." "I've been glued to my desk all afternoon; I hadn't heard the news. Don't let me keep you from faring forth on your honeymoon. Good night, and good-by, *Mrs.* Hunt," he flung over his shoulder from the doorway.

Jane Clifton's chuckle broke the silence which followed his departure.

"Pity to waste that dramatic exit on four persons. I've always maintained that the movie moguls missed a sure bet, when they let Mark Croston escape them." With a sigh she wriggled her feet into the black satin sandals.

"Now that the party's over I'll get into something comfortable. Praise the Lord we won't have the chore of returning the wedding presents, they are all at Lila's, all except B.C.'s and mine, which we had planned to give her after the ceremony. My love, I assume you will shed those glad rags before you return to the Works, as usual, to check up on the night's activities?"

"I shan't stay long, Jane."

"I'll go with you, B.C."

"Greg, not *tonight*," his aunt protested.

Benjamin Clifton caught his wife's arm.

"Come on, Jane. Give our young people

a chance to talk it over. I'll wait for you, G.H."

"The master's voice." His wife chuckled. "Gail, your bags have been unpacked in your room, If you need anything — good gracious, you don't have to drag me, B.C. I'm coming."

Greg Hunt waited until the door closed behind them before he said: —

"When Croston asked if the story of our marriage were true you answered, 'Yes — for the —' He interrupted before you could finish, The word you would have added was 'present,' wasn't it?"

"Yes. Greg, Greg, this marriage is one of those things that just *can't* happen."

"It *has* happened and the world turns on its axis as usual."

She knew that he accepted any given situation as it was, he never wasted time talking or thinking of how it might have been, but this one was different. He *couldn't* leave it as it was.

"I don't like the word 'present,' in connection with our marriage, Gail. Permanent fits my plans better. Don't answer, now. Take off that hat and stay awhile." He lifted it carefully from her head and laid it on a table. "Isn't that a letter sticking from your pocket? Why not sit here and read it?"

She followed his suggestion because she was too dazed to make any other move. Interest in the letter submerged thoughts of self.

"It's from Jess Ramsay," she explained eagerly.

"I remember. At college you and she were known as the Inseparables. Judging from your voice and eyes, I'd say it brought good news."

"It did. Jess is half-Southern. She's not only a grand person but beautiful. A little over a year ago she was staying at Karrisbrooke, her great-aunt Ellen's fabulous plantation in North Carolina, when Vance Trent, major of a parachute battalion from a near-by camp, bailed out into her life. She married him just before he was sent abroad, Destination Unknown. They weren't engaged more than twenty-four hours before the ceremony. I've hardly dared look at a casualty list since for fear I would see his name, but Jess writes: —

"Vance is back, terribly thin, the skin of his drawn face looks like leather and so grim that until he caught me in his arms I wondered if he still loved me, but he's whole. Aunt Ellen and I flew to Washington to see him receive his decoration. The men he had trained came through so magnificently he has been detailed to head the parachute instruction division at a camp here. Am I happy? I'm telling you. Remember Johnny? He'll not come back — ever."

"Who was Johnny?" Greg Hunt asked as she folded the letter and blinked long lashes as if to clear her eyes of tears.

"Johnny Gordon, her stepfather's son. He was great fun. Always laughing and wisecracking. I can't picture him —"

"Don't try. Think of him as you remember him, laughing and wisecracking. That is the way he would want it. This must have been a nerve-racking day for you, all told. I'm off to the Works with B.C. You'd better turn in and get a good night's sleep, if you intend to report at the office in the morning."

"Nerve-racking." She crushed down an hysterical ripple of laughter. "Isn't her wedding day always thrilling for a bride — and can you imagine anything more exciting" — the ripple escaped before she could check it — "than for her to be advised by the groom to get a good night's sleep before she reported for work in the morning?"

A feeling of terror submerged the hysteria as his eyes met hers and his hands gripped her shoulders.

"Do you want it otherwise, Gail?"

"No. No. *No!* The situation just struck me as fun-funny, that's all. Of course I don't want it any dif-ferent."

He laughed and opened the door.

"Don't be frightened. I agreed to play it your way. Only, in future, watch out. Don't rock the boat. Good night and pleasant dreams — my dear."

Chapter 19

Gail stood at the window of her office in the late afternoon fastening the belt of her white gabardine coat. The thick clouds of the morning were drenching the world with glistening torrents of rain. The dimmed lights in the foggy court gleamed through prisms of color.

Thanksgiving. It might be any day in the year instead of a national holiday. Every moment had been occupied taking dictation, getting off letters, answering phone calls. The other secretaries were having the day off, Allah be praised. Otherwise, she would have been submerged by congratulations on her marriage which would have made her feel more of a cheat than she did at present and even that was a little more than she could bear.

She had been too busy to think. Now an upsurge of memory set her pulses thrumming, blood stinging in her cheeks. How could she have consented to Greg's mad suggestion yesterday? Was it only *yesterday* that she had walked up the church aisle with him? She remembered his eyes as he had warned her last night not to rock the boat, and she remembered her moment of terror. She had rated it for the flippancy of her comments. It had been the climax of a day which had begun with Mark Croston so smugly telling her off. Why excuse herself? If Greg had lost his sense of direction from disappointment she should have been level-headed enough to keep hers. She hadn't seen him since his warning, until ten minutes ago, when he had stuck his head into the office and announced: —

"It's raining great guns, Gail. I'll take you home." He had vanished before she could answer. Answer! What answer could she make?

"Don't tell me you're working when you should be honeymooning, Mrs. Hunt." Unheard by her, Mark Croston had entered and softly closed the door behind him. "I was in the court and saw you standing here at the window. Thought you might be wondering how you'd get home in the rain. I'm the answer. I'd be glad to give you a lift."

His voice was slightly breathless, as if he had rehearsed the speech and were hurrying through it for fear he might forget some detail.

"Nice of you, Mark, but I'm waiting for Greg."

"My mistake, I had forgotten the husband."

Of course he hadn't, equally of course he was primed for a showdown. Let it come. The sooner it was over the better.

"Don't be hateful, Mark. We have been good friends. Let's remain so."

"Friends." She shook off his grip on her arm. "How can we be friends when I know you love me and I love you? I drove you into this marriage by the fool things I said about marrying money and influence in this very office yesterday morning, didn't I?"

"You phoned and took it back, remember."

"Cut the sarcasm. It's all over town and the Works, that Lila turned down G.H. at the last minute. The gossips are stumped to figure out why you stepped into the picture. I suspect that in his fury you caught him on the rebound and he caught you when you were sore at me. Right?"

"Resentment is a tricky foundation on which to build a marriage."

Her brother's voice echoed through her memory. Resentment and anger had pitched her headlong into an incredible situation.

The fact that fury at Lila Tenny for letting Greg down had had its part in her consent to his suggestion was no excuse for her.

"That proves you love me, doesn't it?" With the triumphant demand Croston laid his hands on her shoulders. Did he intend to kiss her? His assurance that she loved him must be smashed and smashed hard. Even if she didn't consider herself really Greg's wife, she was legally married to him — for the present.

"Don't." She twisted free. With her desk between them she declared breathlessly: —

"The fact that I m-married Gregory Hunt doesn't prove that I love you, Mark. I'd say that it proves I love him, have loved him ever since I was a little girl."

Dramatizing the situation as usual, aren't you, she scoffed at herself. I must have been convincing, her thoughts surged on, what I said brought that white line around his mouth I've seen before when he was angry.

"You don't mean that, Gail. You can't."

"And why not? Hasn't he what it takes? Family background and a tidy fortune? That combination can do spectacular things for the girl he marries."

Instead of being angry, as she hoped, he laughed.

"That proves it, sweetness. You wouldn't repeat word for word what I said if you didn't love —"

"What goes on here? Ready, Gail?"

She had been too absorbed in preparing an answer to hear the door open. How long had Greg been standing on the threshold? Had he heard her silly declaration that she had been in love with him since she was a little girl? He was looking at Mark now in a way that sent little chills slinking along her veins.

"I'm ready, Greg," she said hurriedly. "Good night, Mark. I'm glad we had this talk. Please go. I want to lock the office."

Greg stepped into the room. Croston paused on the threshold long enough to remind: —

"That isn't all I have to say. I'll be seeing you, Gail. Happy landings, G.H." His laugh implied that they would be the reverse of happy.

Hands thrust into his raincoat pockets Gregory Hunt let his eyes follow him as he stalked along the corridor. When they came back to her they had the look in them she had seen the night in the roadster when he had said, "Someday, somehow, I'll work off a little of the hate which makes me see red when I allow myself to remember." She shivered, but he laughed.

"Theatrical cuss, isn't he? I hope you didn't take seriously that 'I bide my time' threat in his voice, though it was worthy of the best cinema tradition. Ready? Let's go."

Rhythm of rain on top of the convertible. Crystal rivulets on the windshield. Oceans of water under the wheels. Silence in the car. Silence so profound that Gail heard the hard beat of her heart. She tried to think of something to say, something scintillating. The harder she tried the blanker her mind became. If only she could think of some way to talk out the situation with him. It was an ideal chance.

"Rotten weather for Thanksgiving."

His voice at last. She answered eagerly.

"Yes, but why mind rain when we have such grand news from Africa? I've felt all day as if this horrible war were practically over."

"That's the trouble with a victory, people all over the country will think the same and relax their efforts to produce."

"There was no letting down at the Works today. I haven't had a minute to myself."

"You didn't look busy as you stood at the window a few minutes ago. I thought you might be sending out an SSS — submarine sighted, to you — and dashed to the rescue."

"I was ready to leave. I didn't want to keep you waiting."

"Don't do it again."

"Do *what?*"

"Stand at a lighted window. It's an invitation to trouble."

Was he referring to Mark Croston? He had seen her at the window but Greg couldn't know that.

"Hear the rain beat!" To her relief he had changed the subject. "Hope it won't keep the Trevors at home."

"It won't. Johnny is a physician, who, like the U.S. Mail — 'Not snow, nor rain, nor heat, nor gloom of night stays these couriers from the swift completion of their appointed rounds.' Mildred is a soldier, weather shouldn't count with her. Cissie-Lou and Billy are ducks when it comes to rain. I'm sure all of Aunt Jane's guests will answer 'Here' when she calls the roll. She told me she had invited the Selbys and Tom Search as they had no family near."

"Search won't be back until Saturday morning."

"G-Greg. Don't you think we should talk things over?"

"What things?"

"That — that ceremony we went through yesterday for one. It shouldn't have happened."

Even in the dim light she could see the surprise in the eyes that looked down at her.

"You said that before. It did happen. Let's stick to things as they are. Why talk about it? It was as legal as the church and the law could make it."

"That's the trouble."

Even when she was a little girl his laugh had tilted up the corners of her lips in response. Its charm still worked. The situation didn't seem so terrifying.

"Ungrateful gal. You wouldn't want it a phony, would you?"

"Please be serious, Greg. It — it was too sudden to be right."

"Why?" His voice was grave enough now. "Your friend Jess Ramsay's marriage followed a twenty-four hour engagement, you told me."

"That was different. They were terribly in love. Our — that — that ceremony followed in less than two hours your engagement to another girl."

"I hope sometime I'll be able to make you understand about that."

"There's only one explanation. We — we

just went — went cockeyed, both of us. I admit I was the most to blame."

"That's noble of you."

"There's nothing noble about me. I was furious with Mar—" That was a mistake, but having started she'd better finish. "With Mark, and then I had a set-to with Mildred and I was ready for any fool project. The result will be a warning to hold on to my temper which will last the rest of my life."

"You consider marrying me a fool project?"

"Of course it was. You don't love me and I don't love you — we're fond of one another, but you can't build a marriage on fondness."

"And still the wonder grew that one small head could carry all she knew — with a nod to the late Mr. Oliver Goldsmith."

"Greg, please be serious. Please help me." In spite of her desperate attempt at control, her voice quivered. "I feel so lost, so — so — so helpless to set things straight."

In answer he laid his hand lightly on hers lying bare on the rug.

"Suppose you drop the job of setting things straight on my shoulders, Gail. Don't worry about the future. Trust me, won't you? You have trusted me always, haven't you? Here we are at Twin Pines. We'll give our special entrance the go-by this drenching night. The front one is quicker."

She was uneasily aware of him as they entered the spacious hall and he preceded her up the beautiful circular stairway. He opened the door of the living room of the ell apartment, laughed as she hesitated.

"Something tells me you haven't read the headlines in the local paper — to wit — 'The Gregory Hunts will live at Twin Pines for the present.' You're one half of that family, in case you've forgotten."

Her cheeks burned as she entered the room with its blazing fire which set the gold glinting in the bindings of books on shelves along the wall, its rich red brocade hangings and chair covers, its pink chrysanthemums and softly shaded lamps.

"Take off the raincoat, Gail. You appear poised as if to run." He lifted it from her shoulders. "That's better. Come back here after you have changed. I have something important to tell you. Forgot it on the drive home."

"W-what, Greg?"

He laughed.

"It's not what you think it is — but it's

terribly interesting. Hope you brought your yellow dress? I like dark-haired gals in yellow."

She stood for an instant looking at the door he had closed behind him. How could he be so debonair after what had happened? How *could* he, she asked herself again as she entered the room in which she had spent last night wondering, like the Old Woman in *Mother Goose*, if "I be really I." Deciding one minute that she was caught in a nightmare, the next that the marriage ceremony had been only too real.

Backed against the door she looked about her. This room was real. It was a lovely room. No wonder Mrs. B.C. had had the "time of her life" having it done over. Walls and furniture were white, as were the heavy damask hangings drawn across the long French windows which opened on a balcony.

The snowiness of the great fur rug beside the satin, upholstered bed accentuated the polish of the dark floor which reflected the light from two rare Chinese porcelain lamps with rosy shades. Their color was repeated in chair cushions. There were accents of soft green to tie it up with the mirror-lined dressing room and the bath beyond, all sea-green and chrome. Her own silver appointments were arranged on the dressing table; someone had polished them to the nth degree. Exactly in the middle, beside a crystal vase holding two pink Perfection roses, lay a cellophane box tied with silver ribbon. Through its transparent sides she could see a spray of exquisite white orchids.

She stared at it as if it were a time bomb which might go off at any minute. Had Greg put it there? From an envelope addressed MRS. GREGORY HUNT she drew a card. "Too little, but I hope not too late. Greg," he had written. She remembered his disturbed voice when he had said yesterday: "The bride didn't even have an orchid to wear." He was making up for it now.

There was a square white velvet case under the cellophane box when she moved it. Now what? she asked herself. If it was a wedding present she'd better look at it to find out to whom to return it. If she could do nothing else she could refuse presents. She pressed the spring. The cover flew up. She breathed an ecstatic, Oh — o — o! The bracelet had a diamond rose set in leaves of emeralds in the center of a band of smaller diamonds. On the card enclosed was written: —

With love to our niece,
from
AUNT JANE AND UNCLE BEN

What should she do about it? The question occupied her thoughts from shower to the flame-color net frock, which shimmered with opal sequins. As she slipped into it she remembered the day she had seen it in the shop window and remembered thinking that she would need a new costume to wear at the festivities in honor of Greg Hunt's return. She little thought then that she would wear it first as Mrs. Gregory Hunt.

"Life certainly is stranger than fiction," she observed to the looking-glass girl as, seated on the bench before the dressing table in the bedroom, she fastened the orchids at her shoulder. The petals had the opalescent sheen of the sequins on her frock.

She shook her head at the velvet case as she experimented with ear-clips. The bracelet was gorgeous and desirable beyond words, but not for her. Of course she couldn't accept a present for a marriage which wasn't a marriage. Equally of course she would seem horribly ungracious to Mr. and Mrs. B.C. if she didn't. Could she make them understand? Darn! This mess came from not looking before you leap. It went further back than that, it came from letting a tide of anger sweep her into an ocean of tears, into an undertow of furious resentment.

She lifted a diamond circlet from the drawer into which she had dropped it last night when she had pulled it from her finger. Its many facets reflected the light like hundreds of eyes watching her. A wedding ring. Ought she to wear it? *No!*

Who was knocking? Greg? Was he tired of waiting for her to come to the living room? What was the important thing he wanted to tell her? She replaced the ring in the drawer, tightened the screw of a synthetic emerald earclip and dropped a matching chiffon handkerchief over the velvet case.

"C-come in," she answered.

Chapter 20

In response to her voice Billy flung open the door. The case of a portable typewriter banged against his knees as if the machine weren't as precious as the gold of the Indies. The red setter followed him into the room and in one leap planted his paws on her lap and tried to lick her face. In a sudden surge of homesickness she hugged the dog.

"Hey, Mac! Keep your wet feet off that super dress. Charge! Here's the typewriter you phoned for, Gail. Heck, what's wrong? You're red and fussed, your eyes were scared when I barged in. Who you afraid of?"

He dropped the case to the floor, slumped into a rose-brocade-covered wing chair all in one motion, and grinned at her companionably.

"Let me at the guy an' I'll tie his ears back."

For the first time in the last hectic forty-eight hours Gail laughed.

"Scared? Of course not. You know me, pal. If I looked fussed it was because I thought it was Parrock come to tell me that the guests had arrived and I was late. I'm terribly pleased to see you, Billy."

The boy stretched his long legs till they rested on the back of the dog on the floor. He glanced slowly around the room.

"Swell joint you've got here. Like it better than the room you had at our house? I thought that was okay."

"I do *not*." She answered the hint of jealousy in his voice. "I loved that room. I loved being where you and Mac could drop in for chocolate patties."

"Shucks, you got us wrong, we came to see you. I guess now that chocolate's gone to war we won't see many more."

"Cheerio. I have a box of them in my room at home, when I go back to pack up — I forgot, I shan't have to, my belongings will be here tomorrow. Aunt Jane sent her maid, her treasure Sarah, to do it for me." He couldn't know how glad she had been to escape contact with his mother.

"Will you really stay here, Gail? Sure you'll like it? In this set-up I'd think you'd feel as if you were living in a movie world with a camera trained on you."

He had expressed her reaction to her surroundings perfectly.

"I do, but I'll get adjusted to the cinema stage-set in time."

"I was clean bushed when I saw *you* instead of the Tenny menace walking up the church aisle with the Cap. You got a break. Greg will look after you. He's my idea of a swell guy. About as regular as they come, I bet. He'll be bad news for glamour-pants or anyone else who tries to get fresh. I thought Mark Croston was giving you the double rush."

"He was my friend, that's all."

Billy shook his head and frowned at her.

"It gets me how you grown-ups mess things for yourselves. There was Greg all set to walk the plank with another girl when a fella with half an eye could see you were his woman."

"Wrong wave-length, Billy."

"Oh yeah? Then why'd he ask you to marry him the first chance he got?"

"B-because . . . You're too young to understand that, pal."

"Is *that* so! I noticed when grown-ups *can't* explain they wriggle out with that 'too young' stuff."

She ignored his indignant scowl of protest and asked: —

"What has happened at home since what might be called my theatrical plunge into the tempestuous sea of matrimony?"

That brought a laugh as she had hoped it would. It troubled her to see him puzzling over grown-up problems.

"I feel as if I had been away an aeon or two — Mr. Webster — Noah, not Daniel — says that an aeon means an immense period of time — in case you are interested. I'm pos-i-*tive*-ly hungry for news."

"Mom's got Petunia back — that is, she's coming."

"Not *really*, Bill?"

"Uhuh. No kiddin'. She sent for her last evening when we got home from the wedding blowout here. I guess Mom turned on the heat, all right, about Pet's deserting Pop when he was working days, nights and holidays to keep hundreds of people well so they can pass plane parts on to the assembly lines to help save the lives of our boys in the service. Mom's got what it takes when she mounts the soapbox. She had that dame blubbering for fair —

" 'Ah never did think of it that way befo', Mis' Trevor.' " The boy's mimicry of the colored woman's voice was perfect. "Sniff. Sniff. Sniff. 'Miss Gail, she's so smart, Ah thought sure she'd get on all right. Ah'll give notice whar Ah am an' be back here Sunday. Ah 'spect Mr. Doctor,

291

he did miss mah choc'late cake.' "

"I told Petunia all that about your father over and over *and* over."

"Sure you did, but the old girl had picked up the idea she'd be a red-hot rivet in war work."

"*And* she was tired of housework. I don't blame her. For going over and over the same ground, it has a merry-go-round licked to a standstill. I can understand her yen for a change better now than when she left."

"I guess she knew she wasn't much good at the new job and when Mom talked turkey she seized the chance to duck it; besides, Mom upped her pay sky-high. I bet Miss Petunia Judson busts out in mink before the winter's over."

"When does your mother leave, Billy?"

"Dunno. She was up bright and early this morning to get breakfast and got the scare of her life. She called me, 'Come quick, Billy. Your father! What has happened to him?' Relax, Gail, relax. It was nothing but what you and I've seen a dozen times since he's been so rushed. Poor old fella, he had come in, perhaps at four a.m., flopped into a chair without taking off his overcoat and gone to sleep."

"He's been out visiting patients night

after night, all night, after hospital hours, probably."

"Sure, he has. Mom said, 'Billy, he isn't — isn't —' She choked on the word. I knew what she meant; I said: 'Heck no, he isn't blotto. You know he never touches the stuff. He's just plain tuckered out.' "

"What did she say to that?"

"Nothing. She got us a swell breakfast, looked awful cute and pretty in that green-and-white gingham she used to wear. She does everything so darn well. Pop joked about her finding him asleep but she didn't say much. I guess he thought she was mad at him, like she used to be. Heck, you'll never catch me getting married. If there's anything makes me want to crawl under the table it's seeing marrieds fight. Nix on matrimony for me. Mac an' I'll bach it, won't we, young fella?"

The red setter wriggled from under the feet on his back, stretched, yawned a yelp of agreement, rested his chin on the boy's knee and looked up at his master with his soul in his eyes.

"Hear that, Gail? He knew what I said. He's all for the single life, too."

"All married people don't fight, pal." He mustn't believe they did. It was a narrow plank she was walking, to defend matrimony without appearing to criticize his parents. "Your mother and father really love each other, I'm sure of that. Mr. B.C. and Aunt Jane have been married forty years. Of course they have their little scraps — what married people don't? — but I'll wager she has never seen anyone to compare with him and there is no woman in the world who could take him away from her."

"Like the Craven dame is trying to get Pop?"

"*Billy!*"

"I'm not blind if I am only fourteen and a half. Heck, Gail, don't go pop-eyed. Do you think a guy, a junior at High, doesn't know the facts of life? If you do, you'd better get around more. And sometimes I *hope* she gets him."

"*Bill!*"

"So what? Isn't he entitled to a woman he can tell his troubles to, when he comes home all in from visiting sick patients, like I tell you mine? To a *real* wife, a grand guy like him? Working his head off for people who are working their heads off to help win this war? I love Mom, but she's giving him a lousy deal. She can help more in this burg than anywhere else. All the patriotism isn't needed on the war front. I should worry. I suppose they'll fight it out." He swallowed a troublesome obstruction in his throat and blinked his lashes as if his eyes stung. She put her arm about his shoulders.

"You're a dear. Are you too grown-up to allow me to press a chaste kiss upon your brow?"

"Quit kidding. You know I hate to be kissed. Grown-up! I'd better be. Before I know it I'll be old enough for the draft, though you may bet your life I won't wait for that. I'll get in aviation and win a decoration like our Cap. They've put commando technique in High, we're running, climbing over walls, crawling through underbrush to toughen us, besides getting pre-induction courses in math, physics, radio and aviation. It makes school sort of thrilling."

"It must be exciting, Bill. Are they putting in new courses for girls?"

"Yep. Consumer education, they call it. Teaches 'em how to use substitutes for fabrics or foods which may be rationed or no longer available. Gosh, speaking of fabrics, I almost forgot to tell you, Pop's clothes have come back, all cleaned and pressed."

"*What* clothes?"

"The loungecoat and blue suit the guy on our third floor made his getaway in."

"Billy! Who brought them?"

"Search me. About four o'clock I was giving the icebox the once-over for a snack to tide me over till dinner here, when — crack came something against the kitchen window. I figured some crazy kid had thrown a stone and beat it to the back porch to catch him. Stumbled on a suit box outside the door and almost broke my neck. No name on the box. Opened it and there were Pop's clothes."

"Any word, any note with it?"

"Nope. Pop phoned just then and I told him. He was pretty excited." Billy glanced at the crystal clock ticking away seconds on the white mantel behind him. "Isn't it time to eat?"

"In just ten minutes. We'd better go down."

Greg in dinner clothes was standing near the living room door when Gail entered. His smile as their eyes met reassured her.

"Thanks for the orchids, Greg. I did mean to join you and hear what you had to tell me, I really did," she assured hurriedly. "Billy has just told me that Johnny's clothes have been returned."

"That's what I had to tell you. It's okay. I knew Billy was with you, and as I had snitched his girl I thought it only fair to give him a clear field. This is a real family party, isn't it? I'm strong for family parties — when I like the families," he qualified. "Aren't you?"

She nodded. For some silly reason her throat was too tight to permit an articulate reply. Mr. and Mrs. Clifton, he in dinner clothes and she in her sensational pearls and a thin black frock that glittered with jet, stood side by side in heart-warming content in front of the mantel. He was nodding his head in time to the soft music coming from the radio. Somewhere an orchestra was playing, "She'll always remember."

This "she" will, Gail thought and swallowed the lump in her throat before her glance traveled on to Mildred in uniform, now talking to her host. Pat Selby's lovely hair shone copper-red in the lamplight, the silver sequins on her mist-green frock shimmered with every move of her lithe body as she laughed up into Doctor Trevor's eyes, which were regarding her with amused approval. Cissie-Lou in a floor-length evening frock — her first — looked like a Christmas-card angel, a sophisticated angel, in turquoise blue. A quivering silver butterfly poised, as if ready for a take-off, in her hair, satin-soft and yellow as the gold stored at Fort Knox.

"Hi, Gail," Billy whispered. "Watch Cis

slanting her eyes at Joe Selby and giving him her latest model pose. Gosh, he's eating it up." He chuckled. "She sure has what it takes," he added in a voice which revealed his intense love and admiration for the sister whose feet he felt called upon to keep on the ground.

"Hooray, Parrock is whispering to Aunt Jane. Fee, fi, fo, fum! I smell the scent of roast turkey, *umm!* How's that for improvising? I'm a wonder."

"I don't like to talk about myself, *but —*" Gail jeered affectionately.

Later she looked at and listened to Benjamin Clifton at whose left she sat at one end of the long table; at Mildred Trevor at his right; at the bird of paradise centerpiece, the flame-color of its blossoms repeated in the candles in four massive silver sticks and in the pumpkin-shaped candies; at Cissie-Lou seated between her brother and Joe Selby across the table, as secure in her awareness of charm as a Hollywood starlet and yet very sweet and appealing too; at anyone at all except Greg Hunt at her left.

" 'When on others thou art smiling, do not pass me by,' " he suggested in a low voice.

She laughed.

"Copy-cat. You borrowed that quotation from the President."

"Suppose I did. He borrowed it first. You'll have to admit it's pat. You haven't spoken to me since we came to the table." While she was wondering what to reply he confided: —

"I once had an appetite like Bill's. Makes me feel very old, Gail, to see him eat. Where has he put all the turkey Parrock served him? I'd forgotten it was still being done like that."

"*I* hadn't. There were days during this last month when I despaired of making even a dent in his appetite. Guess what? Petunia is coming back to work for the Doctor." She forgot that the man at whom she was smiling was now more than an old friend, forgot that she had been racking her brain to think of something casual to say to him as she met his eyes and laughed. "I turned on high-voltage persuasion to keep her, but it took the Army to round up *that* deserter."

"What thought wiped the smile from your face?"

"I remembered suddenly that Mildred called me a deserter for — for —"

"For getting married? We'll have to do something about that."

"Greg, please don't mention what Mildred said to *anyone*," she begged breathlessly. "Forget it. I told you merely to make conversation."

"Why try to make conversation between you and me? We are too old friends to be afraid of a silence."

Some quality in his deep tender voice did what no amount of her own philosophizing in the last forty-eight hours had accomplished, it untangled her troubled thoughts. Why make a tragedy of an emotional mix-up which at the proper time could be smoothed out, some way, somehow?

She glanced at Mrs. Clifton at the head of the table beaming content at Doctor John at her right and Joe Selby at her left. She was kindness personified.

Women are kind, women are understanding, at times, her thoughts trooped on, but there is something about a fine man which lights little fires in one's heart and soul to warm one through and through.

"I didn't mean that you were to go into the silence, permanently," Greg suggested.

"Sorry. I was thinking what a grand person Aunt Jane is." The picture of a white velvet case flashed on the screen of her memory with a suddenness which took her breath. "Greg, she and Mr. B.C. have given me a diamond bracelet. What shall I do with it?"

He turned to help himself to a piece of the pie Parrock was offering before he answered.

"What does a girl do usually with a diamond bracelet? Wears it, doesn't she? Unless my nose deceives me the mincemeat got itself good and tight before it fell into this pie." He turned to speak to Pat Selby on his other side.

"And that about settles that," Gail told herself indignantly. "Lot of help you are, Mr. Gregory Hunt."

Chapter 21

Greg and Gail stood side by side in the broad hall at Twin Pines speeding the departing guests. Mr. and Mrs. Clifton had said good night in the library. What was the girl beside him thinking as her family departed, Greg wondered, what would she say were he to tell her that when he had seen her sobbing in her office like a tired little girl he had known that he loved her, wanted her for his wife? "A bolt from the blue," he had said. A masterpiece of understatement. The revelation had shaken him. The realization of how near he had come to marrying Lila had turned his blood to ice. Through his mind as he watched her had echoed his aunt's voice, "Not with the kind of love that makes a man take a desperate chance to get the woman he wants."

He remembered that Gail had said he was one of the two men for whom she cared most. Why couldn't "caring" be changed to "loving"? He had made one of his quick decisions, had taken a desperate chance. "Crazy," Gail had called it. Was it?

Only Time could tell and Time had a way of keeping its secrets till the last minute.

"Come out of your trance, Greggy." Cissie-Lou's voice brought him back to the present. "Say good night to the lady like a perfect little gentleman." She offered her hand with an air of sophistication which brought a smile to his lips, an adoring light to her father's eyes and an annoyed frown to her mother's brow.

"Don't forget you are to sing to me tomorrow evening, Cissie-Lou," he reminded. "Shall I send orchids or gardenias?"

"Greg! Do you *mean* it?" She was very young in her eagerness. "I've never had an orchid. Could I have a spray of those green and brown ones? I don't know the name."

"Green and brown they will be. Watch your step. Don't get stage fright."

"Me? Stage fright? I'll eat it up. I — I only hope you'll like my song." A shadow of doubt dimmed the brilliance of her eyes for an instant and was gone. "I'm sure you will. Rhoda Craven says it will be a smash-hit. The house is a sell-out."

"Of course I'll like it." He turned to John Trevor. "Glad your patients allowed you the whole evening off, Doc."

"It was nothing short of a miracle. The party has equaled a year's vacation. I'll go back to the hospital now all pepped up. Don't stand here by the open door, Gail, the rain has stopped and it's cold as Greenland. Good night."

As Cissie-Lou blew a kiss to him from the threshold and the door closed behind the Trevors, Greg's thoughts flashed back to the shadow in her eyes when she had tried to sell her song to him. It didn't look right. Had she doubts about it? He stopped Gail as she started up the winding stairs.

"Just a minute. Do you know what Cissie-Lou has rehearsed for the concert?"

"No." Hand on the stair rail she looked down at him. "She has been very secretive about it. When I asked her the name of the song she said that Rhoda and she wanted it to be a surprise. Something tells me it doesn't add up right."

"Don't worry, she has too much of the Trevor good sense to pull a boner. She said the affair was a sell-out. Where is your seat?"

"With John, Mildred and Billy."

"No place for your brand-new husband?"

"Greg!"

"Why the horror? You have one, or have you forgotten? I'll find a seat. The rain has stopped. The weather-man predicted that the storm would end in a hard freeze. Let's go skating on the pond back of the High School after the concert tomorrow night. We can't take time off in daylight. It's a 'don't dress' affair, I understand; you could wear a skating rig, couldn't you?"

"I could and I will. It's a grand idea. We'll get John and Mildred to join us. It would do him heaps of good."

"That wasn't quite what I had figured out, but, it's okay. Good night — my dear."

The next evening Gail wasn't seeing the white walls of the High School auditorium hung with flags of the United Nations, wasn't seeing the performers at the concert for the benefit of the USO as they appeared on the platform, did their act and took their bows to the accompaniment of loud applause. She was seeing Greg as he had looked up at her from the hall last night. It wasn't playing it her way to say tenderly, "Good night — my dear," as if she really were his dear.

"What you sighing about, Gail?" Billy's hoarse whisper at her right brought a reproving *"Ssh,"* from the seat behind. She caught his hand in a silencing grip as he added: —

"Here comes Cissie-Lou. Gosh, she's a knockout."

She was, Gail admitted, as the young girl in her long blue frock, a spray of green and brown orchids at her shoulder crossed the stage to the microphone and smiled radiantly in response to the applause that greeted her. Rhoda Craven, in gauzy black, glistening with sequins which accentuated the bronze of her hair, took her place at the piano.

Gail glanced at Doctor John seated at her left. The adoration in his eyes and smile as he looked at his daughter tied her throat in a tight knot. Her attention was so entirely given over to her brother's reaction that she missed the master-of-ceremonies' announcement of the name of Cissie-Lou's song.

"Oh, gosh, oh gee, oh *heck*, this is going to be rough." Billy's protest was a whispered wail. His crushing grip on her hand recalled her doubts as to the selection Rhoda Craven had advised.

She felt the little tremor of shock in her brother, heard his wife's dismayed, "Not *that!*" as Cissie-Lou began to sing in the hoarse technique of the successful torch singer, her lovely voice shorn of its music.

As the song proceeded she watched his face whiten, his eyes retreat into their caverns. Once she glanced at Mildred beside him. Her expression was one of angry incredulity. The song their daughter was singing wasn't ribald, it wasn't shockingly vulgar. Billy had expressed it when he whispered: "This is going to be rough." Rough it was.

Why should a girl who had been trained in the best music want to take up with the cheap and shoddy? Rhoda Craven was the answer, Gail told herself, as she glanced at the woman at the piano, who was beaming with possessive pride at Cissie-Lou as she took her bow in response to the thunderous applause. The girl glanced at her white-faced father, who was sitting motionless as a bronze Buddha, arms tightly crossed on his chest. A little frown creased her brow, the laughing radiance of her eyes shadowed. She turned to her accompanist and spoke. Mrs. Craven opened her lips as if in protest but Cissie-Lou returned to the center of the stage. She set the microphone aside and began to sing her father's favorite hymn.

"O God! our help in ages past,
Our hope for years to come . . ."

As the lovely triumphant voice sang the first verse the audience sat motionless as if

307

stunned by the change in subject and technique. It listened in breathless silence through three verses, then with passionate fervor began to sing with her.

"A thousand ages in Thy sight
Are like an evening gone;
Short as the watch that ends the night
Before the rising sun."

In the hush that followed the closing line Gail thought: That hymn was Cissie-Lou's apology to her father.

After "The Star-Spangled Banner" had been rendered with patriotic enthusiasm by the audience and the brasses and strings of the school band, Rhoda Craven swept up to the Trevor family standing in the corridor.

"Greetings, Mildred. Wasn't Cissie-Lou a smash-hit in that first number? What did you think of your daughter, Johnny?"

"What did I think?" John Trevor's eyes were burning black in his white face. "I thought of all the precious things in the world this frightful war is destroying and I thought of what a criminal waste of loveliness it was to use a beautiful voice on a cheap song like that first one. That's what I thought, Rhoda. Let's go, Mildred."

"Not yet." His wife's brittle reply matched the contempt in her eyes. "Not until I've told Rhoda what I think of encouraging a sixteen-year-old girl to sing like a hardboiled night-club entertainer."

"Really!" Rhoda Craven mocked softly. The two voices were in as sharp contrast as the two women, one in olive drab, the other in shimmering black. "If you are so sensitive about what happens to your prized possessions you shouldn't leave them lying round as temptations for someone to pick up."

"Meaning my husband is one of them, I assume?"

"Could be." Rhoda Craven's light laugh slashed. "Don't be a dog in the manger, Milly."

"I, a dog —"

"Mom. Did you like me?" Cissie-Lou with a trail of boys in her wake had pushed her way through the crowd of relatives and friends of the performers. "I know Dad didn't." Color stole to her hair, her eyes flooded with tears, till they resembled nothing so much as violets under water. She slipped her hand under her father's arm and pressed her cheek against his sleeve. "I sang the second song just for you, Daddy."

"I'll tell you what I thought of both of

them later, Cecilia Louise. I'm due at the hospital. Let's get out of here, Mildred. Coming with us, Daughter?"

"You do have the most antiquated ideas, Dad." Cissie-Lou's smile took the sting from her words. "I'm staying to dance, of course. Here's Greg," she exclaimed as Gregory Hunt in skating regalia, red coat, white belt and black tights, joined the group. "My word, you're super in that outfit. Was I box-office, Gregory? *You* weren't shocked at my first song, were you?" She transferred her hand from her father's arm to his and looked up, confident of her charm.

"Shocked, Cissie-Lou? I wonder if that's the word to express my feelings. I only know that I had an almost irresistible urge to mount that platform, take you across my knees and administer the spanking of your life."

"You — you *hick!*" Her eyes blazed. "Guess you've lived in this backwoods city so long you've never heard a swell torch singer."

"I've heard them, liked them, admired them, but their style is not for a sixteen-year-old like you. You still rate chastisement. Better watch your step if you put on this act again."

Rhoda Craven's face flushed with resentment, Mildred's was smugly pleased, Doctor John's approving. Cissie-Lou's quivering mouth was that of a child who has been unjustly censured. Gail said quickly: —

"The hymn was wonderful, Cis. The audience loved it. Notice how they rolled out, 'A thousand ages in Thy sight Are like an evening gone'? You handed us all a stout staff of strength and courage to keep on keeping on when you sang that hymn. How did you happen to think of it?" Cissie-Lou's eyes brightened. She placed her left hand on her hip and shrugged her woman-of-the-world shrug. "I intended to sing that all along as a — a contrast in technique and — and as inspiration, too," she explained loftily. A boy tapped her on the shoulder. "Sure, I'll dance, Nicky. I'll be seeing you," she flung back as she turned away.

"How about our skating party, Gail?" Greg Hunt suggested hurriedly as welcoming neighbors and patients flocked around John Trevor and his wife. "I like your black velvet skirt, quilted jacket and that round cap. Nifty rig, I calls it. Let's get out of this before we are snowed under with congratulations. Is the Doc coming?"

"No. I suggested it but he said he must get back to the hospital. I left my skates in the coatroom. Here come more of our friends. We'd better go if we're going."

The pond back of the schoolhouse shone like a blue mirror, a cracked mirror in some places, in others the ice was like glass where it faintly reflected a few major planets. As they sailed across the moon, mackerel clouds edged with silver made the star-sprinkled sky a deeper indigo in contrast.

"How sweet and pure and balsamy fragrant the air is." Gail drew a long breath. "You were not the only one with the brilliant idea of skating after the concert," she added as laughing couples ran, slipped and skidded down the hill from schoolhouse to pond, stopped to buckle on skates and glided on to the ice.

"Glad you think it was brilliant. Come on."

Arms crossed, hand in hand, they swung off in a swooping spiral. From above drifted the faint music of the school band and young voices singing lustily, "When the boys are home again, all over the world." From around them came the hiss and whine of skates and peals of laughter.

"Something tells me that I joined the

Trevor family group at a crucial moment, right?" Greg asked. He expeditiously swung Gail aside from a woman whose skates had let her down in a huddle in front of them. She was giggling. The man with her rasped, "For Pete's sake, *try* to stand up, Gert."

"To return to your question," Gail reminded. "The crucial moment had occurred a few sixty seconds earlier, when Mildred slashed at Rhoda because of Cissie-Lou's torch song and Mrs. Craven in return suggested that she was a dog in the manger. Those two cultured women were fighting over a man as savagely as two primitive women with knives in their belts."

"Wouldn't you fight for a man you love?"

"No can tell. I —" They were gliding on one skate in perfect timing when she stopped so suddenly she lost her balance. Greg steadied her.

"Don't do that again. You may not be so lucky next time. What happened?"

"Do you see what I see? Ahead of us in white on the shore, having her skates put on."

"You mean Lila? Sure, I saw her when she came down the hill."

"Love's eyes are keen," she flouted, and

would have given Aunt Jane's diamond bracelet, which wasn't hers to give, to snatch it back.

Had Greg heard her sarcastic little dig or was he ignoring it? She had time to wonder before he spoke.

"Thought she was in Washington. Had to come back to see how I was taking it, probably, on the theory that a murderer always returns to the scene of his crime."

"Did she murder something in you, Greg?"

"She did *not*. That quip was just one of the smart-aleck comparisons one makes because it sounds pat. On the contrary, she shocked into glowing life a passion which had been dormant in my heart." He cleared his husky voice and laughed. "That might have been lifted from Sebastian Brent's line. What do you know — Lila is with Mark Croston. She's picked herself a likely lad. Let's speak to them."

"No — Greg — please — I —"

"Still sore because he turned you down? My mistake — he took that back, didn't he?"

"He did."

"Then why avoid him? Can this be love?"

"I'm *not* avoiding him. Come on."

Chapter 22

As they approached, Lila Tenny glided toward them. Except for the brown of her hair visible below her round cap, the pink of her cheeks and the green of her eyes, she might have posed as the snow queen, even her skating boots were white. She held out both hands and miraculously kept her balance.

"Greg! *Darling!* It's wonderful to see you." Her famous smile touched her eyes and lips as she pleaded, "I can explain. No hard feeling, Greg?"

"Not even a sliver, Lila. Just cheers of gratitude. You have heard of my marriage, of course. Remember Gail? My wife."

Into the silence that followed came the ring of skates on ice, the loud report of a bursting meteor, the snap of frost in a twig and a distant voice singing, "There'll never be another you." Lila Tenny laughed.

"Of course I remember your uncle's secretary. Has the time I've been away seemed so long to you, darling? So good of you to pinch-hit for me, Miss Tre— my mistake, Mrs. Hunt."

"It was just part of my wartime work to smooth out the rough places for my boss — Greg's my sub-boss, you know. Canceling all those invitations would have taken more time from the job than I could spare. Filling your shoes was quicker, a whole lot quicker. Let's try scrolling, Mark, and leave Miss Tenny to make the afore-mentioned explanation."

"Sounds good to me." Croston caught her hands. The blades of their skates sang as they struck out for the clear space in the middle of the pond. It seemed to Gail that they skated round and round for hours before he said: —

"That was a long speech you made to Lila."

"I'd say it was long, something in the way of an oration, I calls it. I got started and I couldn't find a place to stop, my mind offered no terminal facility. Let's forget it. Gorgeous night, isn't it? Windless. I like the clear, stinging cold."

"Perfect, *now.*" He emphasized the last word with a pressure of her hands.

"Were you at the concert?" she asked, not that she cared but to turn the current of his thoughts from herself.

"Yes. Wasn't Cissie-Lou a knockout? That youngster certainly has what it takes.

Look here, Gail, let's talk this thing out. Do you intend to stay married to Hunt?"

She'd have to take it. Perhaps it would be better as he suggested to talk the matter out and settle it for all time. She skated backwards that she might meet his eyes with a smile and asked gaily: —

"Just what would you advise, *Mister* Croston?"

"Gail, you're adorable in this mood." She resisted his attempt to draw her closer. "I say, chuck him and marry me."

"I wonder —" She stopped to watch a skater coming at a tremendous pace. Was he coming to her? Had something happened to . . .

"Gosh, Gail, I've been trailing you all over the place." Billy Trevor sent his voice ahead of him. "Miss Tenny wants to go home, Mr. Croston."

"Okay, I'll take you back, Gail."

"I'll take her back," Billy interrupted. "You'll run right along *now* if you know what's good for you. I've seen mad dames before." As Croston shot away, the boy laughed.

"That got him. Looky, Gail, why'd you let Lila Tenny walk in on your date with Greg? I saw you four meet and saw you skate off with glamour-pants. That suited

317

her down to the ground. Why didn't you stay in there pitching?"

"I don't know what you mean, Billy Trevor."

"Sure you know. Don't get on your high horse and *don't* skate so fast. Think you're Sonja Henie? That's better. The Tenny menace skated off with your steady and you let her, that's what I mean."

"My steady, as you call him, appeared to be very well satisfied."

"Oh, yeah, perhaps that's the reason Greg left Lila long enough to tell me to tell Croston she wanted him. I added a little on my own. Here's the Cap now. Ask him. He knows." Bent almost double he was halfway across the pond before she could answer.

"Don't stand still, you'll freeze," Greg Hunt declared. "What say if we go home? I told Parrock to serve hot chocolate and sandwiches in front of the fire in our living room when we came in."

In answer Gail laid her hands in his extended ones. As they glided forward in perfect rhythm she thought: —

You get mixed up with Fate, Destiny or whatever it is that shoots you into the path of a man whose bride has just given him what Billy calls the quick brush-off, and where do you land? In *our* living room. She would sidestep that if possible.

"Hot chocolate before a fire sounds good to me. There are Lila and Mark. I thought they had gone. Let's ask them to come back with us."

A late and somewhat battered moon provided sufficient light for her to see the speculative narrowing of the lids as his eyes met hers.

"What's the idea?"

"I thought — I thought —"

"Having established the fact that 'you thought,' go on."

"That if we invited them it would show we had no hard feelings."

"*We!* No hard feelings!" She hadn't heard him laugh like that since their fishing trips. "That's the funniest thing I ever heard. However, if you want them it's all right with me. Croston or Lila must have a car here. I bet you a twenty-five-dollar war bond they won't come."

To Gail's astonishment and relief they accepted the invitation eagerly. As they mounted the circular stairway at Twin Pines, Mark Croston exclaimed: —

"This is a stunning hall. I've never been upstairs before."

"You and Lila are the Gregory Hunts'

first visitors," Greg said as he swung open the door of the apartment. "All the comforts of home, special entrance at the foot of those stairs, everything we need but the kitchen range."

Gail looked at him and wondered. Unlike him to be so talkative. Was it a cover-up for emotion because Lila was here as a visitor when he had thought she would come as his wife?

Later, as they sat in front of the living-room fire, she wondered if Lila in her turn was thinking that this and the charming bedroom in which she had left her short white fur coat were to have been hers?

She glanced at Greg, who had risen to refill Lila's cup with chocolate. What was he thinking as he looked at the girl who had jilted him? He had told Mr. B.C. he had asked her once to call off the marriage. Had he really or had he said it for the benefit of the girl he had married? He had admitted later that Lila could be alluring. His face told nothing. He was the perfect host.

"The night is young. How about a game of contract?" he suggested.

"I have work —"

"Forget work tonight, Mark," Gail interrupted. "We won't play more than two hours. You can get to bed early and be little bright-eyes for your job in the morning."

"Of course we'll stay, Greg, darling," Lila Tenny declared. "Mark persuaded me that it was my patriotic duty to attend that terrible USO concert. He'll have to stay as a reward to me for being a good girl, that is, if *you* want us, Mrs. Hunt? It's difficult to think of you as Mrs. when you don't wear a wedding ring."

"Lila asked you a question, Gail," Greg reminded as he dropped two decks of cards on the table.

"I'm sorry." The thrust about the ring had wiped the preceding question from Gail's mind. "That name is so new I didn't realize she was speaking to me." She remembered the edge in Lila's voice, remembered Billy's, "Why didn't you stay in there pitching?" and added: "Mrs. Gregory Hunt. Nice name, isn't it? I've always loved it. Forgive that little burst of sentiment. Of course I want you to stay, Lila. Mark and I will take on you and Greg. Right, Mark?"

"Couldn't be better." He placed a chair at the card table Greg had set up. "Sit here, sweetness."

She saw Greg's quick look at him, saw his color rise in response. Mark hadn't intended that term of endearment to slip out, she was sure. During the months they had been friends he hadn't used it to her more than twice. If Greg's expression were an indication of what he was thinking he doubtless inferred it was a habit.

Later as the living-room door closed behind the guests and Greg who had gone down to see them off, she thought, "Lucky at cards, unlucky at love." If this evening is an indication I'm in for a tragic love life. She and Mark had swept everything before them. Lila had been incredulous at first, then resentful. Her "darlings" addressed to her partner had taken on an edge as Lady Luck deserted them and left them flat. Her indignation was excusable; Greg had played carelessly and he was an expert. Why?

Better call this an evening and slip into her room before he came back. He was keen. He hadn't been fooled when she had said that inviting Lila and Mark here tonight would show there were no hard feelings. He might insist on an explanation. What could she tell him except that she had asked them to come to avoid being alone with him? Her hand was on the knob of her bedroom door when he said behind her: —

"Come here. I want to talk to you."

He looked very lean and stern, tall and slim as he stood before the fire. What had he on his mind?

"In that red coat and the black tights you're positively spectacular," she observed in the hope of derailing the train of thought which made his face so stern.

"It's the regalia of my before-the-war Skating Club. A trifle conspicuous but darn comfortable so I dug it out."

So far so good. She glanced at the clock.

"It's late. Won't the talk keep until tomorrow?"

"Sorry, it won't. Sit down. You make me think of the Winged Victory, poised as if ready to fly."

"She had no arms. I have, see?" She held out her hands. The sleeves of her emerald green and silver blouse, which she had worn with her short velvet skating skirt, as a bit of dress-up for Cissie-Lou's concert, came only halfway to her elbows.

"I see. They are very lovely arms. I have been aware of them all the evening. So was Croston. And while we're on the subject, we'll dispose of him first. I won't have him calling you 'sweetness.' Better sit down. I have a lot to say."

"If it's as silly as that choice item about Mark, I'd better." She regarded him defiantly from the depths of a crimson damask chair. "In all the time we have been friends, he has called me that only twice before."

"You must have kept careful count."

"I have not and if I had I consider what I'm called by anyone none of your business."

"I intend to make it my business from now on."

"Don't glare at me as if I were a Kawa 95 you were about to attack. In case you've forgotten, I'm a human being white, free, and twenty-one — if I do happen at the moment to have the misfortune to be Mrs. Gregory Hunt."

Laughter replaced gravity in his eyes.

"Quote. 'Nice name, isn't it? I always loved it.' Unquote. Glad you like it."

She shrugged.

"I don't particularly. Lila started her *banderilla*-throwing act and I said the first thing I could think of to show that her darts made no impression. How can you joke about this impossible situation?"

"It isn't an impossible situation unless you make it so. Why pretend you're a princess imprisoned in a tower? We've been grand friends for years. Why should the few words that clergyman intoned the other day smash that friendship?"

"Greg, you don't understand. I feel like such a deceiver every time I see Aunt Jane. What is there so funny about that to make you laugh your head off?"

"Your belief that you are deceiving Aunt Jane. Now that that subject is nicely washed up, we'll proceed to the examination of the witness. Why don't you wear your wedding ring? Don't you like it?"

Surprise sent the color to her hair.

"Why — why — yes."

"Why not wear it? Wedding rings have been in use for a long time by the best families. You haven't shelved it because you think it's the ring I bought for Lila?"

She thought of the minutes which had seemed hours as she sat in his car in front of the jeweler's shop after they had left the Town Clerk's office that epoch-making afternoon and she remembered her panicky urge to jump out and run and she recalled the pounding of her heart as she had rallied herself, "Don't welsh. Don't be a Lila Tenny."

"You *don't* think that, do you?" he prompted.

"Of course not. Didn't I wait for you while you bought it? It's beautiful, but a diamond circlet is so — so conspicuous and —"

"They were all out of brass wedding rings," he interrupted curtly. "Priorities are forever taking the fun out of life."

"Greg. Let's not fight. I — haven't worn the ring because it made me feel dishonest."

"Don't talk as if it were something you'd stolen. Wear it. That's all."

"May I go now, mister?" He didn't respond to the exaggerated humility of her voice. She hurriedly patted her hand over her lips in pretense of stifling a yawn.

"Even though I didn't have to arise this morning in time to prepare breakfast I was awake at dawn. I'd better turn in as I must be at the office early. Mr. B.C. and I have a full day tomorrow. Tomorrow!" She came close to him and whispered: —

"I'd forgotten. You are to show the picture of the mysterious woman tomorrow, aren't you?"

"Yes."

"Am I to be among those present?"

"Yes. B.C. wants you on the platform with him beside the screen. Have you spoken of the showing to anyone, Gail?"

"I have *not*. Why are you so suspicious of me, Greg?"

"Why? Because something tells me you would have married Croston if I hadn't stepped in, and when a girl loves a man it would be pretty difficult for her to refuse to answer what seem to her to be harmless questions."

"But Mark doesn't ask me questions about the Works."

"Okay." He turned to toss his cigarette into the fire, faced her again. "I'll remind you of what the President said the other day. 'Victory cannot be bought with any amount of money, however large. Victory is achieved by the blood of soldiers, the sweat of working men and women and the sacrifices of all people.' I'll add, on my own, and the absolute loyalty of each worker to his or her job."

"Does that mean you think I'm not loyal to my job?"

"Standards of loyalty may differ. I hope yours and mine are the same. Think it over."

He opened the door of her room.

"You were right when you said we had a full day tomorrow. Better turn in."

She stopped just inside her door and looked up at him in troubled uncertainty. She hadn't set him right when he had said something told him she would have married Mark if he hadn't stepped in. Should she tell him that she knew now that she wouldn't have married Mark Croston if he were the only man in the world?

"What big eyes you have, Grandmother," he said lightly. Bent his head and kissed her parted lips tenderly. "Good night, my dearest."

He closed the door quickly. In the still room it seemed as if the walls echoed his husky voice repeating: —

"Good night, my dearest."

Chapter 23

Jane Clifton, in an amethyst-and-white print morning dress, preceded tray-bearing, pink-frocked Sarah into the ell living room where Gail was checking her wrist watch by the tall clock.

"I like you in that lime-green tweed, my dear. I came up for a chat while you breakfasted. It's wonderful to have a niece in the house. It's the only chance I have to see you. Hope you don't mind?"

"I love it, Aunt Jane." Gail seated herself at the small table which held the tray. "Orange juice, bacon, coffee with *cream,* popovers and raspberry jam. I love 'em all. How'd you ever manage the bacon? I couldn't get any last week!" Was it only last week she had been keeping house for John and the children? It seemed like an episode in her remote past.

"You forget that we have a farm back in the country," Mrs. Clifton reminded after Sarah had departed. "B.C. believes that agriculture is as important in defense work as munitions industries and should be rated and planned for accordingly, that a farm worker should be awarded an F button to wear."

"Sounds fair. Share my breakfast. There is more than enough for one."

"You need it all to prepare for the work those bosses of yours require. I breakfasted with B.C. half an hour ago, if black coffee and melba toast can be called breakfast. If a man goes off to work for his wife the least she can do is to be up and on her job of sending him on his way with a kiss and 'God speed.' Not listening to me, are you, my dear?"

"I am. I can repeat every word you said." She wouldn't confess, though, that the word "kiss" had set her pulses rioting. "Shall I?"

"No. Spare me. I didn't come here to orate on the subject of wifely duty," she chuckled, "I came, first, to ask why you didn't wear the diamond bracelet with that lovely flame-color dinner frock Thanksgiving night? If it was because you thought it was the present B.C. and I had for Lila, you were wrong; or didn't you like it?"

"*Like* it! I *loved* it. Neither of your guesses is right, Aunt Jane. It seemed too much for me to accept when — when —"

"You needn't go on. I understand. I'm

not dumb if I am a stylish stout. Having disposed of the bracelet — I hope you'll wear it soon — I have a human interest story that's too good to keep. After Lila sent the note to Greg telling him the wedding was off, she sat beside the telephone, when she wasn't pacing the floor, waiting for him to come or phone."

"She wrote Greg she was going to Washington."

"She didn't go. Lila's maid told my maid. Sarah adores Greg. She resented that eleventh hour jilt a lot more than I did. When you come down to it, I didn't resent it. I ate it up."

"It's incredible. Perhaps the maid doesn't like Lila and invented the yarn."

"I've seen her. She's not bright enough to imagine such details as 'the bride was dressed in the winter-white costume she'd had made for her wedding,' that she kept looking at the clock, kept asking, 'Did you hear a car stop, Marie?' Oh, no, it's a true story. Our glamorous Lila overshot the mark. Why so serious? I thought you'd think it a joke."

"She came here after the concert last evening. I'm thinking how she must have been hating me."

"You should worry. That break-up was a

direct answer to prayer — or thought transference, take your choice. Each time I saw them together, I would say mentally, 'Throw him over, Lila. Don't marry her, Greg.' I gave the subject the works and see what happened?"

"I see, Aunt Jane. Influencing the lives of others is a pretty ticklish business. Admitting that thought transference works, you may have broken up an ideal marriage."

"Ideal fiddlesticks! Good gracious, Greg, what are you doing at home this time in the morning?" she exclaimed as her nephew appeared in the doorway.

"I'm here to drive Gail to the Works. How else will she get there?"

"I brought my own Ford runabout here yesterday."

"We're pledged to conserve gas. Hereafter, you'll be my passenger back and forth. Finish your breakfast while I pick up some papers in my room."

As he crossed the threshold Jane Clifton said for his benefit: —

"The masterful type. He thinks you're a Flying Fortress under his command, Gail. Watch your step, my dear."

"Thanks for the warning, Aunt Jane. I'll heed it. It's my Nurses' Aide night at the hospital. I won't be here for dinner. I shall go directly from the Works with Pat Selby, who will pick me up there."

Seated beside Greg in the convertible Gail stole a glance at him. The first time she had seen him in the office after his return from the Pacific she had been startled by the change. His face had aged, his mouth, which she had remembered as rather boyishly sweet, was grim, his eyes were fierce as only blue eyes can be. He looked younger today but his lips and jaw were still tense. They hadn't been when he had said last night, "What big eyes you have, Grandmother," or when he had . . . She pushed back the memory, said quickly: —

"Gorgeous morning. Air iced and crystal clear. Isn't the sky blue and hard and cold? Looks like a huge turquoise. Difficult to believe that day before yesterday it was raining great guns. Those are your words, not mine."

"Glad to know that some of the things I say stick in your memory. Did Aunt Jane hand out Sarah's gleanings from Lila's maid as a sort of breakfast cocktail? You needn't answer. Your color tells the story. I wondered when she relayed it to B.C. and me with our coffee if she could possibly resist passing it on to you."

"She told me. What — what are you going to do about it?"

"*Do* about it? Forget it. I have more important things on my mind. One of them, the picture-show this afternoon."

"Have the department heads been notified?"

"Only that B.C. wants them to report in the small assembly hall at four."

"Do they know why?"

"No. You and B.C. will take seats on the platform after the hall has been darkened. Search wants you to watch the faces when the light goes on again. He got back this morning. He has cleared up the Edwards angle. The son for whom the woman was looking was a child by her first husband."

"Then of course his name isn't Edwards. What is it?"

"When I asked Search that question he answered, 'There are some things I don't tell even my boss till I get the pieces of my picture puzzle assembled. One infinitesimal leak and whoosh! our fox will streak to cover; we'll lose him.'

"He's right, of course. A government agent ought to know his business. It sends little shivers over me to think what may be revealed. Suppose the mysterious woman was wrong? Suppose she had made a mistake in the factory?"

"Would she have been so terrified when the guard pointed out the man whose name was the same as that of the son for whom she was looking? I'd like to believe she had mistaken the place, but if my common sense didn't reject the possibility, the information Search has dug up would."

"It means that, soon after four o'clock, someone we have trusted, someone we have thought loyal, will prove to be a traitor, doesn't it?"

"Unless he can fool us. A man who could dispose of another and take his place won't let his expression betray him."

"Greg! You don't mean murder?"

"Could be. In a second after the woman's face appears on the screen a strong light will be thrown on the audience. Observe the men's faces."

"I will. I'll be stiff with suspense. One person I won't have to watch. Remember that since the woman died in the office Mark Croston flew home and saw his mother."

"Remember that this woman is the mother of a man who *should* be a department head here, *not*, if her story is to be believed, one who is filling the position.

Here we are. If I'm tied up and can't take you home I'll ask B.C. to look out for you."

"I shan't need anyone. I'm on duty at the hospital till eleven. Pat Selby and I go together in her car. She calls at the Works for me and takes me home."

"I don't like to have you on the road so late with a woman but it can't be helped tonight. Remember, hereafter you'll go back and forth to the Works with me or B.C."

"The masterful type."

He laughed. "If you've learned that, we're getting on."

The small assembly room was too dusky to make out the faces of the men in the seats when, in the late afternoon, she and Benjamin Clifton sat on the platform one on each side of the screen. The hum of voices ceased as Gregory Hunt spoke.

"A few weeks ago a woman visited several factories looking for a son who had told her before he left home that he had been assigned to an important defense job. She lost the letter and began the rounds to try to find him, with no success. In the hope that one of you may recognize her, if not as your own mother, as the mother of a man you know, we will throw her picture on the screen. Ready."

336

Not a sound from the men waiting. Was each one of them holding his breath thinking it might be his mother? Gail shivered with excitement, then forgot herself as the face of a woman with white hair and dark eyes was flashed on the screen. It was a perfect likeness of the mysterious visitor. Still no sound from the audience.

"The woman died in my office."

With Greg Hunt's blunt announcement a flash-bulb illumined the faces of the men intently watching. One was standing. The sudden light revealed his shocked face. Blackout. From the midst of the darkness came a broken voice: —

"Dead! My God!"

Curtains were hurriedly pushed back. Lights went on. The department heads blinked in the sudden change. Some faces were white as if the shock of that hoarse, "Dead! My God!" still lingered.

"Who spoke?" Gregory Hunt demanded sharply.

Each man looked at his neighbor as if waiting for him to give the name. After a pause a voice answered.

"It was Joe Selby, G.H."

Greg looked down at the faces turned toward him.

"He isn't here. Anyone see him go out?"

"I heard the rear door close softly just before the curtains were pulled back," a man replied. "If the woman on the screen was his mother, must have knocked him cold to learn she was dead." A sympathetic murmur, soft as a gentle breeze, swept the hall.

Selby! Joe Selby! Incredible, Greg thought, even as he said: —

"We've shown the picture as requested. If one of you picks up a clue as to the whereabouts of the missing son — after all, we're only guessing that Selby knew the woman — get in touch with me at once. Company dismissed."

Was it possible that Selby had fooled them all, that beneath that thatch of coarse sandy hair, his brain had worked out a murderous plot? That behind those thick lenses his eyes had been mockingly alert? Greg asked himself as he returned to his office. How else explain the startled exclamation? Was he the son? He couldn't be, there wasn't an atom of likeness between the two faces; besides, there was Patricia — wouldn't the woman have spoken of her, if she had a daughter?

Was he the substitute? If so, why that exclamation, as if it were a shock to learn that the woman was dead? He had been watching another face when the bulb flashed, a face which had shown no recognition of the woman on the screen. Shipping orders went through Selby's department. This morning Search had reported an attempt to hi-jack the motor trucks loaded with plane parts which were to be driven overland for assembly hundreds of miles away. One of his men had received a tip in time to save them.

As he entered his office Benjamin Clifton stopped pacing the floor to explain: —

"Gail and I couldn't wait for you to come to me, G.H., to find out who blurted, 'Dead! My God!' Do you know?" The girl's dark eyes as she stood near the desk asked the same question.

"Sit down, both of you. You're in for a shock." His uncle sank into the one deep chair the room contained and Gail perched on the very edge of one with a straight back.

"Shoot, G.H.," Benjamin Clifton commanded.

"One of the men said it was Joe Selby. Did you notice his face when the bulb flashed, Gail?"

"I did. I hate to believe my eyes, but he was on his feet, staring at the screen as a sleepwalker might who had been startled awake and discovers that he's not where he thought he was."

"A perfect description of Selby's expression. I noticed it too, G.H. I'll go back to my office and get to work. Suspecting Selby of duplicity makes me a little sick. I would have staked my fortune he was straight. Better get started for the hospital, Gail, I don't need you again."

The door closed. Alone in the office Greg clasped his hands behind his head, tipped back in his chair and stared unseeingly at the rapidly darkening world outside the window. He reviewed the evidence against Joe Selby. First, he had recognized the woman on the screen. Second, there had been an attempt to hi-jack a load of plane parts, and his was one of the two departments through which orders were sent for shipments. That tied it.

On his return this morning Search had reported that the fingerprints he had secured at the home of Mrs. Edwards on the Coast were identical with those he had of the sick man who had been secreted by the Pomponis, and later had been moved to the Trevor home. When pressed for more information he had said, "Wait until after the picture-show this afternoon. Even walls have ears these days."

If only the woman had lived long enough to tell which department her son was to head, it wouldn't matter about the name. He, himself, had had a queer, subconscious hunch who it was, but it seemed too fantastic to be possible. He tipped forward in his chair to answer a click from the box on his desk.

"G.H. speaking. A man on the way to my office? You mean he's coming at once? Why the mystery? What? Who's speaking? I am to call him by *what* name? Say it again. Spell it. Who are — Hello!" No answer.

He snapped off the connection. Had the mysterious voice been that of a crackpot or was he someone in the know? At least the informer had known that a man was on the way to his office.

The knob of the door turned. And here he is. It's Selby, I suppose, come with some cock and bull story to explain his exclamation. He pretended to be busy on a paper as the door opened.

"Your secretary told me to walk in. Came to ask if I could help in the hunt for the missing son," Mark Croston explained as he approached the desk. "What's the matter? Have I interrupted a trance, G.H.? You look as if you were seeing ghosts."

Greg swallowed his heart, which was pounding in his throat. It was Croston. He had expected Selby. He stared at the lean, dark-skinned face, the inscrutable, brilliant hazel eyes, the red lips beneath the dark mustache. The vague suspicion he had had of the man crystallized into conviction.

"Do I look dazed, Mark?" Rigid self-control kept his voice steady. "I had just picked up the hot end of a problem when you knocked. Got to nail it while it's sizzling. Take a chair. You'll have my attention in a minute."

"Hadn't I better come back?"

"No. *No*. It isn't so important that I need privacy." As Croston walked to the window and looked out Greg clicked his fingernail against the box.

"Oh, Burt!" he called.

"Yes?" The man at the window wheeled as he answered. As his eyes met Greg's fierce blue eyes his skin turned to chalk. His face settled into the controlled savagery of a man who knows he's trapped and is marshaling all his forces to break through. In one bound he was at the door to the conference room, had seized the key and locked it behind him.

The hot blood of fury surged through Greg's body, his head felt light from shock, his fingers were ice as he snapped the switch in the interoffice phone. Again and again he tried for an answer. It seemed hours before the guard on the first floor spoke.

"Yes, Mr. Hunt."

"Mr. Croston is just leaving the building by our private entrance. An important message has come for him. Stop him. Bring him back. Understand, *Bring him back* to his office. Call help if necessary. Report at once to me when you've found him."

He clicked the shutter on the man's breathless, "Yes, sir."

Who had phoned to tell him to call the man who was on his way to his office "Burt"? Would the guard stop this saboteur masquerading under a borrowed name in a stolen job? He must.

Was that sound a shot or a backfire? He dashed to the window. Light moving in the court. Good God, had Croston shot himself or the guard who had tried to stop him?

He started for the conference room door. Remembered that it was locked. Flung open the other. It seemed an eternity before he reached the unconscious figure on the ground.

"What happened?" he demanded of the guard bending over him.

"I don't know, Mr. Hunt. After you phoned, I had to call someone to take my place. It took a few minutes and as I ran down the steps to beat it to the private entrance, Mr. Croston was just stepping into his roadster. It was almost dark but I saw him swing to the rear of the car, heard a shot, then he was off and this guy was lying on the ground. I thought at first he'd done the shootin' but with that hole drilled in his shoulder I guess 'twas Mr. Croston."

"Have you phoned to have his car stopped at the gate, Sergeant?"

"No sir, I was so surprised —"

"Do it now. Order the hospital ambulance. I'll stay here until it comes. Give me your flash and keep this under your hat."

"Too much noise in the foundries for a worker to hear that shot, Mr. Hunt. I was the only person near."

As the sergeant started off at double-quick, Greg turned the light on the unconscious face. It was that of the third-floor patient, the man he had expected to see.

He stripped off his coat and laid it carefully over the prostrate figure. Dazed eyes opened.

"Get him?" The hoarse voice came with

difficulty between stiff lips, "It was Burt — I — told — you — I did the best I could — before — he — came. Letting out gas — when he caught me. You'll have to — to finish. He's tricky — he'll fool you — he'll go to —" His head fell back. His eyes closed.

Chapter 24

Tom Search lighted a cigarette from a stub and frowned at Greg Hunt seated behind his desk.

"The bogus Croston can't get far. He made his getaway hours ago. Why haven't we caught him? Every road out of the town is blocked. Besides, the man he shot told you he had let out some of the gas.

"*Some*. Doubtless the tank was kept filled for just such an emergency. May have been enough left to reach a haven. There must be one or two persons in this city aiding him or he wouldn't have been sent here. These saboteurs leave nothing to chance. While we stop to draw breath, tell me what you discovered on the Coast."

Seated on the corner of the desk Search drew within reach the large bronze ashtray, already piled with stubs he had contributed.

"I called on the neighbor who had set Major Brent on the woman's trail. Explained my errand and authority. He turned over the key to the house next door and okayed my investigation. I had taken the precaution first to get in touch with the local FBI."

"Find any letters from the son or pictures of him?"

"Nary a one. The place had been stripped. Someone had been through the house before I arrived. Had destroyed all letters, all pictures that would show what the boy looked like. If I hadn't been sure before that there had been foul play that would have convinced me. I cautiously cross-examined the neighbor. Didn't tell him what I had found. He said the only person he had let into the house was a man with an order to turn off the gas. I asked him if it was the one who usually came. He said 'No,' but he had a badge to show who he was."

"Know when this gas man showed up?"

"The neighbor couldn't remember for sure, thought it was the last week in October."

"The last week in October! The bogus Croston, Burt to you, flew to the West Coast at that time. He has scored. He blocked you on the fingerprints you expected to get from the letters."

"I got 'em all right, if not from the letters. The son's room was full of them. Easy enough to raise them with silver nitrate solution. They matched up with those of the patient who vamoosed from Doctor Trevor's."

"Have you figured what happened?"

"I dope it out like this. The real Mark Croston was recommended for the Clifton Works. His credentials were approved and he was hired. Somewhere on the way East he was shanghaied, a subversive substitute, the man we've known as Mark Croston, primed with his case history, was sent on to take his name and position, to pull what dirty work he could and to make his getaway at the first hint of suspicion."

"Can you get data on this man Burt?"

"I have it. Ten minutes after you told me that the so called Croston had answered to that name I was in touch with Headquarters. In half an hour I had the man's dossier. An engineer apparently named Burt was drowned while fishing on a river last summer. Overturned boat, oilskin case holding draft registration and letters, the last badly stained, were found on the bank for identification."

"No body?"

"No. The man's background was looked up by the police of the town near which boat and papers drifted ashore. Orphan.

Good family. Graduate of a Western college for engineers. Decent-living guy. Fishing enthusiast. Demise was announced in papers. No answers. Marked off as accident."

"The murderers, of course, figured they had disposed of their victim permanently."

"That's where they're fooled. We've got him now, safe in the hospital, thanks to the fake department head's bullet. Since my visit to the Coast I've known that the guy we knew as Doc's patient was the real Croston. When Joe Selby came out with that hoarse, 'Dead! My God!' I felt as if a flash-bulb had gone off in my brain. What the devil did he mean by it? I've been trying to get in touch with him but he hasn't been home."

"He had me fooled. I thought he was the man we were after. I can believe almost anything in the way of subversive activities but a shift such as you've described would seem impossible to put across."

"This man Burt wasn't the only man on the job, remember. The substitution was protected at every point by organized saboteurs. It's been done before in these last few years. This time they didn't get away with it."

"The substitute department head couldn't

have had a hand in the damaged plane parts. That filthy work must have been done before he came."

"Sure it was, but whoever was back of it evidently decided to have the new man put on a different act. Hi-jacking the latest shipment of plane parts for a starter. Orders for shipping went out from his and Selby's offices, remember. We've got to get that guy and no fooling. I'll shoot back to the office. One of my men is seated outside our special patient's door at the hospital to phone me the moment he regains consciousness. Doc Trevor is Head there now and has agreed to let me talk with the real Mark Croston. We want his story. We got him away from the Works into Receiving and whisked into a private room so quietly that only the night intern, the surgical intern and a nurse know he's there."

He held the knob of the door in his hand long enough to warn: —

"Keep away from the hospital, G.H. It may ball things up if you go. Go home and stay there. The bogus Croston may be hanging round to take a crack at you. It isn't a secret that you married a girl he was crazy about. He'd have nothing to lose by putting you out of the running. He must know his goose is cooked. Will you go home?"

In spite of his tense anxiety Greg laughed. "Sure, I'll go — for a while. Hold on, Search. Gail is on Nurses' Aide duty tonight. The man we know as Croston may try to contact her when she leaves the hospital in an attempt to have her help him. I must bring her home."

"I'll look after her. I promise. Go home. I've got to know where to reach you."

"Okay, I'll go."

As he entered the hall at Twin Pines Greg glanced at the tall clock. Only ten? It seemed as if he had been on the move talking, following clues, listening for hours. He wouldn't be here now if Search hadn't made such a point of it.

"Mrs. Hunt home yet, Parrock?" he asked as the white-haired butler appeared. Wishful thinking. Of course she wasn't.

"No, Mr. Greg. The Madam said at dinner that this was Miss Gail's evening at the hospital."

"Right. I'd forgotten. Bring up a tray. I haven't eaten since — come to think of it, since breakfast. I'm hollow. Perhaps that's why I'm low in my mind." He stopped on the third stair to inquire, "Any phone messages?"

"Mr. Selby telephoned several times, Mr. Greg. Very anxious to talk with you. I couldn't tell him when you'd be back, so he said he'd come and wait for you. He's in your living room now. Hope it was all right to let him go up?"

"Sure. Double everything on the tray, he may be hungry too. Any other calls?"

"Not on the phone, sir. Mr. Croston stepped in for a minute."

"Croston!" Greg's heart turned over. Search had said it wasn't a secret that the man was crazy about Gail. Had he come for her? *"Croston!"* he repeated. "At what time?"

"I'd say it was about — well, between four and five, nearer five, Mr. Greg. Madam hadn't returned from the movie, you know she goes every Saturday afternoon."

"I know all that, Parrock. What did Cros— Mr. Croston want? How long did he stay?"

"He inquired for Madam and Miss Gail — beg pardon — Mrs. Hunt — but he really came to use the telephone. Said his car had broken down not far from here, and he wanted to phone for a mechanic."

"Did he get one?" *I know he didn't because we found the abandoned car,* Greg reminded himself.

"I presume so, Mr. Greg. He told me not

352

to wait, that if he couldn't get a mechanic he'd call a taxi. When I came back to the front of the house he had gone. You look anxious. I hope I didn't do wrong letting him come in?"

"Of course not, Parrock. Mr. Croston has been here as a guest dozens of times. Rustle up that supper, will you?"

His thoughts were in a turmoil as he went up the stairs. Search's men had been quietly on the hunt for Mark Croston since they had received the news of the man's revealing "Yes" in answer to the name of "Burt" and his dash for liberty. That last would have been a confession of guilt if there had been nothing else. He had been in this very house. Lucky Gail hadn't been here when he called. She must have been on her way to the hospital at the moment of the shooting. Had Croston — hard to think of him by his right name — succeeded in getting a cab? The taxi company would tell the story.

The living room was rosy with fire and lamplight as he entered and threw his hat and topcoat on a chair. Joe Selby looked up from a magazine. In spite of Greg's smarting anxiety he swallowed a laugh. Selby's coarse red hair reared on the right side of his head like a scalplock, he swung his heavy shell-rimmed spectacles in one hand while his shortsighted eyes blinked like those of a schoolboy about to blubber. Indubitably he had something weighty on his mind.

"Thank the Lord you've come, G.H. Hope you don't mind —"

"Darned glad you're here, Joe. Just a minute, I've got to phone — pronto."

He entered his bedroom and closed the door. Dialed the hospital. Inquired if Mrs. Hunt had reported for work.

"Mrs. Hunt — Oh, you mean Miss Trevor that was?" The operator giggled. "Sure, she's here. Just passed along the corridor with a tray. Want her paged?"

"No." One anxiety checked off. He had been tense with fear that Croston might have threatened Gail's safety.

He called Search's office. Reported the bogus Croston's call at Twin Pines, that he had ordered a taxi, suggested that he might have knocked out the driver and taken his cap and the wheel himself. Next, he contacted the taxi company.

"Gregory Hunt at Twin Pines speaking. Did you receive a call from this house for a cab this afternoon?" Good Lord, was the man looking back through the year's records before he could answer?

"You did? Shortly before five. That's right — Did you send the cab? . . . I *know* you're dependable. I wanted to make sure it came, that's all. Do you know where the driver took the passenger? He's out with another fare? Check and give me a ring when he comes in, will you? I'm trying to reach the man who ordered it. Want to pass on an important message which he should have. Okay, never mind if it is late. Give me a ring, I'll be here the rest of the night."

"Sorry to be so long, Joe," he apologized as he entered the living room. "Couldn't get connections."

"You look all in, G.H. I won't take but a few minutes of your time."

"I'm mighty glad to have you here. I — Here's Parrock with eats."

The butler snapped down the legs of the laden serving table he had brought in and removed silver covers in varying sizes. As he placed two chairs he explained: —

"I thought hot roast-beef sandwiches, beef, nice and rare with plenty of dip, green salad, crackers and cheese, would taste good, Mr. Greg. The milk that came from the farm today is especially fine. I knew you wouldn't drink coffee. Here's a fresh fruit cup and angel cake — will that be sufficient?"

Greg's tired face brightened in a grin.

"Looks to me to be a regular lend-lease menu. How about you, Selby?"

"Am I in on this? I'll manage to make way with my share. I've been so busy trying to contact you I forgot to go home to dinner."

The butler solicitously rearranged the flat silver. On the way to the door he picked up Greg's topcoat and hat.

"Leave that where it is, Parrock," Greg protested. "I may want it. I've left my convertible in the drive at the side entrance. *Don't move it.* I may have to leave in a hurry. Understand? *Leave it where it is.*"

"Very good, Mr. Greg. I won't touch it."

Greg laughed as the door closed.

"Now I've hurt his feelings. I was too loud and emphatic but I had to be to get the idea across. He's so darn orderly that leaving my coat and hat on the chair will probably bring on a nervous breakdown. He'd put the car up himself rather than have it stand in the drive." Seated across the table from Selby he reminded: —

"Let's have it. What's on the little mind, Joe?"

Selby set down his tall glass of milk with a thud and drew a ragged breath of relief.

"Thank the Lord, you haven't gone haywire because I went melodramatic on you, with that 'Dead! My God!' act. I was practically driven from my office to escape condoling department heads, who assumed that the picture on the screen was that of my mother."

"Wasn't it? You gave me an awful jolt, Joe."

"My mother died years ago. I saw that woman once, that's all."

"She must have made a deep impression or you wouldn't have been shocked into that exclamation when I said she died in my office."

"She did make an impression. She was chock-full of that indefinable something they call charm, for want of a better word. I met her one blustery afternoon in October when I was coming from the railroad station. She was struggling along ahead of me against the wind. Her hat blew off and I caught it. She was breathless and a little blue about the lips when I returned it. I remember thinking, 'You're taking a chance, buffeting a wind like this, lady.' Her eyes and voice were so friendly and attractive as she thanked me that I laughed and said: —

" 'Never bother to chase a hat, Madam. There's sure to be a man near to rescue it.'

" 'My son tells me that.' Worried lines in

her face replaced the smile.

"The wind was fierce. I linked my arm in hers to help her keep her feet. As we walked — struggled would be a better word — she told me she had come to New England to see her son who was in defense work. She was planning to stay at the Inn. Just then my head timekeeper called to me from his car.

" 'You can't walk alone in this gale, madam,' I said. 'I've got to leave you.' I hailed a taxi. 'Hop in and tell the driver where to take you.' The last I saw of her she was smiling and looking out the cab window and saying, 'Thank you.' "

"I recall that wind. I stood at the window watching the workers chase their hats. You didn't hear the address she gave the driver?"

"No. I assumed it was the Inn. The episode slipped from my mind — you don't need to be told the vital problems I've had to tackle — I haven't thought of it again until I saw her face on the screen today. Then I remembered the woman's charm, her breathlessness, her wistful eyes. When you announced that she had died in your office, I was stunned. I thought that had I stayed with her it might not have happened. I felt in a way responsible. That was when I blurted, 'Dead! My God!' "

"Forget that part of it, Joe. She didn't register at the Inn. She must have dismissed the taxi. Probably didn't want it known she was coming here. She was terribly excited when she came into my office. She was living on borrowed time. The post-mortem showed that her heart was worn out."

"Did you know who she was?"

"No. Not until today when we showed that picture — I should say after — because for a few minutes I thought you were impersonating the woman's son, Joe. There's a story behind that picture."

"Sure there is. I'm not dumb if I am nearsighted. Croston's tied up with it, isn't he? I've had a hunch that some day when we arrived at the Works he'd be missing. Nothing definite, just a feeling that he would bear watching. I told Search. Asked if I'd better tell you. He said, 'Not yet. Keep your eyes on the ball, that's all.' Mark's been terribly upset about his mail, jumpy and irritable lately and evidently expecting letters that didn't come."

No wonder he was anxious, Greg thought, with no letters coming from the woman whose son he was pretending to be.

"Before long you'll get the whole story,

Joe. Meanwhile, everything I've said is off the record."

"I get you. There's the phone. Answer it, G.H. I'll shoot along. Good night."

"Good night."

In his bedroom Greg answered the call. Not the cab company. It was one of Search's men to report he had contacted his boss at the hospital and passed on the information that the man they were after had left Twin Pines in a cab in the late afternoon. How had the fake Croston got by so long with the deception? Why hadn't someone detected it? Suddenly on the screen of his mind flashed a picture of Croston standing beside the roadster in which sat Cissie-Lou, again he felt the man stiffen under the hand on his shoulder. Had he thought the FBI had caught up with him? Of course. It was plain as daylight now.

He changed to a brocaded green lounge-jacket. For hours he had been on the move. It would be heaven to drop down and relax for a few minutes. Why not? He wanted to speak to Gail when she came in, to assure himself that she was safe at home. He would hear her enter the living room even with his door closed.

He moved the telephone stand close to

the chaise-longue. The taxi company ought to report soon.

With a sigh of relief he stretched out, groped for the light afghan and pulled it over his shoulders.

"This is the l-life," he said drowsily. "This is the —"

He would have sworn he hadn't closed his eyes when a sound on the door brought him up standing. There was something about the hurried *tap-tap* that set his heart pounding. Gail! In spite of Search's watchfulness was she in danger? He flung open the door.

Chapter 25

In the dressing room at the hospital Gail furtively observed Pat Selby as they changed from street clothes to Nurses' Aide uniforms. She had been unusually quiet as she drove her small car. Did she know that her brother was impersonating someone else?

What other explanation could there be of Joe's startled exclamation when Greg had announced the death of the woman whose face had been flashed on the screen?

The suspicion was incredible. Pat was too grand a person to assist in criminal deception. Besides, she wouldn't dare be engaged to a government secret agent if she were helping her brother. But, neither she nor Joe knew he was a secret agent, Greg had said. They thought him a reporter who was in town to write up the personnel of Clifton Works.

"What's on your mind, Gail? You've barely spoken since we left the Works."

The wall mirror reflected the auburn-haired and the dark-haired girl as they stood side by side facing it; reflected the insignia of a red cross on a white triangle in a dark blue circle on the left sleeve of each of their white blouses, and on the facing of their snowy caps, the jumper-top of their full-skirted light blue dresses; it gave back, also, Gail's smile as she met Pat's eyes and answered: —

"Funny, I was thinking at that very moment that you were not as chatty as usual."

"I'm low in my mind, hope I haven't seemed a little gob of gloom. Tom told me today that the Clifton Works writeup had been okayed, that he was ordered back to Washington by his boss."

Gail's heart stopped, picked up and thudded on. The recall of the secret agent must mean that the job here was finished, that he had his man. Poor Pat, the discovery that her fiancé had been on the trail of her brother would mean the end of the world for her for a while.

"Good heavens, now I've plunged you into gloom." Pat linked her arm in Gail's. "I can take it. Think of the thousands of girls and women whose men are on the fighting fronts. I'm terribly ashamed of my wail. Come on. Time to report."

As they walked along the corridor she added: —

"You're one of the lucky ones to have

your beloved in defense work. I — I — haven't had a chance before to tell you how happy Joe and I are that you married Greg. We adore him. We were threatened with heart failure as his wedding day to Lila drew near. Sorry. Not very tactful to remind you of that."

"Why? Everyone knew they were engaged. Let's forget it. I love the clean, antiseptic smell of a hospital. I love our work, too. I love making patients comfortable and trying to cheer them when they are frightened. In my next incarnation I shall be a trained nurse."

"You may have it. Not for me. I don't like knowing so much about the human body at close range. I don't like taking TPR's — temperature, pulse, respiration to you. Only patriotism and the fun of saying, 'Yes, sir,' humbly to the cocky young interns, while I suppress a giggle as they regard me patronizingly, keep me on the job. They sure feel their oats. There's one at the desk now. Watch the student nurse adore him."

Pat was right, the girl's heart was in her eyes, Gail thought, as she approached the desk to report. The white nurse seated glanced up from a chart. It was Hilda Speed.

"On time as usual, Miss Gail — 207 has refused to eat her supper until you give it to her. She knew it was your night here. She says you're the only Aide who feeds her without missing her mouth."

"I will get her tray at once, Hil— Miss Speed. See you as the clock strikes eleven, Pat."

She walked along the corridor past doors that were closed, past doors that were open, from which came voices and the scent of flowers. It was visiting hour. Almost collided with the chief resident who dashed around a corner. Picked up a hot-water bottle for a student nurse who dropped it as she came out of the supply room with her arms full.

"Thanks. Drowning case. Fell through the ice. Just brought into Receiving," the pink-cheeked, blue-uniformed girl announced in pleasurable, if breathless, excitement and hurried on.

Gail fed 207, carried trays, took temperatures, made up an ether bed, bathed hands and faces, soothed a frightened child who missed his mother. Wheeled a patient to the operating room. At leisure for a moment she dropped into a chair in the corridor and stretched out her white-shod feet to rest them. Golly, they were tired.

"Calling Doctor Trevor. Calling Doctor Trevor," boomed a loud speaker in the corridor.

Hilda Speed's uniform crackled with starch as she hurried toward her.

"Himself wants you to report at once, Miss Gail."

John Trevor was pacing the floor of his office as she entered.

"Thought you'd never get here." He handed her a pad and pencil. "They've just called me. That means that the man who was shot at the Works —"

"What man? *Greg?*" Was Johnny trying to break bad news to her gently? After seeing the woman's face on the screen the man who was impersonating her son might attempt escape. It would be just like Greg to try to stop him.

"Greg! Are you crazy? Of course not." He laughed. "It's an ill wind that blows nobody good. Your white face settled some doubts in my mind. Sit down till your knees stop shaking."

His tone brought the color surging back into Gail's face.

"Thank you, my knees are not shaking, Doctor Trevor. What are your orders, sir?"

"Come with me." As they walked along the corridor he explained: —

"The man who was shot at the Works is our late third-floor patient."

"Who shot him?"

"I don't know. I pulled a bullet out of his shoulder. He was brought down from Surgical two hours ago. Search is here. He was notified as soon as the wounded man regained consciousness. The patient is very weak but insists that he must tell what happened to him, that many lives are at stake. Your job is to take stenographic notes of what he says. Type it later for me, tonight if you can. Here we are."

A NO VISITORS card hung on the door he opened. The air of the room was heavy with the scent of ether. Tom Search, who had been slouched in a chintz-covered armchair, stood up. A white nurse who had been checking the patient's pulse rose from the straight-back wooden chair beside the bed.

"It's stronger, Doctor. He wanted to talk. I told him he must wait until you came."

"I must — talk, Doctor." The voice was faint and halting.

"Take it easy and your strength will hold out. That will be all for the present, nurse."

Gail, seated on the edge of the chintz armchair, saw the woman's eyebrows arch like the back of an angry cat as she glanced in her direction. Was she wondering why a Nurses' Aide was taking the place of an R.N.?

"Ready, Gail." Her brother's voice recalled her to the present. She rested the pad on the arm of a chair and gripped her pencil. She had the curious feeling that she was in a theater waiting breathlessly for the rise of the curtain on a drama which would unroll the story of the mysterious happenings of the last weeks. The doctor was seated at one side of the bed, Tom Search at the other, deep lines of concentration were etched from his nose to his lips.

"All set, boy. Get the load off your mind. Don't go too much into detail. Mr. Search will fill in. Don't hurry. You have all the time there is, remember."

"I'll take it easy as I can, sir, but — don't let me slip — away till I've told my story. It's terribly important, Doctor. Promise."

"I promise. You can help by making that story as short as possible. Go on."

"After I left Tech I started at — the beginning in a — foundry and worked — to the top." The patient's voice gained in strength and control as if a desperate urge overcame physical weakness. "Because my record was A1 I was recommended for a department-head job at the Clifton Works.

My credentials were approved, I was hired. On my way East I was shanghaied. I got this." He tried to raise his hand to the deep scar above his right ear. The Doctor caught it and laid it gently back.

"Keep your hands still. Conserve your strength. Go on."

"The next I knew I was lying on the bank of a river half in the water, staring up at a million stars. Slowly I became aware of my head. I touched it. My hand came away sticky. I lay there trying to make out what had happened. When the dawn came I saw that the suit I had on was not mine. Then I knew I had been put out of the way that someone might impersonate me. Sabotage, of course."

For a few minutes the only sounds in the room were the patient's heavy breathing, the faint, far siren of an ambulance.

"I knew I must lie low," his voice was stronger. "I hid in the woods. They had done a thorough job. In my pocket, in an oilskin case, were the draft registration, engineer's license and letters addressed to Sidney Burt. Whoever had thrown me overboard had counted on publicity being given to finding the body. I left those credentials on the bank."

Doctor John raised the patient's head

and held a glass to his mouth. Gail watched the pale face breathlessly. Would he slip away before his story was finished as had the mysterious woman in Greg's office?

"I won't try to tell of the hectic weeks and months that passed before I fell flat across the Pomponis' threshold," he went on. "During that time I lived in a fever of fear that I would be recognized by some member of the gang which had tried to put me out of the way. I determined to get near the Clifton Works. I knew if I were caught, disposing of me would be thorough this time and the saboteur in my place would keep on with his dirty job. I realized that I must be clearheaded before my story would be credible. I didn't write to my mother — God knows where she thinks I am."

He dozed. In the corridor the elevator door opened and closed. The sound roused him.

"You took me in, Doctor, just in time, for a man had begun to drop in at Pomponi's. Once I heard Louis call him by name, my name. At last I had found the impostor. He must have been well paid to take the risk. When I heard his voice downstairs I would break out in a cold sweat for fear he suspected I was there, or

370

that the family might reveal my presence.

"Pomponi was one of his timekeepers," the weak voice struggled on. "He brought the kids presents. You tried to get my story, Mr. Search. I put on a dazed act and kept it up while I was at the Doctor's. I knew you were FBI but I had to play a lone hand. One day the kind nurse helped me to the living room for a change. 'It will do you good,' she said. 'But, I may lose my head for it.' She went to the kitchen. I phoned from the hall to the one man I knew in this town. He agreed to get me away. I told him to say he was one of Search's men. I borrowed your clothes and car, Doctor."

"How came the blood in the back seat of the sedan?"

The ghost of a grin touched the wounded man's lips.

"My friend — I won't tell his name for fear I'll get him into trouble with the gang which shanghaied me — had picked up a revolver somewhere. He wasn't used to handling a gun and shot himself in the leg."

Gail remembered the evening in the sedan, remembered Greg's voice saying, "Right. It's blood." To her it had meant murder. To the man in the bed it now spelled comedy.

"I've had a job cleaning windows at the Works for two weeks. I trailed the man filling my department-head position. I could see he was getting a little uneasy and wondered why. I tipped off Search's men that motor trucks were to be hijacked. I was working in the office which was to have been mine when I heard the fake department head tell a man in the corridor that he was going to G.H.'s office at once to ask if he could help."

"Don't try to sit up or you won't finish this," the Doctor warned and pressed the bandaged shoulders back on the pillow.

"Okay. I spoke to Mr. Hunt on the inter-office phone. Told him to call the man who was coming to his office 'Burt' and see what happened. I was letting the gas out of Burt's car when he shot me. That's — about all."

His eyes closed, his head rolled weakly on the pillow. Search bent over him.

"Just a minute, fella," he pleaded. "One minute more. Sign this story I've written. Then we'll go after the guy that's been filling your place."

The patient's eyes opened. Thin, capable fingers groped for the pen.

"Sure, I'll sign. You know my name already, but there it is, Mark Croston."

372

"Mark Croston." The hoarse whisper kept up a repetitive echo in Gail's mind; kept time to the rhythm of the wheels as Search and Pat drove her to Twin Pines; followed her as she stole up the circular stairway and tiptoed across the living room. It was still with her as she entered the mirrored dressing room.

She pulled off her fur jacket, slipped out of her green tweed frock. She would change to a housecoat and type her shorthand notes before she went to bed; Johnny wanted them.

Mark Croston. The Mark Croston she had known was a saboteur. She had wondered if she loved him! — Suppose she had married him.

"You didn't. Don't let your imagination run away with you, silly," she flayed herself. She opened the wardrobe door. In the middle of a cleared space hung a white velvet housecoat, a glass cabochon in the buckle of the broad gold kid belt blinked in the light like a huge green eye. A card was stuck in a gold sandal on the floor beneath it.

I ordered this for Lila. Hope you won't mind wearing it.

AUNT JANE

"Mind! Mind wearing that adorable thing? I'll say I won't," Gail exulted. She changed to a white slip, kicked off her shoes and tucked her feet into the sandals, brushed her hair till it shone, freshened her make-up, slipped into the velvet coat and gold belt.

The mirrored walls gave back her flushed cheeks, her glowing dark eyes, her parted crimson lips. She shook her head at the looking-glass girl, said aloud: —

"I presume that's what is technically known as a plunge neckline." Her reflection grinned back at her. "Some plunge. If Hilda Speed could see that, she'd class it with Rhoda Craven's perfume. 'Downright sinful.' Clothes certainly make the woman. I didn't realize you were so good-looking, Miss Trevor."

A hazy outline appeared in the mirror beside the looking-glass girl. Her heart stopped. It couldn't be —

"I could have told you that," said a low voice behind her. She whirled. Clutched the back of a chair to steady herself.

"Mark!" she whispered. *Mark!*"

"Don't say it again." The man closed the door behind him softly. A bluenosed revolver glistened in his right hand. "You've *got* to help me get away."

It came over her in a flash that this man's name wasn't Mark Croston, that the real Mark Croston was lying in a bed at the hospital, that the gray-faced man regarding her with burning eyes, whom she had liked enough to wonder if she would marry him, was an impostor, a saboteur. She shrank back as he came nearer.

"I know what you're thinking. Don't worry. I won't say I wouldn't like to stay with you, you're hard to resist in that white stuff, but I must get away. I can tell by your eyes you know what's happened. You've got to get me out of here."

"I can't. I won't." She drew her right hand across her eyes as if by the gesture she could brush away the cloud of horror which seemed to be closing in on her. Was this just another phase of the dream world in which she'd been living the last few days?

"Then you'd rather have your *husband* come in and find me here? He's in his room."

Greg so near . . . If only she could make him hear. He wouldn't believe what Mark was intimating. If only she could reach him. The pressure of the revolver against her arm halted her forward step.

"Nothing doing. Listen. I've been here

since five. Told Parrock I wanted to use the phone. When he left I stole upstairs into this room. I was almost caught when the maid came in to open the bed. Hid on the balcony. Heard G.H. come in. Heard him tell Parrock to leave his coat on the chair, his car in the drive, knew that getting hold of it was my one chance to escape. Who would look for an escaping saboteur in Gregory Hunt's convertible?"

"You acknowledge that you are a saboteur? Oh, Mark. M—ark!"

His face settled into haggard lines. It was a terrifying thing, she thought, when a man who had had all the benefits of civilization lost his sense of direction and sold himself to the devil for thirty pieces of silver.

"Cut out the sob stuff. Go into G.H.'s bedroom. I heard him close the door after Joe Selby left. Keep him till I make my get-away in his coat and car. It won't be hard to interest him, looking as you look now."

The suggestion in his eyes and voice sent a hot tide of blood surging through her body. Also, it swept away the pity she had felt for him.

"I shall not. You'll stay here till I hear a movement in the house, then I'll scream 'fire.' "

"I'll shoot you at the first sound."

"All right, I have but one life to give to my country. That's been said before but it's still tops to express what I mean."

"Putting on the twinkle-twinkle act — it won't work — I've a better idea than shooting you. I'll knock on Greg Hunt's door. When he opens it, I'll shoot *him*."

"*Mark!* You wouldn't."

"That got across. Love him, don't you? Will you keep him in his room till I get away, or shall I knock and use this?"

She looked from his hard eyes to the gun in his hand, back at his eyes.

"I'll go."

"Be quick. Leave your bedroom door open. My gun will be leveled on him. If you play a trick, I'll get him. I'm not fooling with a prison door swinging open. Keep him interested till you hear the car start. Go."

It seemed to Gail that years passed as she crossed the living room. She raised her hand to tap at Greg's door, dropped it. Suppose he should insist upon coming out? A slight sound behind her stiffened her courage. She tapped hurriedly.

It seemed hours until the door was pulled open. Hours that Greg stood looking at her incredulously. Color burned up under his skin.

"Gail!" he said. *"Gail!"*

"May I come in? I'm — I'm terribly lonesome. Besides, I thought you would like to see Aunt Jane's latest present, this costume. Swish, I calls it." She brushed by him. As he closed the door she leaned against it. Put her hand behind her and turned the key. Now he was safe.

"Sorry you're lonesome. We'll have to see what we can do about it." His eyes swept her from head to foot. "You're looking very lovely. Aunt Jane's present is a knockout on you. Don't stay at the door. Here's a comfortable chair."

His voice drove back the cloud of horror of the last few moments, brought with it the certainty that honor, courage, integrity, self-discipline — the qualities she had been taught are the basic principles of right living — still prevailed in the tortured world.

She listened tensely for the sound of footsteps crossing the living room. Silly, of course she wouldn't hear them. The rug was thick. She had better pay attention to Greg or he might suspect why she had come.

"Nice room you have, G.H." Her eyes traveled from the bed with the sheets turned back to the mahogany highboy, to the model of a plane on the mantel.

"Did you make that model?" She glanced at him standing before the fire-place. Her eyes shifted away from his which were narrowly regarding her.

"No. What is it all about, Gail? You're colorless. You're shaking. Come away from that door — or shall I come and get you? Just a minute till I answer this." He picked up the phone. "Gregory Hunt speaking."

Would the car never start? She bit her lips to steady them. She would probably go to prison — if nothing worse — for helping a saboteur escape. What if she did? What would that count against saving Greg's life. Mark had taunted, "Love him, don't you?" She did. Terribly, achingly. That was why no other man had measured up to him in her heart. It had taken the threat of danger to him to make her realize it.

"Taxi company — Yes — Call for cab was canceled almost immediately? Sure about that? Okay." As he thoughtfully cradled the telephone Gail heard the whir of an engine in the drive below.

"Who the devil started that car?" Greg demanded. She watched his eyes. Curiosity changed to surprise, surprise flamed into fury, fury to comprehension. In one stride he was beside her.

"It's Croston! *Croston!* He didn't take a

taxi. He's been hiding in this house. That's why you came in your bridal white? To keep me here so he could escape? It won't work. Get out of my way."

She shook her head and dropped the key into the front of her coat.

"I shan't let you out, Greg."

For a split second he stared at her incredulously, then seized the phone and dialed.

"Police Headquarters? Gregory Hunt speaking. A saboteur has stolen my car. It just shot out of Twin Pines drive. Put every man on the force to stop him. Okay. I'll be there in ten minutes." He cradled the phone, flung off his loungejacket, slipped into his tweed coat and faced Gail.

"Do you want me to take that key myself or will you hand it over?"

"You can't have it until he's safely away."

"Love the man you're protecting, don't you? I thought so."

"Yes. I love the man I'm protecting. So desperately that I intend to make sure he's safe."

"You double-crosser! You *little* double-crosser!" he whispered hoarsely.

She stood immovable as a stone girl as he slipped his hand inside the deep V neck of her coat. His face was darkly red as he held up the key.

"I have it. I'm on my way; but first —"
He caught her in his arms and crushed her
mouth under his.

"That seems to take care of that," he declared fiercely and thrust the key into the
lock.

Chapter 26

"That's all. We'll call this a day, Gail."

Benjamin Clifton removed his eyeglasses, tapped them gently on the green blotter while he thoughtfully regarded the girl in the thin-wool gray frock seated beside his desk. His eyes lingered on the bunch of deep purple violets tucked in her belt before they came back to her face. He cleared his throat.

"Just a minute," he said as she snapped the band about her notebook. "Neither your Aunt Jane nor I wish to butt into your personal affairs — sit down again — what I am about to say is nothing from which you need run away."

Gail sat rigid in the straight-backed chair. It seemed as if the familiar office walls were closing in on her. She had been expecting this, even had rehearsed an answer which would have just the right light touch. Now that it had come, her heart pounded like a foundry engine. She attempted a smile.

"I wasn't running away, Mr. B.C. These

letters should be in the mail tonight."

"The letters can wait. It will be three weeks tomorrow since you left Twin Pines to stay with your brother's family."

Three weeks! As if she needed reminding. Twenty-one days with Greg's contemptuous, "You double-crosser! You *little* double-crosser!" echoing through her mind; the feel of his hand against her flesh when he seized the key, the savage pressure of his mouth on hers, sending hot blood chasing through her veins. Could she have told him after that, that when she had defied, "I love him so desperately that I intend to make sure he's safe," she had meant the man she had married? She couldn't. Of course she couldn't.

"I felt the children needed me, Mr. B.C., while their mother was away getting her honorable discharge from the service."

"We are all glad that Mildred has realized where she can do the greatest good. My assurance that she was needed here had some influence in Washington. I understand she will return tomorrow. We would like to have you come back to Twin Pines, my dear, before Greg returns. You know, of course, that the saboteur who was impersonating Mark Croston has been taken into custody?"

"I haven't heard a whisper about him at the Works or outside."

"There have been no whispers. Search and his men work silently, but the papers will have the story tonight. In the hope of lightening his sentence the saboteur Burt, I still think of him as Croston, tipped us off as to the identities of the gang which placed him here, also of the man who previously had damaged the plane parts. Greg has been on their trail for three weeks. I suspect that the hunt worked off a little of his fury at the machine-gunning of his bombardier. You know, of course, that he nabbed the runaway just one hour after the man left Twin Pines?"

"If you know that, you know I helped Mark — the man Burt — get away. I wouldn't have cared if he had shot me, Mr. B.C. — perhaps I would have later — I didn't then, but when he threatened to shoot Greg unless I went to his room and kept him there, I — I — just couldn't take it, that's all. I argued to myself that he was bound to be caught, that meanwhile I must keep Greg out of range of his gun."

"So, that's the way it was? I didn't know you knew that the man we called Croston had been in the house."

"I knew all right. I've expected any

minute to feel a hand on my shoulder and hear a voice thunder, 'You helped a spy escape. The U.S. Government wants you.' "

"After all these years you don't know Greg very well, do you, if you think he would drag you into this mess? That's all, Gail, except that your Aunt Jane and Uncle Ben want you back at Twin Pines. Christmas is very near. We would like to have our children with us. Don't answer now. Think it over. That's all till Monday morning. Get home before dark, my dear."

Gail drove her runabout slowly through the city. The air was clear, cold and scented with balsam. Not yet dark enough for the dimout. Wreaths and holly and red ribbons in shop windows. The river a still, dark streak of blue mirror. One star like a big gold button. Music from a car radio, "I hear America singing." The late Saturday afternoon crowd spending its pay . . . Laughter . . . Girls in smart frocks hanging on the arms of men in uniform. . . . They were packing today full of gaiety and happiness.

I hope each one of you has the good sense to know when you love a man. I didn't, she flayed herself.

Mr. B.C. didn't say that Greg wanted me back, Gail thought, as after dinner she sat on the broad sofa in the Trevor living room, elbows on her knees, watching the fire.

She had no intention of returning. Would it mean that she would lose her job? So what? Washington and her senator hovered in the offing. He had said he would welcome her back with open arms. Mr. B.C. had noticed the violets in her belt. She had been tempted to tell him they were a farewell from Sebastian Brent who had written. "Off to 'Destination Unknown.' Keep your fingers crossed for me. You will, won't you, even if you are married?" She would, of course she would.

"Billy Trevor! Don' you go fer to touch them fresh cookies." Petunia's voice echoed through the hall, followed by a deep, rich chuckle. "Ah 'clare, Ah don't know where you's puts all you's eats. Ah guess you's hollow."

"What's a cookie to a growing boy, Pet? Hand over that panful."

"You take jes' one. Ah says *one!* Don't you waste mah cookies on that dog. Now clear out of mah kitchen — quick."

"You shouldn't tease Petunia, pal," Gail protested as Billy entered the living room with a cookie in each hand and the red setter at his heels. "Someday you'll get her good and mad and she'll give notice."

He flopped into the wing chair beside the fireplace with an abandon which set the springs creaking. Leaping flames cast rosy shadows on his laughing face.

"Not with her present pay. She's got her eye on that nifty yellow dress you're wearing. She confided just before I seized the cookies, 'Ah's a-goin' to get that dress she's wearin' off Miss Gail someday.' Can you beat it? She must be a perfect forty. Where's Cis?"

"She answered the office phone a few minutes ago. One of her specials, I judged, by the haste with which she slammed the door so we wouldn't hear the conversation. Here she is."

Cissie-Lou's violet eyes were big with excitement, her cheeks as pink as her smocked crepe frock. Left hand on hip she posed in the doorway.

"Heard the news? Nicky phoned there's an Extra out. What do you think?" She waited for a split second before she dropped her bomb. "Mark Croston was a spy!"

Gail sensed Billy's quick look at her before he exclaimed:

"Now what d'you know about that! You'd better beat it out of town, Cis. When they find you went bicycling with the guy, they may arrest you." His teasing voice was faintly tinged with anxiety. His sister's face lost a trifle of its lovely color.

"Nuts to you, Billy Trevor. I didn't go with him many times. I got fed-up with his questions. He was always pumping me as to what Gail said about business at the office and if men from Washington ever came to see her. If they arrest anyone as a conspir—"

"I, as in spirit," Billy prompted with a grin. His sister wrinkled her nose at him.

"If they arrest anyone it will be Gail. She fell hard for him, didn't you, Gail?"

"I liked him very much, Cissie-Lou, I liked the man I thought he was."

"Heck, there's the doorbell. I gotta answer it, I suppose. Something's always taking the joy out of life." Billy pulled himself out of the chair and sauntered through the hall, the setter at his heels. Gail heard the door open.

"You want him *now?*" The boy's shocked query sent her to the hall, Cissie-Lou behind her. A man outside on the steps touched his cap.

"The Army wants Mac, Miss. He's the keenest dog in town. There's a truck waiting at the firehouse for him and some others."

Billy's face was white. His throat contracted before he said: —

"Okay." He bent and pulled the setter's silky ear.

"You're in the Army now, Mac."

Gail heard Cissie-Lou's sob, heard her run back to the living room. She was tempted to slip her hand into Billy's, but his head was up, he didn't need her comforting touch. As the fireman slipped a leash into his collar the dog looked up at his master. Billy brought his hand to salute.

"On your way, Mac."

Gail stood beside him in the doorway and watched the setter trot down the path to the piano accompaniment of "Stars and Stripes Forever" coming loudly from the living room. As he reached the fire department car the dog stopped and looked back. Billy drew a long unsteady breath.

"It's okay, soldier. I'll be seeing you," he called. Big tears rolled down his cheeks as he closed the door. He started for the stairs. Impatiently brushed his hand across his eyes.

"Jeepers, anyone would think I was a kid and couldn't take it. It was Cis's 'Stars and Stripes' that got me. Didn't know she cared so much about M—Mac. Come along, Gail, I'm okay now. The show must go on."

In the living room he backed up against the mantel. Cissie-Lou, her lashes like wet fringes, whirled on the piano bench, threw him a kiss and announced dramatically: —

"And this, my children, is the Spirit of Young America."

"Nuts, Cis, I'm no hero. Where were we when the Army broke in?" he asked with a valiant attempt at the light touch. "I remember. Talking of glamour-pants — that was. Darned lucky you didn't marry him, Gail. Guess you'd be in a hot spot right now. Wonder what J. Edgar Hoover would have done to you?"

"Why wonder, Bill?" Greg Hunt spoke from the threshold. "She didn't marry him. I'm the lucky guy."

"Hi, *Cap!* When did you get back?" Billy's exuberant surprise, expressed by a loud laugh, provided an outlet for his suppressed emotion. Gail hastily uncurled from the sofa corner and stood up. Cissie-Lou patted his sleeve.

"Greggy, we've missed you terribly. Sit down and tell us where you've been," she urged.

He looked over her head. His eyes met and held Gail's.

"Sorry, can't stay, youngsters. Just reached town. Dropped in to take Gail home."

"I'm *not* —"

Billy's startled eyes, still showing the hurt of the loss of his dog, stopped what had started to be an angry refusal. Through her memory had echoed his voice saying, "If there's anything that makes me want to crawl under the table, it's seeing marrieds fight." Bill adored Greg. He mustn't think that he and she were fighting.

"I'm not packed," she explained quickly.

Had she imagined it or had Greg drawn a long breath of relief? Hadn't he known she would refuse to go back with him after his contemptuous "You *little* double-crosser!"?

"Toss your things into your bags and be quick, Gail. B.C. is expecting me at Twin Pines for my report."

She conquered the temptation to change from the mimosa yellow frock, to take her time packing. She and Greg would have to come to terms sometime — hers — why not get it over?

"I'll carry the bags down, Gail." Billy spoke from the threshold of her room. "Looky, you do want to go with Greg, don't you?" His troubled voice tightened her throat. "You've been so — so sort of queer since you came back I was afraid something had happened. Heck, for a minute just now, you looked as if you hated him. He hasn't been giving you a raw deal, has he?"

"Now, who's being foolish?" Gail settled her black velvet beret more firmly and slipped into her fur jacket. "Of course I want to go with him. I just hate to leave you, pal."

"Don't you worry about that. You'll be seeing me plenty." He picked up a bag in each hand. "This way to the taxi, lady."

Sky, dark velvet punctured with stars. Air, crisp and tingling. Rhythm of tires on hard macadam road. Whir of wings overhead. Dimmed street lights. Greg's voice saying: —

"You didn't think I would let my wife walk out on me, did you?" Without waiting for an answer he asked: "You've heard what happened to the man we knew as Mark Croston, haven't you?"

It was characteristic of him to come straight to the point, she thought, before she answered: —

"Yes. Mr. B.C. told me today."

"I'm sorry for you."

"That's nice of you" — with an attempt at aloof indifference. "I'm terribly sorry for him. You are sure there is no mistake?" Silly question. Hadn't Mark admitted that he was a saboteur?

"Not a chance. I wish I could think there was. I never liked the man, never trusted him. Almost had heart failure when I thought you loved him. That was one reason, not the biggest, I urged you to marry me. Not that I, for a moment, suspected he was what he turned out to be. His youth was spent abroad, he was brought up on poisoned doctrines, trained as an engineer and for the sort of job he pulled at the Works. He would have been caught in time but he missed the bus when he left out of his letters to the real Croston's mother her son's tenderness and affection, and aroused her suspicion. He hadn't received letters from her for weeks, became uneasy and in the guise of a gas company employee got into her house and destroyed all pictures and letters of the man he was impersonating."

"Johnny told me that the news of his mother's death set the recovery of the real Mark Croston back for a few days, but he rallied and would be ready to work soon. Mr. B.C. told me that you found

Ma— Burt, but not where."

"At Pomponi's. Louis was head time-keeper in his department. I knew Croston had granted him unusual privileges. Often wondered why. When I heard my car shoot down the drive that night I had a hunch where he'd gone and followed. When I saw my convertible standing behind shrubs on that lonely road and heard the soft hum of the heater fan, I knew I was not far behind the man I was after. While the police were stopping every car on the roads out of the town, he had doubled back to hide there."

"I'm surprised that Louis would take him in."

"Louis knew only that his boss had dropped in to talk over the next night's work with him. You should have seen his face when I walked in with one of Search's men."

"Greg! Did he try to shoot you? That night — in my room — He swore he would — unless I — I went to you and —" A stifled sob blocked the next word. She sensed his quick look at her.

"My God! The heel had been hiding in your room? I *see*, said the blind man in a blaze of light; and *was* he blind?" He cleared his husky voice. "Let's write off that episode forever. Something tells me it will be fair tomorrow. Sunday. No work for you or me. How about a skating party, Gail?"

"Not interested. Now that you have straightened out the mix-up at the Works we'll straighten out yours and mine, Greg."

"It sure needs straightening — Mrs. Hunt. Here we are at Twin Pines. I find myself suddenly and unromantically hungry. We'll have Parrock bring up a tray."

"For you, not for me. I'll say good night to Aunt Jane," she announced as she stepped from the car. "You must know that I wouldn't have come back here if it hadn't been for Billy?"

"Billy Trevor! How come?"

"I didn't want him to think we were fighting marrieds."

"We are not, are we?"

The gravity of the question set the blood rioting in her veins. Why, why had she said "Yes" that day in her office? she asked herself as they entered the house.

"Brought your girl home, Aunt Jane," he announced to Mrs. Clifton standing at the door of the library with her husband beside her.

"*My* girl!"

"Oh, she's mine too," he acknowledged lightly.

"*Hmp,* that's better. Gail, I didn't know I could miss anyone as I've missed you, my dear. Greg, darling" — his aunt blinked away tears and steadied her wobbling chin — "Good heavens, I must have picked up that 'darling' from Lila. Don't shush me, Ben Clifton, Greg can bear the mention of her name especially when he hears she has closed her place here, put it on the market and, to quote her maid, 'Shaken the dust of this country city off her feet.' "

"I can bear anything now, Aunt Jane, I'm so glad to be home. How spicy the Christmas greens smell. Tell Parrock to rustle up a snack. So anxious to get here I didn't stop to eat. After I've freshened up we'll be down to have it with you and B.C. while I tell all. Come on, Gail."

"I'll wait here."

"Not a chance. I want to talk to you. Tell your secretary to obey her sub-boss's orders, B.C."

"I won't tell her anything. I'll merely suggest that even a high hill isn't nearly so insurmountable as it has seemed from a distance."

"Hear that, Gail? We've got to talk this situation out. Come."

At the head of the stairs he looked down and saw his aunt and uncle looking up at him wistfully. She was wearing a frock as silver-gray as her hair. Her husband's arm was around her waist, her head was against his shoulder. His eyes prickled as if filled with sand, he had to swallow a lump in his throat before he called: "We'll be down in ten minutes."

He flung open the apartment door. Picked up Gail in his arms and carried her across the threshold.

"This time we'll do it right," he said gruffly. He kept an arm around her after he set her on her feet. He pulled off her hat and flung it on the table. "Take it off and stay awhile." He put his finger under her chin and tilted up her face.

"Know I love you, don't you?" he asked unsteadily. "Know that I went haywire when I thought you were helping Croston escape because you loved him? Don't talk." He pressed his mouth hard on her parted lips.

"Remember you flared that you would do anything to keep the man you loved safe? I didn't know until a few minutes ago that you meant me. Right?"

"Remember what you called me?" She bit her lips to keep them steady.

"Do you think I could forget? That memory hasn't been scraping my heart raw every minute since? I came to the Doc's for you because I couldn't bear it another minute."

"You came not knowing that Mark wasn't the man I loved?"

"I came because when my furious jealousy cooled, I knew that no matter how much you loved a man, you wouldn't help a traitor escape."

She looked up at him through tears.

"I couldn't let anything happen to you, Greg. I planned to telephone the police the moment I heard the car start, but you — you knocked every idea out of my mind with your fury."

"I'm sorry." He caught her close in his arms. "Forgive me?"

She nodded, her head against his breast. He released her quickly.

"Then that takes care of that." His eyes and voice belied the practical words. "I'll change, then we'll join B.C. and Aunt Jane in the library. They've been pretty anxious about you and me. My throat tied itself up in a hard knot when I looked down and saw them looking adoringly up at us. Put on the white coat you wore the other night. I like it and it will please Aunt Jane. Leave your door open, it seems a lot more friendly." He crossed the living room whistling, "My wonderful, wonderful love." The lilting waltz tune rose and fell and faded in the distance.

Ten minutes later in the white velvet housecoat Gail intently regarded herself in the mirror of the dressing table in her bedroom. Surprising that heartache hadn't grayed her hair and lined her face in the twenty-one days which had seemed like as many years of hoping, praying, that Greg would come back or send some word that he understood. And here he was. His lips had been on hers, his arms hard around her.

"Happy?" a husky voice inquired. Without waistcoat and coat he stood on the threshold adjusting the knot of a dark green tie between the points of the collar of a fresh white shirt. Her breath caught. Her eyes, wide and shining, met the caressing laughter of his in the mirror.

"My heart's so light it's fluttering round the room on little silver wings. Hear it?" Would he notice the quiver in her voice?

"I've caught it."

Heavenly nonsense. Shutting them into an enchanted rose-color country of their very own. For a little space shutting out the terror and conflict of a warring world.

"Finding's keeping?" the deep unsteady voice demanded.

She turned from the mirror to face him. "For as long as I live, Greg."

"That promise can't be properly answered at this distance," he declared in a voice infinitely tender. "I'm coming in."